MW01135268

BROKEN WORLDS: CIVIL WAR

(1st Edition)

by Jasper T. Scott

JasperTscott.com
@JasperTscott

Copyright © 2018

Cover Art by Tom Edwards
TomEdwardsDesign.com

CONTENT RATING: PG-13

Swearing: PG-13, mild with made-up euphemisms

Sex: mild references

Violence: moderate

Author's Guarantee: If you find anything you consider inappropriate for this rating, please e-mail me at JasperTscott@gmail.com and I will either remove the content or change the rating accordingly.

ACKNOWLEDGMENTS

Editing is the least satisfying part of writing, and it also happens to be the part where I need the most help. As such, I'm grateful to have such a great group of editors and advance readers. Among the former many thanks go out to my editor, Dave Cantrell, my volunteer editor, William Schmidt, and to my proofreader, Ian Jedlica. You guys are amazing.

As for the advance readers, I'm always amazed how each and every one of them finds something different. I can go through a dozen sets of feedback, fix a hundred typos, and somehow advance reader number thirteen will still find something new to fix. It's a case of the more eyes the merrier when it comes to editing, and my heartfelt thanks go out to: B. Allen Thobois, Chase Hanes, Dave Topan, Davis Shellabarger, Donna Bennet, Gary Matthews, George P. Dixon, Gregg Cordell, Harry Huyler, Ian Seccombe, Jacqueline Gartside, Jeff Belshaw, Kenny Harvey, Lisa Garber, Mary Kastle, Michael Madsen, Paul Birch, Peter Rouse, Ray Miles, Raymond Burt, Rob Dobozy, Ryan Nelson, Shane Haylock, and William Dellaway—you all make me look good!

To those who dare,
And to those who dream.
To everyone who's stronger than they seem.
—Jasper Scott

"Believe in me / I know you've waited for so long /
Believe in me / Sometimes the weak become the strong."
—STAIND, Believe

DRAMATIS PERSONAE

Main Characters

Darius Drake "Spaceman"
Human male
Cassandra Drake "Cass" / "Cassy"
Human female, 12 years old
Tanik Gurhain "Scarface"
Human male
Dyara "Dya" / "Hottie"
Human female

Acolytes

Thessalus Ubaris "Arok"
Lassarian male
Flitter
Murciago male
Seelka
Vixxon female
Gakram
Banshee male, deceased

Secondary Characters

Trista Leandra
Human female
Buddy
Togran male
Gatticus Thedroux "Slick" / "Metal Head"
Male android
Admiral Ventaris
Human male
Blake Nelson
Human male
Yuri Mathos
Lassarian male

Minor Characters

The Augur
Human male, deceased
Feyra
Keth female
Vartok
Keth male
Kovar
Male Cygnian (Ghoul)

PREVIOUSLY IN THE BROKEN WORLDS SERIES

Broken Worlds (Book 2): The Revenants

WARNING: The following description contains spoilers for *Broken Worlds (Book 2): The Revenants.* If you haven't read that book, you can get it from Amazon here: http://smarturl.it/brokenworlds2

After the battle at the Crucible, Darius and his daughter, Cassandra, are stranded on the other side of the Eye with the crew of the *Deliverance*, and their enigmatic leader, Tanik Gurhain.

While stranded behind enemy lines, Tanik trains Darius and Cassandra, along with a handful of other Acolytes rescued from the Crucible, to become Revenants to fight the Cygnians and defeat the Union. Darius learns that he is special, a so-called Luminary, whose powers can influence other Revenants.

While Tanik trains the Acolytes on Ouroborous, a planet long-abandoned by the Keth, he is reunited with his long-lost wife, Samara Guhain.

Darius begins to suspect that Samara isn't who she claims to be. He begins to have visions that lead him to discover the truth: she isn't Tanik's wife, but rather Nova, the new leader of the Revenants. He further learns that she is using her abilities to control Tanik.

Nova foresees the same thing Tanik has, that Darius will someday defeat the Cygnians and depose her as the leader of the Union. She tries to kill him before her visions comes to pass, but he escapes.

Darius learns that Nova has taken control of everyone on Ouroborous, including his daughter, and she has brought her fleet of Revenants to support her.

Darius slips into the old fortress where everyone has been training, and manages to kill Nova, thus releasing her hold over Tanik and the others. Darius and Tanik convince Nova's fleet to join their war against the Cygnians and the Union.

While preparing for their war, Darius has visions of Cassandra being killed by the Cygnians while negotiating for peace. When he finds out that his daughter and Tanik are in danger, he uses his powers as a Luminary to force the Revenants to go after her and attacks the Cygnian fleet preemptively.

Darius arrives too late to save his daughter from being poisoned by a Cygnian, and the only antidote dies with the alien. With no immediate way to save her, Tanik freezes her in Cryo.

Blinded by rage and a thirst for revenge, Darius destroys the Cygnians' home world with a ZPF bomb, but he has to force a young pilot to sacrifice his life to do so. The decision leaves him feeling guilty and conflicted. He struck a deadly blow against their enemy, but at a terrible cost.

Unknown to Darius, Tanik returns to Ouroborous and his real wife, a Keth woman named Feyra. We learn that Tanik was an orphan of the war between the Revenants and the Keth, a human boy stranded on Ouroborus and raised by the Keth. Like Darius, he is also a Luminary, and he was only pretending to be under Nova's influence. We also learn that Tanik is an assumed identity used to infiltrate the Union as part of a long-term plan to avenge the Keth.

Tanik secretly obtained the antivenin to cure Cassandra and intends to use it to control Darius when the time is right. In the meantime, he and Feyra plan to enjoy a well-deserved break from war and fighting while Darius unwittingly pursues their agenda of defeating the Cygnians and destabilizing the Union.

Broken Worlds (Book 1): The Awakening

WARNING: The following description contains spoilers for *Broken Worlds (Book 1): The Awakening.* If you haven't read that book, you can get it from Amazon here: http://smarturl.it/brokenworlds1

In the year 2045 AD, Darius Drake and his daughter, Cassandra, were put into cryo-sleep to await a cure for Cass's cancer. They expected to sleep for fifty years, maybe a hundred, but instead awoke fourteen centuries later, and not on Earth.

They found themselves aboard a giant spaceship, the *Deliverance*, with hundreds of other cryo-sleepers, and in orbit around an unfamiliar planet, Hades.

The ship's biological crew were all dead, ripped apart by vicious alien predators called *Phantoms.* Only Gatticus, an android, survived the slaughter but with most of his memory corrupted.

Gatticus helps Darius and the others solve the mystery of where they are and why. They learn that Hades is a hunting ground of the Cygnians, which turns out to be the proper name for the Phantoms.

Cygnians hunt humans and other species for sport, and they do it with the approval of the Union, an interstellar government formed to keep peace with the Cygnians. The Union sends criminals and innocent children to designated hunting grounds.

Children from every species are sent to the Crucible when they come of age. They have no memory of the experience, but each receives a mark on the underside of their right wrists: the seal of life, or the seal of death. Those with the seal of death are sent to designated hunting grounds, such as Hades, while the ones with the seal of life are returned to their parents. A small percentage of children never return and are presumed dead— they are known as Revenants.

Hades is populated with those sentenced to be hunted. A society has formed on the planet and does its best to defend against Cygnian hunting parties. Darius and some other cryo patients go down to the planet to find fuel for the *Deliverance* in the hope of escaping the system before the Cygnians show up again.

But they're too late. The Cygnians arrive. Cassandra is captured, and presumed dead, while Darius and the others are forced to flee with the help of a man named Tanik Gurhain—an exiled war criminal with mysterious powers.

After leaving Hades, Tanik assumes leadership of the band of survivors and declares his plan to use the *Deliverance* and its frozen cargo of patients to fight a war against the Cygnians and their empire—The United Star Systems of Orion (USO). He wakes all of the cryo patients and cures them of their various diseases using nanites.

Darius is surprised when the entire group agrees to go along with Tanik's plans. He learns from Dyara Eraya, Tanik's right-hand, that she has misgivings about him, and that Tanik might in fact be controlling the recently-awoken crew by supernatural means.

Dyara and Darius seem to be the only ones able to resist Tanik, so they plot to overthrow him. The coup fails, and Dyara is arrested.

Gatticus learns that Tanik had a role in the death of the *Deliverance's* original crew, but before he can warn the others, Tanik disables him and sends him into deep space on a transport ship to cover up his actions.

Tanik doesn't arrest Darius for plotting his overthrow, because he believes Darius is the key to defeating the Cygnians.

Believing his daughter to be dead, Darius only cares about revenge and wants no part of Tanik's war. He changes his mind when Tanik tells him the Cygnians actually took Cassandra to the Crucible to be tested and marked like all of the other children.

Clinging to hope, Darius joins forces with Tanik to find and rescue his daughter from the Crucible. They succeed and manage to rescue a handful of other children as well, none of which had been marked. The Crucible is heavily defended, and the *Deliverance* is forced to flee. Tanik takes them to an abandoned world to hide and reveals the true purpose of the Crucible. It's part of a eugenics program, designed to breed more Revenants for a war against an enemy called the Keth. The children returned to their parents show signs of being able to breed new Revenants; the ones marked for death are sent to designated hunting grounds to prevent them from propagating, and the ones who never return are conscripted and trained to become Revenants.

Tanik says he's going to train Darius, Cassandra, and all of the children they rescued to become Revenants, but not to join the war against the Keth. They're going to fight the Cygnians instead.

Darius isn't pleased about joining a war with his twelve-year-old daughter, no matter how good the cause, but with no fuel and the way back to Union space blocked by Cygnian patrols, he has little choice but to go along with Tanik's plans.

PART 1 - DESTROYER OF WORLDS

CHAPTER 1

Dark blue lines spidered the day side of Gaharr's rocky gray surface, while the dark side of the planet gleamed with the lights of its ten billion residents. It was the fourth Cygnian world the Revenant Fleet had attacked in as many months.

So much for ending the war before it began, Darius thought. After they'd vaporized Cygnus Prime, the Cygnians hadn't been frightened into submission. If anything, they were more hostile than ever.

The bright silver hulls of Cygnian warships gleamed against the dark side of Gaharr. Darius smirked at the sight of them. By now the Cygnians knew what they were up against. Word of what had happened to their last three planets had spread far and wide. But it didn't matter. These Cygnians had never encountered Revenants before, much less a whole fleet of them.

"Commander, are you ready?" Admiral Ventaris asked from the command station beside Darius. "Our fighters will arrive any second now," Ventaris added.

Darius tore his gaze away from Gaharr and nodded to the admiral. The hint of a smile tugged at the corners of Ventaris's lips, and the skin around his eyes crinkled.

The admiral had been Darius's mentor for the past four months, ever since Tanik had mysteriously disappeared. Darius had learned a lot since then, both about his powers, and the galaxy that he'd woken up in. At first, he'd been horrified at having sent a man to his death to win the battle at Cygnus Prime. Now he realized that it had been a necessary evil, but he was in no hurry to turn anyone else into a suicide bomber. Fortunately, there were other ways of defeating the Cygnians.

Darius closed his eyes and relaxed against his acceleration harness. He opened his mind to the zero-point field and used his Awareness to find the commander of the enemy fleet.

It didn't take him long to zero in on a particular bright and shining presence aboard one of the Cygnians' three ring ships. The commander was a Ghoul, as usual. Darius zipped inside the alien's mind and took over. The bridge of the alien ship snapped into focus. He saw a dark, gleaming deck surrounded by curving panoramic viewports arrayed in a circle around five command stations. The Ghoul commander's station lay in the center of the other four. Banshees, rather than Ghouls, sat at the other stations, recognizable from their smaller size. Darius raised all four of the Cygnian commander's arms and flexed giant hands with wicked gray claws. He felt an insatiable hunger gnawing inside of him, along with an inexplicable need to rip something apart with his teeth, to feel hot blood spurting into his mouth and running down his chin...

This was what it felt like to be a Cygnian: always hungry, always burning with violent, blood-thirsty desires. It was almost enough to make Darius empathize with them. They couldn't help being the ruthless predators that they were. It was part of the Cygnian condition. *All the more reason to exterminate them*, Darius decided.

One of the Banshees growled something urgently. "King Dahgurr, enemy fighters just jumped in at a high velocity on the far side of Gaharr! Should we send our squadrons to intercept?"

"It's a trick," Darius growled back, speaking in Cygnian. "Let our ground defenses deal with them.

We have to focus all our forces on keeping the enemy fleet away."

"But master, what if they have their secret weapon aboard one of those fighters?"

"Do you really think a weapon capable of destroying an entire planet could be carried aboard a fighter?" Darius countered.

"I do not know, master. Surviving witnesses from the prior attacks were unable to determine what caused the destruction. Perhaps we should send a few squadrons of our own to intercept them to be safe."

"Are you challenging my orders, *Keeper?*" Darius said, pouring as much malice into his voice as he could.

The Banshee's four black eyes widened and slowly blinked at him, first the upper set and then the lower. "No, Master."

"Perhaps you think you should be the one to lead us into battle!"

"I meant no disrespect, My King." The Keeper inclined his head in a gesture of submission.

"Good, then let me know once our fighters reach the enemy fleet."

"Yes, master."

Darius watched the Revenant Fleet through the Ghoul King's eyes—all four of them. He counted

eighteen capital ships, although at this range they were barely larger than pinpricks and much duller than the average star.

"Our fighters are ten *blinks* from firing range with the enemy fleet," the Keeper announced. "The enemy does not appear to have launched any fighters to defend themselves. It will not take us long to devour them."

Before Darius could reply, the Revenants' ships all went from a dull gray to shining brighter than the stars. The Revenants had just begun shielding their vessels with the zero-point field.

"Something is wrong," another Banshee growled. "The enemy fleet is radiating some kind of energy in the visible spectrum."

"It is the Divine Light," Darius mused, to which the four Banshees on the bridge began muttering and growling amongst themselves. The *Divine Light* was the deity that all Cygnians worshiped. It was just another term for the zero-point field, or ZPF, but no Cygnian this side of the Eye had ever seen physical proof of it before. To physically see it for the first time, and to find it accompanying their *enemies,* must have been a shock.

"How do you know this?" the Keeper asked.

"Because *I* am a Revenant," Darius said, and

bared the Ghoul King's jagged gray teeth at the Banshee.

The Keeper stared uncertainly at him, even as the other three glanced his way.

"A Revenant, My King? You are one of the children who never returned from the Crucible? We have been with you for many *orbits*. Why are you only revealing this now?"

"It was not important until now," Darius explained. He detected ripples of shock and fury roiling just beneath the surface of the Ghoul King's thoughts. King Dahgurr was resisting him, but without the strength of a real Revenant, he stood no chance of breaking Darius's mental hold on him.

The Banshee held his gaze a moment longer before turning back to his displays. "Our fighters have engaged the enemy fleet, My King."

Darius waited a few seconds, already anticipating the exclamations of shock and disbelief to follow.

"Our weapons are having no effect!"

Darius smiled inwardly. "It will take time to break their shields. Keep firing!"

"Their shields, My King?"

"They are using the Divine Light to shield their vessels. That is why they are radiating light."

"Such a thing is possible?" one of the other Banshees asked.

"Yes," Darius replied. "Keep firing."

"The enemy fighters we detected earlier have just reached the surface of Gaharr. They are also radiating light. Our ground defenses are proving ineffectual against them."

"They will not last long," Darius assured them.

The next few minutes passed in silence, followed by: "The enemy fighters are withdrawing to orbit, and their fleet is turning to leave!"

"Chase after them!" Darius growled.

"We are getting strange readings from Gaharr," another Banshee said.

"What kind of readings?" Darius demanded.

"Thermal. The planet is—"

A flash of light interrupted the Banshee, and Darius felt a brief wave of searing pain. Suddenly he was back on the bridge of the *Harbinger* with Admiral Ventaris. He blinked his two human eyes open and stared into the roiling fireball that had been Gaharr.

"Another planet down," Admiral Ventaris said. "That's four."

"Five more to go," Darius replied.

"Enemy fighters are breaking off!" Lieutenant Hanson called out from Flight Ops.

"Sensors, get me a tally of surviving capital ships in the Cygnian fleet," Admiral Ventaris said.

"There's... none, sir," the officer at the sensor station replied.

Ventaris flashed a wicked grin. "Then their fighters have nowhere to run." Cygnian Blade fighters, unlike the Union's two-man Vultures, did not come equipped with warp drives. "Flight Ops—launch our fighters to intercept, and have the squadrons returning from the planet join them."

"Yes, sir."

"How many of those fighters survived?" Darius asked.

"All pilots accounted for, Commander," Lieutenant Hanson replied.

Ventaris turned to Darius. "It seems you were right. This is better than using suicide bombers."

Darius nodded stiffly but gave no reply. It wasn't common knowledge that he'd *forced* an officer to sacrifice his life in order to destroy Cygnus Prime. The official story was that the pilot and copilot had both volunteered for the mission. Darius preferred not to talk about it for fear that one of the bridge crew might reveal the truth. That would be particularly bad for morale. The Revenants all knew that he *could* take control of them, since he was one of the so-called *Luminaries*

— 24 —

who could influence the minds of other Revenants, but so far none of them had reason to suspect that he might have actually used that power.

Darius gave the admiral a tight smile. "Do you need me for anything else, sir?"

Admiral Ventaris shook his head. "You are free to retire to your quarters. I'll contact you if we need you for anything else."

Darius released his acceleration harness and stood up. His mag boots clunked resoundingly on the deck as he went. The marine corporals sitting to either side of the bridge doors saluted him as he left.

Darius's quarters were on the command deck along with the bridge, so it didn't take long to get back to them. Once there, he walked straight over to the glowing blue cryo tank standing along the far wall. He placed a hand against the frosted glass and scraped away some of the ice to see his daughter's face. His hand lingered on the freezing glass, as if to cup her cheek. Waking her was out of the question. She was frozen on the brink of death, with enough Cygnian venom buzzing through her veins to stop her heart in seconds upon waking. He'd spoken with every medic on the Revenant fleet about her condition and had them run tests, but none of them had been able to offer any encouragement. Without a sample of the venom from the particular Cygnian who had poisoned her, they couldn't synthesize an antivenin, and that Cygnian was long dead.

Darius scowled and removed his hand from the cryo tank. Walking over to a particular storage compartment he opened a drawer and withdrew a transparent flask of luminous water, alive and dancing with glowing specks of light—the Sprites. *Living water*, that's what the Revenants called it. It was teeming with the symbionts that gave Revenants their powers. Gazing into the tank, Darius warred with himself, but only briefly, before raising the flask to his lips and depressing the button to release the contents into his mouth. Cold water coursed down his throat, leaving his tongue and the inside of his cheeks tingling, as if he could actually feel the incessant scurrying of the Sprites.

Darius's eyes drifted shut, and a sigh escaped his lips. A world of tension and exhaustion faded away, replaced with a feeling of raw power. It was a feeling of security and safety, the banishment of restless fears and anxieties. If only he could live on this high all day long.

This must be what drug addicts feel, Darius thought. That was a good analogy. Admiral

Ventaris had told him that repeated dosing with Sprites would make him stronger, but that it would be addictive, and that if he took too much, too frequently, it could literally disintegrate him on a molecular level. Darius likened it to heroin. He wasn't sure if they still had that drug on Earth, but it seemed to have all the same properties: euphoria-inducing, addictive, and deadly if overdosed. The difference was that Heroin didn't confer supernatural powers to its users.

Darius walked back over to his daughter's cryo pod and clinked the flask of living water against the glass cover of her pod. "Cheers, Cassy," he said, and released another stream of the luminous water into his mouth. By the time he lowered the flask his head was buzzing, and he was smiling in spite of himself—smirking, perhaps. "I know you wouldn't approve, but I'm making them pay for what they did to you." He took another sip from the flask and sighed with pleasure. The sense of euphoria the Sprites conferred on him was so compelling that he almost got carried away and finished off the entire flask.

With a physical effort, he lowered the flask from his lips and returned it to the storage compartment. It wouldn't be a good idea to overdose now. As long as he had a shred of hope to someday revive his daughter, and as long as there were still Cygnians to kill, he still had a reason to live.

A knock sounded on the door, and he waved it open without bothering to check who it was.

"Darius?"

He recognized Dyara's voice and turned to face her. She startled at the sight of him, and a wary look flashed across her face. She must have seen the Sprites dancing in his eyes.

"Never mind," she said. "I'll come back later."

"Wait!" he said. She jumped at the volume of his voice, and fear replaced the wariness in her eyes. "Sorry," he added. That was another problem with dosing on Sprites—increased aggression.

"We can talk tomorrow," Dyara said. "When you're feeling more yourself."

"Dya..." he took a few steps toward her, but she retreated quickly into the corridor and disappeared from sight.

He scowled, wondering if he should *make her* come back. It was infuriating that she reacted this way when she *knew* that the only reason he was using the Sprites was to win this war faster and save more lives. He was literally sacrificing himself for the good of others. She should be grateful, not treating him like a leper!

Darius's hands closed into fists, and he lashed out at the nearest wall with a kinetic attack. The storage compartments buckled and crumpled inward with a metallic shriek. The compartment with the flask of living water in it popped open invitingly.

Maybe just one more sip. He'd earned it.

CHAPTER 2

—TWO WEEKS LATER—

Hagrol was a beautiful world, green and blue with streaks and swirls of white clouds. It looked a lot like Earth but for the shape and number of its continents. *No wonder they call them terran-class worlds*, Darius thought.

This was the fifth Cygnian planet they'd visited. It was almost a pity they'd come to destroy it, but once the Cygnians were all gone, they'd be free to explore and colonize the Galaxy. There'd be many more worlds like Hagrol.

"Admiral, the enemy fleet is setting an intercept course," the officer at the sensor station announced.

"Make a show of trying to go around them, but without getting too close," Admiral Ventaris replied.

Not getting too close was key. They couldn't afford to get caught in the blast wave when the planet disintegrated. The Revenant Fleet had yet to lose even a single capital-class vessel in the fighting. Better to keep it that way.

Darius smirked. The war had devolved into a boring routine. The outcome was never in question from the moment they arrived to the moment they left.

"Commander, are you ready?" Admiral Ventaris asked, glancing at him.

Darius nodded. "Yes." He relaxed into his acceleration harness and allowed his eyes to drift shut. Casting his mind out into the swirling energies of the zero-point field, he soared through space in his mind's eye, to a gleaming fleet full of bright and shining lifeforms. They were all Cygnians from the size and shape of their bodies— four arms and two legs, or *six* legs, in the case of the Banshees.

There were also a few dozen smaller ships crewed by smaller beings. They were lurking on the far side of the planet, hidden in its shadow. Darius frowned inwardly at the sight of those ships and drew closer for a better look. They weren't Cygnian vessels. They were Union ships, and some of those crew looked... *human.*

These people were much brighter presences than the Cygnians, some of them so bright that they shone like miniature suns. Darius felt a mind reaching back for his, seeking to take control of *him.* He recoiled from it and blinked his eyes open. Suddenly he was back on the bridge of the *Harbinger,* trying to decide what he'd sensed. There was only one possible explanation for it.

"The other Revenants are here," he decided. "Someone re-opened the Eye to let them through."

Admiral Ventaris turned to him with glazed eyes and an unsettling smile. "Are you sure?"

Before he realized what was happening, Darius's acceleration harness crumpled in around him, constricting his ribs and chest, making it impossible for him to breathe. He gasped for air and reached into the ZPF to push back. He pushed as hard as he could, and the acceleration harness exploded, sending pieces of it clattering to the walls and ceiling of the bridge. Sucking in a hasty breathe, Darius leapt out of his chair.

"All ahead full!" Admiral Ventaris yelled. Darius barely had enough time to register those words before he went flying backward, sailing toward the doors of the bridge.

He pushed back with his powers just as he

would to survive a fall in gravity. That cushioned the impact, but he still heard and felt the bridge doors shudder like a drum as he slammed into them. He lay against the doors, dazed and pinned by five *G*s of acceleration. White-hot rage sang inside of him, making his whole body tremble. Clearly, there was another Luminary in the system, and he'd taken control of the admiral—perhaps the entire bridge crew. The question was *how?* Tanik had shut the Eye. There was supposedly no way for any of the other Revenants to follow them.

Darius saw the Admiral's chair rotate, his sidearm drawn and aimed. Darius summoned a shield just a split second before the barrel of the weapon flashed. The laser bolt splashed harmlessly off his shield, the energy dissipating with a hissing roar.

"Kill engines!" Admiral Ventaris said in a strained voice.

The immense pressure pinning Darius in place suddenly lifted, and he gasped. "Who are you?"

"I am Kovar," Admiral Ventaris replied. "You must be Darius Drake. I have seen you in my visions."

Darius gingerly probed his aching ribs with his fingers, wincing at the sharp stabs of pain that action provoked. He rolled his shoulders and drew on the ZPF to deaden the pain. "Kovar. A Luminary?"

"Yes," he said and released his acceleration harness to join Darius in standing.

The rest of the bridge crew slowly rotated their chairs to watch the growing confrontation. Their eyes were all glazed, just like the admiral's.

"How did you get here?" Darius asked.

"We came through the Eye," Kovar said as if the answer should have been obvious. "Is that not how your fleet came to be here?"

"Yes, but we shut the Eye after we flew though from Revenant space."

"You mean Keth Space," Kovar said, while casting about. "That's an interesting story. The wormhole wasn't shut when we arrived, but I don't sense that you are lying. That is troubling." Kovar's gaze fell upon the weapons locker beside the bridge doors, and he thrust out a hand toward it. The locker flew open, revealing seven gleaming black swords on a rack. All of them leapt out of the locker, and the crew raised their hands as one to receive the weapons. Hilts found waiting palms with a quick succession of meaty *slaps*. Two swords sailed into the Admiral's waiting hands. One of those weapons belonged to Darius.

"You're fighting the wrong enemy," Kovar

said while flourishing the blades. All five of the bridge crew released their harnesses and rose from their stations to join the Admiral in standing. The pair of Marines guarding the doors, one to either side of Darius, did likewise and drew swords from the sheaths on their backs.

Darius glanced briefly at each of them. He was outnumbered seven to one.

"The Cygnians are just a convenient means to feed our army with soldiers," Kovar went on. "The Crucible, the seals, the Cygnians and their hunting grounds, it's all designed to weed out unproductive bloodlines and favor Revenant births."

"I know," Darius growled, and waved his hand to dismiss further explanations.

Kovar cocked his head—Admiral Ventaris's head—to one side. "Then why are you trying to exterminate them?"

"Because they're part of the problem. We can't change the way things are until they're out of the way. We already tried reasoning with them." Darius experienced a momentary burst of rage at the recollection of how Cassandra had ended up in her current condition: she'd gone to negotiate with the Cygnians, to warn them what was coming and get them to back down before anyone had to die.

Instead of heeding her warning, they'd attacked her.

"If you eliminate the hunting grounds and the Cygnians, you'll dilute the pool of future Revenants. Our army will be whittled away to nothing, and then the Keth will come and kill us all."

Darius's mind raced, trying to come up with a way to fight off seven Revenants at once without a weapon. "How do you know that?" Darius asked, buying time to come up with a strategy. He probed the minds of the Marines flanking him, trying to wrest control of them from Kovar. He felt Kovar pushing back, so he pushed harder. The Luminary's hold on them was strong, but it wasn't strong enough. Just before he broke through, Darius gave up and pretended to be exhausted by the effort.

Kovar grinned. "Nice try. As for how I know that the Keth would kill us all if given half a chance, I know what they are like—I ought to after fighting them for the past nine centuries. Have you even met one of them yet?"

Darius shook his head. "No, because they're all dead. You're out there chasing shadows while the real enemy is at home sleeping in your bed."

"The Keth are hiding, not dead," Kovar

replied. "Their numbers are likely few by now, but they are a cunning enemy. If we had not used the Cygnians and the Crucible to swell our numbers, they would have slaughtered us long ago."

"If they're so powerful, how did you conquer their homeworld?"

Kovar smiled. "As I say, their numbers are few. In addition to that, their technology is leagues behind our own."

Darius frowned. "Then why are you so scared of them?"

"Because we have all foreseen the Keth's plans. We know they are planning to wipe us out."

"Why would they want to kill us—besides the fact that you've spent nearly a thousand years killing them."

"Because they don't want to share their power. The more beings there are drawing on the ZPF, the weaker each individual becomes. It's a finite pool of energy. That's the other reason for the Crucible and using the Cygnians to send everyone there. Breeding and training more Revenants as fast as we can diminishes the Keth's strength without us even having to fight them. All of the Keth used to be able to open wormholes, but now no one is strong enough, and the Eye is the only way to reach us. We managed to bottle them up on their side of the galaxy, and we'd like to keep it that way."

"Tanik Gurhain might be strong enough to open wormholes," Darius mused.

Kovar's eyes narrowed swiftly. "Tanik Gurhain? What does he have to do with this?"

"You know him?"

"I did. How do *you* know him?"

"We met him on a world called Hades. He trained me and convinced Admiral Ventaris to go to war with the Cygnians, but after we destroyed Cygnus Prime, he disappeared without a trace. You said—or *the Admiral* said—that he may have opened a wormhole to disappear like that."

Kovar scowled. "Tanik Gurhain is dead. I felt his presence fade during the battle for Ouroboros twenty years ago."

"He said he faked his death in order to escape the Augur's influence," Darius replied.

"Did he now?" Kovar replied. "Assuming that's true, why would he abandon a fight that he started? And how did he open a wormhole? The Augur was the last Revenant who could do that, and he died the same time Tanik did."

"Tanik said he wasn't strong enough to open a *traversable* portal."

"And yet he disappeared without a trace from

one of your ships. Not even I can do such a thing. You're telling me that a lowly Advocate somehow managed to do something that a Luminary cannot?"

"I don't know," Darius admitted.

Kovar sneered. "I'll find out. In the meantime, you have a choice to make: join me, and help me clean up the mess that you've created, or die."

All seven of the Revenants on the bridge began glowing in the light of ZPF shields, and their swords became wreathed in shimmering light.

Darius glanced at the Marines standing to either side of him, then back to Kovar, and he gave a slow smile. "I have a counter proposal—you release my crew and agree not to interfere with my fleet, or I'll hunt you down and kill you myself."

CHAPTER 3

Kovar laughed in Darius's face. He flourished his glowing swords and grinned. "Goodbye, Darius."

The entire Bridge crew began advancing on Darius at once. The two Marines standing to either side of him were just a few paces away, nearly close enough for their swords to reach him without even taking another step.

Darius took a deep breath and drew on the ZPF. As he let out that breath, he released a shock wave of energy. Everyone went flying into the holo panels around the edges of the bridge—all except for Kovar, who deflected the assault.

"Impressive," he said.

Darius cast outward, reaching for the minds of each of the crew. He pushed against Kovar, forcing the Luminary's presence out of the ship and into space.

Admiral Ventaris started, then blinked. His eyes were no longer glazed. "What..." Realization dawned. "The Revenants found us."

"Yes," Darius replied, nodding.

"We have to retreat. We're not prepared to face Revenants," Admiral Ventaris said.

"Kovar is weak," Darius said.

"Is he?" Ventaris demanded. "He just took control of me and my bridge! You don't know how to defend us against psychic attacks. He could turn our own ships against us! For all we know, he already has. Comms!" Ventaris whirled around.

"Sir?" The comms officer, along with the rest of the bridge crew, were just now strapping back in at their stations after Darius had tossed them into the holo panels to buy himself time to break Kovar's hold on them.

"Give the order to retreat," Ventaris ordered.

"Yes, sir," the comms officer replied.

"Wait," Darius said. "We still have a chance. Their fleet is on the far side of the planet. Our fighters are already inbound. If we destroy Hagrol now, we might be able to take out their fleet with it. Tell me how to defend us from him. I can do it."

Admiral Ventaris turned to regard him once more. "If we lose our fleet now, the war will be over, and this will all have been for nothing."

"And if we win here, even the other Revenants will be afraid of us," Darius said. "Give me a chance."

"Very well. Close your eyes and cast your mind outward."

Darius did so, and stars swirled around him.

"Find our fleet and all of our crews. Focus on them."

Thousands of bright and shining silhouettes appeared through the hulls of their ships. "Now what?" Darius murmured.

"Fill their minds with your own. Imagine that they have all become a part of you, each of them like a finger or a toe, an extension of yourself that you can feel and move around at will."

Darius tried that, and whispering voices echoed through his mind in an unintelligible roar. Thousands of different scenes flickered before him. Countless sensations and emotions colored his perception in a confusing swirl. He had become the hub for a kind of hive mind, a collective entity of enormous power, but it made him feel stretched thin, like an overinflated balloon about to pop. But along with that sense of tenuousness came euphoria that swelled inside of him, making him feel invincible. He had become a god. He could feel every one of the Revenants in the fleet as if they were a part of him. With the slightest whisper of a thought, he could compel any one of them to do whatever he wanted.

"Now tune out all of the voices and the sensations, but don't allow your awareness to shrink," Admiral Ventaris directed. "Keep your mind open to all of the others."

As Darius followed those instructions, the whispering voices and flickering images disappeared.

"Now, open your eyes," Admiral Ventaris said.

"Wow..." Darius breathed as the bridge snapped back into focus around him. "That's—"

"What it means to be a Luminary," Ventaris said. "Can you still feel everyone?"

"Yes." Darius nodded. He didn't even have to check. It was like knowing whether you still have all of your fingers and toes. No one has to tell you to check, you just know. You can *feel* the blood pulsing through them.

"Good," Ventaris said. "Now if Kovar tries to take control of one of us again, you'll feel it instantly and be able to stop him. Did you find the fighter pilots headed for the planet?"

Darius blinked. "No, I—"

"Find them," Ventaris snapped.

Darius bristled at the order and narrowed his eyes at the Admiral, but did as he was told. Closing his eyes once more, he cast his mind back into space and searched for the three squadrons of Vulture fighters that they'd sent to Hagrol...

But he couldn't find them. Darius opened his eyes once more. "Flight Ops!" he bellowed. "Have our fighters jumped into the system yet?"

"Yes, sir, but I can't find them anywhere."

"We're too late," Ventaris whispered.

"What do you mean you can't find them?" Darius demanded. He stalked up behind Lieutenant Hanson's station and leaned over his shoulder to look. The man's screens were all blank.

Hanson began shaking his head and pointed to his sensor display. "Sensors logged a gamma radiation burst consistent with a ZPF warhead exploding five minutes ago. All three squadrons disintegrated in the blast."

"Kovar must have made them fire on each other," Ventaris said.

"Kak!" Darius roared.

Admiral Ventaris shook his head. "We have to retreat. It would take too long to set up another attack run."

"We can worry about destroying Hagrol later," Darius said. "Right now we have a more important

— 44 —

target. If we kill Kovar, I can take over his fleet and add it to ours."

"That's an ambitious plan," Ventaris said. "But between the Cygnian fleet and Kovar's fleet, we're outnumbered. We need to get out of here while we still can."

Darius nodded. "Go ahead. Give me four squadrons of Vultures, and I'll come back with Kovar's head."

Ventaris frowned. "If you get yourself killed, the outcome is the same as if our fleet is destroyed. None of us can resist the influence of a Luminary on our own. After he kills you, Kovar will hunt us down, and take control of us, adding our fleet to *his*."

"I'm not asking for permission," Darius replied. "I'm leading from the front like any good commander should."

"There's a time and a place for that, and it's not here or now," Ventaris said. "You seem to have forgotten that I outrank you."

Darius smiled thinly at him. "Maybe it's time we did something about that. Lieutenant Hanson! Have our Vulture pilots ready and waiting in their cockpits. Tell them to bring their swords. We're boarding the enemy flagship."

"Belay that order!" Admiral Ventaris replied.

"Yes, sir."

"Major Becker!" Admiral Ventaris directed his gaze to the ranking Marine of the pair seated to either side of the bridge doors.

"Sir?"

"Take the commander to the brig."

"Yes, sir..." The major released his acceleration harness and rose from his chair.

It took a supreme effort for Darius to control the black tide of rage that surged inside of him. They couldn't arrest him! Who did Admiral Ventaris think he was?

Darius rounded on Major Becker as he approached. The man's eyes glazed over and his stride faltered, as if he'd suddenly forgotten what he was supposed to be doing. Darius experienced a brief flash of guilt at overriding the man's will, but this wasn't the same as what he'd done the last time. He wasn't making anyone sacrifice their lives. In fact, removing an inept leader like Ventaris from command would likely *save* lives.

"Admiral Ventaris is no longer fit to command this fleet," Darius said. "Take *him* to the brig."

"Yes, Commander," Major Becker replied.

"Not Commander—*Admiral*," Darius said. He turned back the other way to find Ventaris staring at him in shock. He held out his hand. "Your rank insignia, please."

"You don't want to do this, Darius. You need my experience to command this fleet."

A murmur of agreement rose from the bridge crew. "You Luminaries are all the same," one of them said. It was the comms officer—Lieutenant Grifton, if Darius remembered correctly. "All you want is power, and to hell with the people you have to hurt to get it."

Darius pointed at the man, and Grifton's hand hovered up beside his cheek. The man stared at it in bemusement, and Darius made Grifton slap himself with an echoing *smack.*

"Would anyone else like to comment?" Darius asked, his eyes flashing around the bridge. A brittle silence answered him. "Good. I'd rather not have to compel your cooperation."

Major Becker reached Admiral Ventaris and bound his hands with stun cuffs.

"Who's going to be in command while I'm in the brig and you're boarding the enemy fleet?" Ventaris asked.

"*I'm* in command," Darius replied. "But you're right, someone needs to be on the bridge to relay my commands. Lieutenant Hanson!"

"Sir?"

"I'm awarding you the brevet rank of

Commander," Darius said. "You'll be in command of the *Harbinger* when I'm not on deck, and you'll see that my orders are properly relayed to the Captains of the other ships."

"Yes, sir."

"This is a mistake," Admiral Ventaris said again.

"Major Becker, stun the admiral."

The major's sidearm discharged with a flash of blue light, and Ventaris's eyes rolled up in his head.

"Much better," Darius said. "Now, as I was saying—Hanson, have our pilots waiting in their cockpits. We have a Luminary to kill."

"Yes, sir."

Darius turned in a quick circle to address the rest of the crew. He noticed Admiral Ventaris floating along as Major Becker dragged him by his arm toward the bridge doors. "Hang on, Major." Darius crossed over to them and snatched the rank insignia from Ventaris's upper left sleeve. He removed his own insignia and went back to the Flight Ops station to give it to Lieutenant Hanson. "Just so there's no confusion about who's in charge," Darius explained, as he clipped the admiral's insignia to the magnetic plate on his upper left sleeve—a gleaming golden triangle with two stars at the top.

Lieutenant Hanson nodded uncertainly as he clipped the commander's insignia to his own sleeve.

The bridge doors swished open, and Major Becker dragged Ventaris off the bridge. Darius could feel the crew's outrage pulsing off them in waves as they watched.

They'll get over it. "Mark my words, by the time I return, there will be twice as many ships in our fleet, and Hagrol will be nothing but a cloud of dust. For the Union!" Darius cried. But no one took up his rallying cry. Darius gritted his teeth. "I must be hard of hearing. What did you say?"

"For the Union," the crew mumbled.

"We'll work on it." Darius snorted and shook his head as he strode toward the bridge doors. Someone cleared their throat. "Admiral..." It was Hanson.

Darius hesitated at the doors, but didn't turn around. "Yes, Commander?"

"What should we do while you're boarding the enemy flagship, sir?"

"Engage the Cygnian fleet. Pin them between you and the planet, but don't get too close yourselves. I don't want to lose any of our ships when we take out the planet."

"Yes, sir," Hanson replied. "Good luck, sir."

Darius smirked. "Thank you, but I won't need luck."

CHAPTER 4

Tanik watched petals of sunlight dance over Feyra's face as the wind waved the tree branched outside their bedroom window. He smiled and brushed her sparkling white cheek with the back of one hand. Sprites milled through her veins, glowing visibly through her transparent skin. Removing his hand from her cheek, he stretched quietly beside her, being careful not to disturb her sleep. She needed to rest after last night.

They'd spent the past four months here on Ouroboros together, basking in the success of their plot to get the Union to tear itself apart in a civil war. Even after four months it still felt like they were on their honeymoon—not that the Keth observed such customs.

Tanik got out of bed and walked down the hall to reach the kitchen. On his way there, he caught a glimpse of a human face staring at him from the mantle above the fireplace. Tanik frowned at the stuffed head—the Augur's head. He understood why Feyra had kept it. There was something satisfying about staring into the wide and terrified eyes of the man who had butchered their people, and knowing that those eyes were now made of glass.

It had been a long time coming, but the former leader of the Revenants had paid in blood for all the Keth that he had killed.

Now that the Revenants had gone to deal with the civil war, the Keth had finally come out of hiding and returned to Ouroboros to rebuild. It would take a long time to return to their former glory, but thanks to Tanik they had all the time they could possibly need.

After the last Revenant ship had flown through the Eye, Tanik had used his abilities to shut the wormhole leaving them no way to return and threaten the Keth. The Augur had been the only Revenant powerful enough to open and shut wormholes, and his head was stuffed and hanging on Tanik's wall.

Tanik smirked and looked away from the trophy. He went to the kitchen sink and filled a cup with water from the faucet. Gazing absently out the window as he drank, he spied pairs of Keth children sparring with glowing swords in a nearby field.

There were a few dozen children dueling out there. Tanik heard people cheering as one of the fights concluded. The parents of the victor ran in and congratulated their... *son,* Tanik decided, while the parents of the loser silently carried their daughter's body off the field.

Almost any other species would say that the Keth's system of training was barbaric, but the Keth weren't like other species, whose only goal seemed to be flooding their worlds with their progeny. For the Keth, life was not a right, it had to be won. Children earned their place and proved their worth.

It made sense on a certain level. Why waste a limited pool of power by sharing it with the weak and unworthy? That was also why the Revenants had to die—besides the fact that they'd been the ones to start the war all those years ago.

Another cheer sounded as a second fight concluded. Tanik felt arms slide around his waist and glanced over his shoulder to see Feyra standing there behind him.

"Good morning, my love," she said.

He turned to her and kissed her. "Good

morning," he mumbled against her lips. She pulled away, distracted by the children dueling in the field.

"They started the Letting ceremony already?" Feyra asked. Her eyes skipped to his and tightened with accusation. "Why didn't you wake me?"

"I'm sorry, darling," Tanik replied. "I just noticed myself. We slept later than I'd thought."

"We'd better go. We don't want to miss any more of the ceremony than we have to."

Feyra turned and strode for the door to their cabin. It blew open before she reached it, moved by unseen forces. Tanik ran out after her and caught up just as she emerged from the woods where their cabin lay and crossed the sunny field to reach the sparring children and their on looking parents. Feyra and Tanik reached them just as another fight came to an end. A young Keth girl cut her opponent's sword arm off in a fiery burst of glowing embers. The injured boy stumbled away. To his credit, he didn't scream or cry, but instead used his abilities to summon his fallen sword to his other hand, and backpedaled hurriedly to put distance between him and his opponent.

The girl made a horizontal leap of ten feet to close the gap between them. Her sword flashed down, and the boy blocked, but he must have been weak from the loss of his other arm, because she batted his sword away easily. His eyes widened in horror, and he said, "I choose ex—"

But the girl cut him in half before he could finish. Tanik frowned. Everyone here could fill in that blank. *Exile.* The coward's way out. Just as well he hadn't had enough time to bring that shame upon his parents.

The boy's parents went to collect their son's remains while the victor's parents congratulated their daughter and led her off the field. For the losing family's sake, no one said anything about their son's cowardice.

"Tanik," a familiar voice whispered.

He turned to see Master Vartok standing behind him. Vartok stood a head taller than the average Keth, and about three inches taller than Tanik himself. He was also thicker across the chest than most, with a more developed musculature. Where most Keth were thin and bony, Vartok was a veritable Colossus. His physical strength complemented his affinity for zero-point energy field, making him the strongest surviving Keth. By default that also made him the leader of their people.

Of course, if Tanik were allowed to challenge him for that position, the Keth would have had a new leader a long time ago. Unfortunately, they'd never allow a *human* like him to lead them. It was a miracle that they tolerated him among them at all, but he'd proven himself time and again, starting with a *Letting* day ceremony just like this one.

"Master Vartok," Tanik said. "Do you need something from me?"

"A word," Vartok intoned.

Feyra tore her gaze away from the dueling children to regard Master Vartok with blazing blue-white eyes. "Can it wait until after the ceremony?" she asked.

"I suppose," Vartok replied.

Tanik nodded. "I will look for you."

"See that you do." Vartok stalked off, his loose black tunic pasting itself to his body as a wind gusted through the field, revealing a narrow waist and broad shoulders.

"I wonder what that's about," Tanik mused.

"I don't like the way he looks at you," Feyra replied.

Another victor emerged from the sparring children and cheers erupted from the assembled parents, interrupting their conversation.

"After everything you've done for us, you deserve more respect," she went on, shaking her head.

"I understand it," Tanik replied. "The last time your people encountered a human as powerful as me, it was the Augur, and look how that turned out."

"But you killed him," Feyra said. "That should be enough to prove whose side you're on. When will it end?"

Tanik shrugged. "Maybe never." Feyra scowled, but Tanik wrapped an arm around her shoulders and pulled her close to kiss the top of her hairless head. She was a remarkable woman. No other Keth had ever shown any romantic interest in him. He was far too ugly for any woman to love. And yet, Feyra had fallen in love with him anyway.

Tanik smiled, his chest swelling with his affection for her. It was a pity they could never have children of their own. He could only imagine the pride the winning families felt today as their children slew their opponents and took their place in the *Kibiksa*.

When the Letting ceremony concluded, the victorious children and their parents gathered together and started down the trail to the living water springs, where they would bathe together in the Sprite-infused waters. The losing families would have to abstain from that ritual until one of their current or future progeny emerged victorious on another Letting day.

Tanik trailed after the winners, walking hand-in-hand with Feyra. They had no children, so they had never lost the right to bathe in the pools.

Master Vartok emerged from the group, having stopped to wait for Tanik and Feyra to catch up.

"You did not come find me," Vartok accused.

"I apologize, master," Tanik said. "I did not realize the matter was so urgent."

"It is."

"Tell me about it," Tanik urged.

"I have foreseen the death of the human you left to fight your war for you."

"What? When?" Tanik asked, genuinely shocked by that revelation.

"Last night," Vartok replied. "As I slept in my bed, I saw him die, and I saw the Union re-born, stronger than ever before. That cannot be allowed to happen."

"How is that possible?" Tanik wondered. "I have foreseen him on a throne, ruling over the broken ruins of the Union as the last surviving Revenant."

"Perhaps you foresaw that because of your coming intervention."

"My intervention?" Tanik asked, regarding Vartok with eyebrows raised.

The Keth leader flashed pointed white teeth at him. "Yes. You must go join the war in order to ensure that it kills the Revenants as you predict."

"Hasn't he done enough?" Feyra demanded. "He killed the Augur, and he got rid of the Revenants. They can't come back, so what does it matter whether they die or not?"

Vartok's eyes darted to her. "It matters very much, young Feyra, and watch how you speak to me. I have been more than patient with this abomination of a pairing that you forced me to accept. No other *Duma* in the history of our people would have allowed his daughter to choose a mate outside of her own species. I have made my peace with it, but do not challenge me again, and do not interfere when I ask something in return for my tolerance."

"I'll do it," Tanik said. "But when they're all dead, and the Union is shattered beyond repair, I would like something in return."

"And that is?" Vartok asked.

"It is the tradition of our people that when a Duma's children pass their Letting day challenges and choose a mate, they are allowed to leave and start their own *Kibiksa*."

"Yes, but Feyra cannot bear your children, so how will you do this?"

Tanik favored his father-in-law with a thin smile. "I will choose a worthy *Aroketh* to bear children for me."

Feyra's eyes widened with shock. This was the first she had heard of the idea, but he'd given it a lot of thought over the past few months, and it was the only way. Tanik would never stop having to prove himself to Vartok as long as they were living in his Kibiksa.

"That is an interesting proposition..." Vartok said slowly. He glanced at his daughter and appeared to notice her horrified expression. He flashed another grin at Tanik. "Very well, I accept, but you must not delay. I sense that you do not have long if you wish to save your pet."

"I will leave at once," Tanik replied.

CHAPTER 5

Darius slammed into the back of the pilot's seat as his Vulture shot out into space at five *G*s. Eleven other Vultures appeared to port and starboard. The *Harbinger* could launch an entire squadron at once with its twelve launch tubes.

As soon as his fighter cleared the ship, the crushing weight of acceleration lifted, and Darius sucked in a deep breath. Air rasped noisily through his oxygen mask and air hose. He heard an echo of that sound from Dyara in the seat behind his. With her experience, she should have been piloting her own fighter, but this was a particularly dangerous mission, so he'd ordered her to fly as his co-pilot. It was the only way he could guarantee her safety.

Keying his comms, Darius said, "Alpha wing, this is Blue Leader. I've marked the enemy flagship on your navs. Set a course and stay in formation."

Acknowledging clicks echoed back over the comms. No one dared to offer a verbal reply, possibly because they'd already heard about the recent change of command and this was their passive aggressive form of protest. That, or because they privately agreed with Ventaris's assessment that this was a suicide mission. Regardless, Darius wasn't going to tolerate any passive aggression from his pilots. "Squadron leaders, acknowledge receipt of orders, over," Darius prompted.

"Green Leader here. Five by five, acknowledged."

"White Leader acknowledging, loud and clear... *sir.*"

Darius was about to reprimand the ape-like Selarian for her disrespectful tone, but the leader of Black Squadron chimed in before he could.

"Acknowledged, Blue Leader. Black Squadron has your back."

"Good. Shields up everyone. I'll update your orders as we draw near. Blue Leader out," Darius said.

"I'm assuming that means you have a plan," Dyara said.

"More or less," Darius replied as he drew on the ZPF to envelop their fighter with a shield. The inside of the cockpit began radiating a dim light. A moment later the shield brightened as Dyara added her strength to his. He targeted the enemy flagship and aimed the nose of his fighter to one side of Hagrol to fly around the planet. Reaching for the throttle, he pushed it up to two Gs.

"Do tell," Dyara said, her voice hitching briefly with the sudden pressure of acceleration.

"We're going to fly in with our shields up, dodging enemy fire as best we can; then we'll fly inside the flagship's hangar and clamp our fighters to their landing pads. We'll use our swords to cut a way in, and fight through the ship to reach the bridge and Kovar."

"In other words, charge in blindly and hope it works," Dyara said dryly. "I meant where's the hidden genius to this mission that's going to keep us from all getting killed."

Darius ground his teeth. "Let me worry about the mission, you just focus on being a good co-pilot, understood?"

"Yes, *sir.*" Dyara's voice dripped with sarcasm, making Darius wonder how much insubordination he should tolerate from her before meting out punishment. Their personal relationship had ended in a slow fade of mutual withdrawal over the past four months, and now there was more than enough tension between them to make them hate each other. Darius tried not to let his personal feelings color his attitude toward her, but she wasn't making it easy.

"Cygnian Blades are moving to intercept," Dyara announced. "Bearing three ten, mark twelve. They must think we're trying to reach the planet. ETA to firing range, five minutes, nine seconds."

"We'll have to outrun them," Darius said.

"They're *Cygnians*, Darius! They can take twice as many Gs as other humanoids. You'll turn us into pancakes before you outrun them."

Darius grimaced. She was right. They had to stop and fight. Their shields gave them an edge, but not as much as Darius would have liked since technically they couldn't fire through their shields. If they dropped their shields to open fire, they'd be giving the enemy a window of opportunity. There was, however, a messy compromise that involved some tricky synchronized flying.

Darius keyed the comms. "All squadrons, adjust course to bearing three ten and prepare to engage pursuing Cygnians. Break into wing pairs and adopt scissor formations, over."

Acknowledging clicks came back over the comms.

"We're outnumbered," Dyara pointed out. "There's only so many of them we can get in the first pass."

"Then we'll make a second pass!" Darius snapped. He keyed the comms once more. "Blue Leader to *Harbinger*."

"*Harbinger* here," Lieutenant Grifton replied.

"Launch all fighters and maneuver the fleet between us and the Cygnians. They cannot be allowed to interfere with our mission."

"Yes, sir. Right away, *sir*," Grifton replied dryly.

That was it. Darius had had enough. An example had to be set. He reached out to the *Harbinger* and took control of Lieutenant Grifton. The bridge snapped into focus around him. Suddenly he was sitting at the comms station. Wasting no time, he made a fist and punched himself in the face as hard as he could. His nose exploded with a sickening *crunch,* and a crimson spray of blood. A stabbing, throbbing pain pulsed between his eyes, and bright ribbons of blood snaked from his broken nose. Of course, it wasn't his nose that was broken. It was Lieutenant Grifton's.

"Major Becker!" he called out, and spun his chair to face the marine seated to the left of the bridge doors.

"Sir?"

Becker's eyes widened in alarm at the sight of him. "Kak! What the fek happened to you?"

"Lieutenant Grifton has been relieved of duty and duly reprimanded for insubordination," Darius said in a nasal voice. "He is no longer fit for duty. I assume you know how to man a comms station?"

"Uhh..." Major Becker trailed off. "Mr. Drake, is that you?"

"*Admiral* Drake," Darius confirmed. "Is that a yes or a no? Can you man the comms station?"

"Y-yes, sir."

"Good—helm, kill thrust while the Major trades places with Lieutenant Grifton."

"Aye..."

All eyes were on Grifton. A few of the crew reached for the helmets stowed under their chairs to avoid accidentally inhaling free-floating globules of his blood.

As soon as he felt the ship's forward acceleration stop, Darius released Grifton's acceleration harness and stood up. He walked by the Major and strapped in at the now-empty guard post. Brevet Commander Hanson stared at him in shock. Darius met that gaze and nodded once to him. "Don't hesitate to contact me if there are any more disciplinary problems," Darius said, and with that, he released Grifton's mind.

The bridge vanished, and the Vulture's cockpit appeared with all of its glowing screens and control panels.

"Darius!" Dyara kicked the back of his seat. "Wake the fek up!"

"I'm back," he said.

"From where?"

"Never mind that. How long before we reach weapons range with those Blades?"

"Two fekking minutes, that's how long!" Dyara said.

A thought occurred to him, and Darius shut his eyes once more. He reached out for the Cygnian pilots racing toward them and tried to take control of them. He was hoping to make them turn on each other, or to turn around, but there was some kind of mental barrier that he couldn't get past. Kovar must have already cemented his influence over them.

Scowling, Darius opened his eyes and grabbed the flight stick. Targeting his wingman, he pulled up hard and stepped on the left rudder pedal to activate the Vulture's maneuvering jets. The friendly fighter swept into view with bright blue thruster trails. Darius increased the throttle to catch up. As he did so, he keyed the comms and said,

"Blue Two, One here. I'll be the slicer, over."

"Nice of you to show up. Roger that, lead. Slice away," Blue Two replied.

When he was trailing just a few meters behind Blue Two, Darius rolled so that the twin laser cannons at the end of each wing were peeking out above and below his wingman's fighter. To an outside observer, their wings would look like an open pair of scissors.

Darius targeted the Cygnian Blade directly in front of his wingman and counted down the remaining seconds to firing range. His targeting reticle never turned green to indicate a target lock, since there was a friendly fighter in front of him, but he did see enemy lasers splashing off Blue Two's shields with bright flashes of light.

"Drop our shields, Dya!" Darius ordered just as he stopped shielding their fighter. The inside of their cockpit stopped glowing, and Darius pulled the trigger. Two twin streaks of gold shot out, flashing safely around Blue Two. The first shot missed, so he adjusted his aim by a fraction of a degree. After that, the second shot hit its mark, vaporizing his target. *Must have hit a missile,* Darius mused. Streams of gold stuttered out from Alpha wing, and whole squadrons of enemy fighters either exploded or sailed on as derelicts, having suffered critical systems failures.

"Nice one," Dyara said.

"Blue Two, line up with our next target!" Darius shouted over the comms.

His wingman clicked out an acknowledgment and drifted into line with another Blade. Darius followed that maneuver closely, using Blue Two's shields like they were his own. They might not be able to fire their weapons while they were shielded, but this was the next best thing. Darius squeezed off two pulses from his lasers in quick succession. This time both shots hit, stabbing his target full of holes. The enemy fighter didn't explode, but it immediately stopped firing. He'd probably hit the pilot.

Darius smirked. "Next target!"

CHAPTER 6

Tanik kissed Feyra goodbye under the umbrella-shaped *colari* trees that grew around their cabin. The fabric of his old Revenant uniform clung to his body, squeezing the sweat from his pores and distracting him as they ran in itchy lines down his back.

"Be safe, my love," Feyra said as he withdrew. "May you return victorious—and *soon*."

"I will," he said, then turned and strode into the field where the Keth children had been sparring minutes ago. His mag boots felt too heavy and too tight, but they'd be weightless soon enough. Tanik hesitated in the field, taking a moment to savor the sights and smells of his world before he left. Keth cabins peeked through the colari trees standing around the field. Tanik sucked in a deep breath. The sharp scent of the colari trees' cone-shaped leaves made his nostrils flare. He slowly let out that breath and looked up to a clear, dark blue sky. The color was deepening with the fading light of day. Ouroboros was remarkably similar to Earth. If something ever happened to the Keth's homeworld, they had a ready replacement waiting on the other side of the Eye. Maybe that was why the Augur had been so driven to wipe out the Keth.

"What is it?" Feyra asked. "Is something wrong?"

"No," Tanik replied. "I'm just homesick. That's all."

"You haven't left yet," Feyra said, her eyes twinkling with a combination of amusement and Sprites.

"No, but I didn't get to stay long enough."

"You don't have to leave. I can convince my father to let you stay."

"And justify his reservations about me?" Tanik shook his head. "No, this is the only way to elevate myself to your level, to become a Duma and start our own Kibiksa."

"One you will populate with false heirs?" Feyra challenged.

Tanik favored his partner with a wan smile. "Not false heirs. *Your* heirs. Your blood will run in their veins, even if mine cannot. Don't worry, I'll let you choose the Aroketh to sire our children. But—" Tanik raised a finger and jabbed it at her. "—if you replace me with him, I will kill you both and mount your heads beside the Augur's."

Feyra grinned, and a warbling laugh bubbled up from deep inside her throat, like the croak of a frog. "You had better leave before you entice me further and start something that you have no time to finish."

Tanik turned away with a thin smile. Closing his eyes, he cast his mind out across the light years, searching for a particular presence... After just a minute, he found Darius—in the cockpit of a fighter, of all things, in the middle of a heated battle. He had his fleet pinned between enemy Revenants and Cygnians. Tanik scowled. Vartok was right. Darius was about to get himself killed.

Summoning the energies of the ZPF, Tanik opened a wormhole to one of the lower decks of the *Harbinger*. He opened his eyes to see that deck on the other side of a shimmering portal.

"It's a pity you can't come with me," Tanik said.

Feyra smiled. "As your Keth prisoner?"

"As my Keth lover," he corrected.

Her smile broadened and her eyes danced.

"I'm sure I would enjoy the looks on the Revenants' faces when you introduce me as such, but I don't think now is the right time to reveal yourself to them."

"No, I suppose it isn't," Tanik replied. "Goodbye, Feyra." He leaned in for a final kiss and then dashed through the portal. As soon as he reached the other side, his magnetic boots snapped against the deck, but the lock broke almost instantly as the effects of the *Harbinger's* acceleration set in. He pitched forward and went flying head-first down the corridor. The end of the corridor rushed up to greet him, fifty meters of bulkheads and doors blurring by him in an instant. Tanik drew on the ZPF to slow his acceleration, but there was no time to re-orient so that he'd land on his feet. He arched his back to hit the wall shoulder first, and got the wind knocked out of him as the rest of his body followed.

Wincing, he pushed himself up into a sitting position. It wasn't easy. He needed to get to a fighter to save Darius, and in order to do that, he needed Admiral Ventaris to kill the engines.

Reaching out for the bridge, Tanik searched for the admiral's presence. But he didn't find Ventaris. Instead, he found Lieutenant Hanson from Flight Ops sitting in the command chair. Even more curious, a Marine Major was sitting at the comms. *You've certainly been shaking things up, haven't you, Darius?*

Tanik found the officer at the helm and planted a suggestion in his mind that the engines were malfunctioning dangerously and could not be fired again until the problem was diagnosed and solved.

Almost immediately the pressure of acceleration lifted, and Tanik sprang to his feet. He walked down the wall to the floor and looked down the corridor, first one way, then the other, wondering which way to go. What level was he on? Glancing behind him he saw bold white letters on the wall—S09. He was just four levels above the flight deck. He needed to get down there to steal a ship and join the action.

Tanik mentally activated his extra-sensory chip and connected it to the ship's network. He queried the ship's computer to find the nearest bank of elevators. A schematic flashed before his eyes, revealing that the elevators were twenty meters away, down the left side of the corridor he stood in. Tanik took off at a run, his boots drawing metallic thunder from the deck.

As soon as he reached the elevators, he waved the nearest one open and walked inside. He hesitated with his finger hovering over the button

F05. A vision flashed unprompted through his mind's eye, and he realized that there was something else he needed to do before he went down to the flight deck. He stabbed the button labeled *C18,* and the elevator shot upward, heading for the command deck.

CHAPTER 7

Darius rocketed around the night side of Hagrol with the thirty-nine remaining Vultures in his wing. They'd lost nine fighting the Cygnians who'd tried to intercept them—almost a full squadron. They hadn't even reached Kovar's fleet yet, let alone boarded his ship.

"We should have a visual on the enemy fleet soon," Dyara said.

Darius nodded absently, mentally preparing himself for what was to come. He watched stars creeping out from behind the featureless black crescent of Hagrol's night side.

"We've got visual! Wow, that's a lot of ships..." Dyara breathed.

Darius stared at his sensor display in shock. There were forty-three capital-class warships, and more than a *hundred* fighter squadrons already launched and waiting for them. By contrast, Darius's fleet only had eighteen capital ships and less than forty squadrons of fighters. Kovar's fleet was more than twice as strong. Suddenly Darius wondered at the wisdom of charging out with just four squadrons of fighters to deal with Kovar.

"We need to turn around," Dyara said.

Darius shook his head. "We're not going to get another chance at this."

"We never had one!" Dyara replied. "These aren't Cygnians. They're Revenants, like us. They'll be shielded, like us. And if they're even half smart, they'll figure out the same scissor move that we invented so they can shoot at us from behind those shields."

"So we jink hard and fly fast. All we have to do is kill Kovar, and I'll do the rest. They won't be able to fight us once I'm controlling them."

"And you won't be able to control them if your dead. Use your brain, Darius! What's left of it, anyway."

"What's that supposed to mean?"

"It means you're not yourself, and you're not thinking straight. Ever since you started guzzling Sprites, you've been acting like a completely different person! You need to snap out of it before you get us all killed!"

Darius focused on his breathing to quell the rising tide of anger that Dyara's lecture provoked. "Are you done?" he asked quietly.

She blew out a breath. "This is not going to end well, Darius."

"We'll see about that." He keyed the comms and said, "Squad leaders, this is Blue Leader, listen up: do not engage enemy fighters. We're going to fly in fast and land inside the target's hangar. From there we'll set up a portable airlock and cut our way in. Set throttle to five Gs and follow me, over."

Acknowledging clicks sounded through the cockpit speakers, and Darius set his own throttle to five Gs. Thrusters roared deafeningly in his ears, and the sheer force of the engines threatened to rip his hands off the controls.

Darius nudged the stick until the enemy flagship drifted under his targeting reticle. ETA to reach it was just over fifteen minutes. That was a long time to spend dodging lasers and missiles from all those enemy fighters. They were going to take heavy losses on their approach.

Glancing at the sensor display, Darius found all one hundred squadrons of enemy Revenants angling toward them. They'd reach firing range in... five minutes and twelve seconds. Outnumbered twenty to one, Darius could only imagine how many lasers would be converging on them when that happened. Dyara was right. They didn't stand a chance.

Unless...

"Dya, I need you to take over for a minute."

"Gladly."

Darius shut his eyes and reached out into space with his mind. He found the enemy fighters and their pilots. Their luminous silhouettes outshone the stars. Kovar would be expecting him to try to take control of their minds, so Darius didn't even try that.

Instead, he decided to take a more subtle approach. He summoned an image to mind of a massive fleet of fighters and capital ships jumping into the system right between Alpha wing and the enemy fighter squadrons. He used all of his strength to project that image to the minds of the enemy. For all they knew, that fleet was real.

"What the hell?" Dyara exclaimed. "Where did those ships come from?"

Maybe he'd projected his ghost fleet a little too over-zealously. Even Dyara saw it. Not opening his eyes for fear of breaking his concentration, Darius imagined his illusory fleet opening fire on Kovar's fighters with a hailstorm of lasers and missiles.

"They're breaking off!" Dyara said. "This was

your plan all along. You knew they were coming."

Darius smiled. *Not exactly.* "Take us in, Lieutenant Eraya," he said, addressing her by her rank and last name. He struggled to keep the illusion fixed firmly in his mind.

"The enemy fleet is turning to run," she said. "I'm detecting gamma rays. Their warp drives are spinning up."

"By the time they can jump away, we'll already be docked inside their hangar," Darius replied.

"It looks that way," Dyara agreed. "But what if they jump out with us on board? We'll be cut off from our fleet—or *fleets*."

Darius gave no reply, it was getting harder and harder to maintain this illusion with so many people watching. Several minutes crawled by with Kovar's ships fleeing and their warp drives charging. In all that time none of the enemy fighters succumbed to fire from Darius's ghost fleet. That would be suspicious, but there was no way to actually destroy enemy ships with an illusion. Darius felt Kovar's presence join his among the stars, probing the illusion, looking for real, physical presences of pilots and crew to accompany the illusory ships, but of course, Kovar wouldn't find anyone.

A split second later, Darius saw the enemy

fleet and fighters turning back around. He let the illusion fade and opened his eyes.

"Um... what just happened?" Dyara asked.

"I bought us some time," Darius explained. "How far are we from the target?"

"Those ships weren't real," Dyara guessed.

"How far?" Darius pressed.

"Six minutes, fifteen seconds," Dyara replied. "Hang on, we're being targeted! Going evasive!"

Dyara sent their Vulture skipping and jumping on a randomly weaving course just before bright red lasers came snapping out from Kovar's flagship. Two heavy lasers slammed into their cockpit one after another, provoking a loud roar of dissipating energy from their shields. A dozen more laser bolts went wide, flashing by to all sides—some missing by a wide margin, others by a hair.

"Five minutes!" Dyara announced. "We're taking heavy losses, Darius!"

Another laser hit them, followed by a second, and then three more. The repeated flashes of light dazzled his eyes, even though those visuals were simulated by the fighter's combat computer.

As soon as Darius stopped blinking the spots from his eyes, he noticed a damage report flash up on one of his secondary holo displays. He scanned it. Weapon systems were offline, ailerons offline—along with rudder, elevators, and flaps. They didn't need atmospheric control surfaces in space, but the extent of the system failures made Darius wonder how badly they'd been hit. He glanced out the side of the cockpit to look for physical signs of the damage—

The starboard wing was missing. He checked the other side. The port wing was gone, too. That might not have been a problem, but the fighter's magnetic docking clamps were located under the wings.

The comms lit up with traffic. "Black Leader here, I'm down six pilots from the approach! I've only got three left. Permission to abort! Over."

"This is White Two, I've lost lead. I've lost... fek! They're *all* dead! I'm pulling—" The transmission died in a suspicious burst of static.

"Green Three to Blue Leader, my squadron is down by nine, including lead. This is suicide, over. We have to turn back."

Darius opened the comms for a reply. "Blue Leader to Alpha Wing, hang on! It's easier to keep going than it is to turn back."

"Two minutes!" Dyara announced. "We've got a problem, Darius. We can't dock. Our mag clamps are gone."

Darius rocked his head against his headrest, watching the enemy hangar bay loom before them—a rectangular prism with the ends cut off. "Match target velocity," he ordered. "As soon as we're in position, I'll pop open the canopy. If you get us close enough to the hangar deck we, can jump to reach it."

"Our acceleration and theirs makes that a problem. As soon as we clear our fighter, the hangar will go sliding out from under us at two point five Gs. It will be moving too fast by the time we hit. Even if we still had our mag clamps, this still wouldn't work. We can't board them while they're under way!"

Dyara was right. That was a problem. His sheer lack of planning for this mission was beginning to show. Nevertheless, he did have an idea. "Hang on, I'm taking the controls," Darius said. He gripped the flight stick in a tight fist and flew an evasive path toward the enemy hangar as planned. Enemy lasers flickered around them as they closed the last half a dozen kilometers to reach Kovar's flagship.

Mentally activating the comms, he said, "Blue Leader to Alpha Wing. Change of plans, we're going to fly straight through the hangar to the other side. We'll gain access by flying in through the launch tubes, over."

"Are you *goffity?* That's not possible! We'll hit the sides of the tubes and break apart inside the ship!"

Darius had to check his comms panel to identify the speaker. It was Black Leader. "It's our only shot," Darius insisted as another pair of lasers hit his fighter "Besides, it's too late to abort now."

"You don't sound too upset about that," Black Leader quipped.

Darius offered no reply, instead devoting all of his attention to the challenge ahead. The enemy hangar swelled to fill their entire view, and a dozen different landing strips stretched into the distance before them. Darius swooped inside. Illuminated landing strips blurred by underneath them as they raced through the hangar. At least in here, enemy lasers couldn't reach them.

The sharp hiss of an impact said otherwise. "What was that?" Darius asked, and threw them into a spiraling roll to avoid subsequent lasers.

"We've got two interceptors on our six," Dyara replied in a tight voice, straining to speak against the Gs they were pulling.

"Just two?" Darius growled. "Don't we have friendly fighters flying in behind us? Why aren't they helping us?"

"They all broke off," Dyara said.

Darius's head grew hot. His pulse thundered in his ears. He considered forcing the other pilots to come back, but there was no way they'd survive a second approach. They probably wouldn't even survive their cowardly retreat. He'd deal with the survivors when they got back to the *Harbinger*.

They reached the end of the hangar and shot back out into space. Using a rear camera and intuition to guide him, Darius located the opening of the nearest launch tube and fired the maneuvering thrusters to line up the back of the Vulture with the opening. The pair of interceptors that had been chasing him shot out behind him and flipped around on the spot to continue firing. Darius winced as enemy lasers raked over them in stuttering golden lines. He pulled back on the throttle, and the walls of the tube closed around them, blurring by to all sides. The open end of the launch tube shrank rapidly as they retreated into the enemy flagship.

"Darius!" Dyara's voice rose sharply as they rocketed backward down the launch tube.

With both of the Vulture's wings sliced off, it was surprisingly easy to stay away from the sides of the launch tube. Keeping an eye on the rear-view camera, Darius watched the sealed doors of a vehicular airlock rushing up fast behind them. He nudged the throttle up just before they arrived to buffer the impact, but they still hit hard. Darius's teeth clacked together and his guts clenched. The lights in the cockpit flickered but didn't die. Another damage report flashed up.

"Are you okay?" he asked.

"I'm fine," Dyara groaned.

Scanning the damage on his secondary holo display, Darius found that almost every system was marked *offline*. The canopy seemed to be intact, but there was a loud hissing sound coming from somewhere inside the cockpit, and cabin pressure was dropping steadily. At least they had a self-contained air supply.

"Now what?" Dyara asked. "It's the two of us against... four thousand plus Revenants."

Darius gasped dramatically. "That many? I thought there'd be less."

Dyara ignored his sarcasm. "This is a Colossus-class carrier. Same as the *Harbinger*, so yes, *that* many. Oh, and Kovar's ship is still accelerating at two and a half Gs, so unless you're planning to crawl to the bridge under that much force, we're going to be stuck in here until our air runs out."

Darius ground his teeth, considering their situation. Dyara was right. Getting out of their fighter and cutting a way in would be the easy part. After that, they still had to find a way to negotiate the ship's corridors while resisting significant forward acceleration. That would mean falling most of the way and using the ZPF to cushion those falls. And when they weren't falling, they'd have to crawl through the ship while weighing the equivalent of four or five hundred pounds each.

"I never should have gone along with this mission," Dyara said. "None of us should have. We lost all of our pilots just getting here!"

"Shut up!" Darius snapped. "I need to think."

"Fek you!"

Darius almost lashed out at her with a kinetic attack, but he managed to stop himself. A flash of guilt followed that impulse. Maybe it was time to stop dosing with Sprites for a while.

"Are our missile launchers still functioning?"

"No," Dyara said. "And even if they were, you can't shoot missiles in here. You'll blow us up long before you take out the carrier."

"Maybe not," Darius said. "How many missiles do we have on board?"

"A full complement. Eight Hornets, and six Stalker torpedoes. Even if you could fire all of them safely, that's not enough to take out a ship this big—especially not since the crew are Revenants, and they're all still shielding the ship."

"We don't need to destroy the whole ship," Darius replied. "Just its engines, but you're right... we don't need missiles for that. We just need to gain physical access. Our swords will do the rest."

"Do you know how far we are from the engine room?" Dyara asked.

Darius shook his head. "No, but I have a feeling it will be easy to find."

"How's that?"

"The engines are pushing us. If we follow the axis of that force, we'll find them."

"What are you going to do, cut through all of the bulkheads between here and there?"

"Exactly," Darius replied.

"Are you insane?"

Darius pulled the release lever for his acceleration harness and then hit the open/close canopy button. The cockpit canopy groaned reluctantly open, and the remaining air in the cockpit whistled out in a condensing white stream of vapor. Darius grabbed the portable oxygen tank from under his seat and switched his air hose for the one trailing from the tank. Leaning forward with great difficulty, he clipped the tank to the magnetic plate on his back and then took his sword from a specially designed rack in the side wall of the cockpit and clipped the scabbard to his back beside the tank.

The direction of their shared acceleration with Kovar's flagship was coming from directly behind their Vulture, so Darius climbed out over the back of his chair. "Are you coming?" he asked as he braced his feet to either side of Dyara's headrest.

She glared up at him. "Do I have a choice?"

CHAPTER 8

Darius stood on the wall, breathing hard as he used his sword to draw a molten circle at his feet. Once the glowing blade returned to its starting position, a severed chunk of wall went tumbling down the adjoining corridor with a thunderous clank and clatter.

Standing on the edge of a hundred foot drop, Darius mentally prepared himself to jump. Even just standing upright was a challenge while resisting two and a half times standard gravity. Falling several dozen meters and somehow surviving the landing should have been impossible. But Revenants specialized in the impossible.

"Ready?" he asked, glancing at Dyara. She was lying flat on the wall beside him to save her strength. She nodded wearily and heaved halfway up into a sitting position—then she appeared to think better of it, and began rolling like a log toward the hole he'd cut. Darius snorted and shook his head. "Creative."

She reached the edge of the opening and rolled straight through, falling in a clumsy butt-first drop which she managed to correct in the air. Darius sheathed his sword and stepped through the hole feet first. The walls of the corridor rushed by as he fell, faster and faster. Before he could pick up too much speed, he used the ZPF to slow his fall. Glancing down, he saw Dyara already waiting for him on the wall at the end of the corridor. His landing was coming up fast. Darius's boots hit with a *thud*, and he bent his legs to further cushion the blow. Not wasting any time, Darius drew his sword and set to work the next wall.

So far his plan was working. No one seemed to realize that they'd made it on board. Darius was using his concealment ability to keep the enemy Revenants from sensing them, but that didn't hide them from the ship's sensors and internal security systems. Either the ship's security settings were unusually lax, or Kovar already knew they were on board. The question was, why wasn't he doing anything about it?

Darius finished cutting the hole. "Drop three,"

he said, and this time he jumped through first. Air whistled by the external audio pickups in his helmet as he picked up speed. Just as Darius reached out to slow his fall, something happened: his precisely aimed drop down the center of the corridor shifted, and he slammed into what should have been the ceiling.

He slid by exposed conduits until his foot hooked behind one of them and twisted his ankle before popping free. He cried out in pain and reflexively grabbed his ankle. His cry ended suddenly as he hit the frame of the blast doors at the end of the corridor and got the wind knocked out of him. His head spinning, he lay against the doors with his ankle throbbing painfully, listening to his own heartbeat and willing his lungs to suck in a breath.

Dyara rocketed down toward him, going too fast for a safe landing. His diaphragm recovered, and he drew in a quick breath just as she hit the door frame. Her knees buckled, and she screamed in agony.

"Where are you hurt?" he asked.

"Knees. Ankles. Oh, fek, that hurts!"

"Do you think you'll be able to keep going?" he asked.

She pushed up onto her elbows to glare at him

from behind the faceplate of her helmet. "Can *you?*" she challenged.

Darius tried rolling his injured ankle, but an explosion of pain left him shaking and sick to his stomach. "No."

Dyara snorted and shook her head. "Nice job, Darius. Now all we can do is surrender. You wanted to add Kovar's fleet to yours. Now, thanks to your recklessness, he's going to add ours to his! That includes me. You've single-handedly lost the war! How does that feel?"

"It's not over yet," Darius insisted.

"Isn't it?"

Just then, the crushing weight pinning them in place lifted. They were in zero-G again and floating up near the ceiling. Darius sucked in a deep breath, his ribs aching with the echoes of the force they'd been under a moment ago.

Dyara raised her arms and fluttered her fingers in front of her face. "They killed the engines..."

"Why would they do that?" Darius gritted out. The return to zero-G did nothing to fix the throbbing pain of his twisted ankle.

"Maybe because we're incapacitated, so now it's safe to come and capture us," Dyara suggested.

A new voice joined theirs. "Welcome aboard the *Nemesis*, Darius, and... Dyara. Please stay where you are while I send a team to escort you to the bridge."

Darius had never heard that voice before, but he assumed it had to be Kovar. The voice was strange, gravelly and deep, thick with an alien accent that drew out the *Rs* and *Ss*. Darius guessed that Kovar might be a Sicarian, a species of reptilian humanoids.

"Well," Darius said. "That saves us the trouble of finding a way to reach Kovar. He's going to bring us right to him."

"You say that like it's a good thing!" Dyara roared. "We're injured, and we'll be surrounded by enemy soldiers. What exactly do you think you're going to be able to do to Kovar like that?"

Darius didn't have an answer ready for her. His veins were burning, his brain buzzing with the indiscriminate need for violence and bloodshed. It reminded him of what it felt like to take control of a Cygnian. He was becoming like the monsters he sought to destroy.

CHAPTER 9

Six Revenants came for them, all wearing matte black suits of power armor with four glowing red eyes, and four arms.

"Cygnians?" Dyara whispered.

They walked on two legs, but several of them stood head and shoulders shorter than the rest, making Darius think they must be Banshees.

Darius and Dyara floated above them, watching their approach in stunned silence. Darius reached for his sword, but one of the Cygnians gestured to him, and the weapon flew from his back into the Cygnian's waiting hand. Dyara's sword followed, and then so did they, carried down from the ceiling by unseen forces. The Cygnians glared at them in silence for a long moment, holding them frozen in mid-air, with their feet dangling just above the deck. Darius didn't bother trying to resist. Defeating these six wouldn't help them, but they were a means to an end. He had to get to Kovar.

"Well?" Darius prompted. "Are you going to take us to the bridge, or not?"

One of the Cygnians hissed at him. That was the only reply they got before the Cygnians sent Darius and Dyara drifting down the corridor ahead of them.

"I hope you're not planning some kind of suicidal last stand," Dyara said over their comms. "That's not going to change anything."

Darius said nothing to that. He wasn't going to win an argument with her right now, and he didn't need his mind filled with negative thoughts right before his battle with Kovar.

They reached the nearest elevator, and one of the Cygnians waved it open. It was only big enough for two of the Cygnians to squeeze in with them. The other four took a second elevator. One of the two in Darius's elevator leaned over his shoulder to press the button marked *C18*. The alien could have done that telekinetically, which made Darius think that he was goading him.

Sensing that Dyara was tensing for action, Darius caught her eye and gave his head a slight shake. *Don't*, he thought at her. She subsided, but he could feel resentment radiating from her in waves.

The elevator doors opened, and they floated down the corridor to the bridge with the six Cygnians once again clomping along behind them. As they arrived at the bridge, another pair of Revenants greeted them. They wore the same matte black suits of armor, with the same four arms and glaring red eyes. A suspicion formed in Darius's gut. Revenants were made up of all different species, so why hadn't they seen any other than Cygnians?

The doors parted to reveal a familiar-looking bridge. Holo panels lined the walls, floor, and ceiling, giving a perfectly uninterrupted view of surrounding space—uninterrupted but for the four-armed Ghoul who stood in the center of the dimly-lit space, waiting for them. The Ghoul wore nothing but a pair of overlapping sword belts that formed a black X over the brown skin of his chest. Four short swords dangled within reach of his hands, and massive jaws gaped open in a jagged grin of nine-inch gray teeth that shone like knives in the starlit gloom.

"At last, we meet face to face, Darius. I am Kovar, but you may call me *master*."

Darius gaped at Kovar as the Ghouls behind

them used the ZPF to send him and Dyara floating into the bridge. Darius swung his feet down and activated his mag boots to plant him on the deck. He was determined to stand before his adversary. The lack of gravity made that possible despite his throbbing ankle. Following his example, Dyara planted her feet on the deck beside him.

"You're speaking in Primary, not Cygnian," Darius pointed out.

Kovar nodded slowly—a human gesture. "Surprised?" he asked.

"I am," Darius admitted.

"I was trained by a human—the Augur himself, in fact."

Darius arched an eyebrow at that as he glanced around the bridge. Chairs turned in unison to face him, revealing that the bridge crew were all Cygnians, too. "Where are all the other Revenants?"

Kovar tilted his giant head to one side. "Other Revenants? They're here, all around you."

"The other species," Darius clarified. "You can't have crewed your entire fleet with just your own people. I was told that Cygnian Revenants are rare."

"Rare is a relative term, but there are other species on my other ships. I find there are fewer internal disputes when each ship is crewed by just one species."

"I see... Are you the only Luminary who followed us through the Eye, or did the others join forces with you?"

Kovar offered another gaping smile and took a few steps toward them. "Why do you want to know?"

Dyara caught his eye. Her gaze was wide and terrified behind the faceplate of her helmet. "Darius," she whispered over their comms. "If you don't surrender now, he's going to kill us."

Not if I kill him first, Darius thought at her.

"Darius... don't."

"I want to know so that I can figure out who I have to kill before I can take control of your fleet."

Kovar stopped approaching. His smile faded dramatically, and his jaws clamped shut. All four of his eyes pinched into thin, angry slits.

Then his shoulders began to shake, his lips parted, and a hissing laugh whistled out between his teeth. "I like you, Darius. I'm almost sorry that I have to kill you. As for the whereabouts of the other luminaries, you'll be going to join them soon enough." Kovar drew all four of his swords, and they began glowing brightly in the light of a shield.

"They're all dead?" Darius asked, blinking in

shock as he backed away from Kovar. "How do you know?"

"Because I killed them," Kovar replied.

CHAPTER 10

"You killed them?" Darius asked, still backing away. His twisted ankle screamed in pain with every step, but he didn't care.

"Oh, yes. I picked their bones clean," Kovar replied with a flash of his alloy-enhanced gray teeth. "If only you had arrived an hour earlier. I've already eaten. I may have to eat you more slowly than the others. I hope you don't mind."

"Won't I be too dead to mind?"

"I prefer my meat fresh."

Darius nodded agreeably as he back into one of the curving holo panels running around the bridge. He reached out to the guards who'd escorted them and snatched back his and Dyara's swords. They sailed into his waiting hands and glowed to life as he summoned a shield to envelop himself. Drawing on the ZPF to suppress the pain of his twisted ankle, Darius sprang off the deck and sailed over Kovar's head.

The Ghoul tried to pull him down, but Darius resisted and unleashed a kinetic attack that sent Kovar staggering backward. Darius landed behind Kovar, his mag boots *thunking* loudly as they clamped him to the deck once more. Advancing steadily on Kovar, he swung both of his swords at the same time. Kovar blocked with two of his own blades and swung his remaining ones in a scissoring motion toward Darius's neck.

Darius leapt back and slapped the swords away before they could slice his throat. Kovar hit him with a kinetic blast, and Darius pushed back, but it still staggered him.

They were evenly matched—except for the fact that Kovar wielded twice as many swords. This was going to be harder than Darius had thought.

Dyara looked on from the entrance of the bridge, radiating concern and a faint, desperate hope that he might somehow succeed.

"Is there something else you'd like to try, human?" Kovar asked, while twirling his swords.

Darius feinted left, then dashed right and thrust one sword straight at an opening between the Ghoul's arms. His blade kissed Kovar's ribs with a flash of light and a burst of fiery ashes.

Kovar spun away, hissing in pain, his side now black with charred flesh.

Darius gave the Ghoul a smug look.

Kovar replied with another telekinetic blast. It was much stronger than the last, and Kovar followed that attack with two more. Darius went flying as the mag lock of his boots gave way. He tried to push back and regain his footing, but he had too much momentum, and Kovar continued hitting him with kinetic attacks. Darius hit the far wall of the bridge hard enough to crack the holo panel. He lay there, pinned in place by Kovar's fury.

"How shall I punish you?" Kovar asked, while striding casually toward him. "What do you fear the most, human?"

Darius felt Kovar's mind pressing against his, probing and questing from all sides at once, like some tentacled monster. He struggled to resist, even as he reeled with shock. "That's not... possible," he gritted out. "I'm immune."

"Immune?" Kovar asked. "Not to me."

"Luminaries are immune to each other," Darius insisted.

"Oh yes, we are. I can't take control of you, or override your will, but reading your mind is not the same. If you were stronger than I, perhaps you could resist me, but you are not." Kovar fixed him with an ugly sneer.

"Get out of my head!" Darius growled.

"Leave him alone," Dyara said. "We surrender."

Darius was surprised to hear her arguing his case.

"Your daughter..." Kovar said slowly, his fist-sized black eyes closing to slits as he concentrated on beating down Darius's mental defenses. "She's sick... poisoned. She's... on board the *Harbinger? Yesss,* your flagship, of course. You thought she'd be safe there." Kovar's eyes snapped open. "You thought wrong. Elder Tokara, instruct our fleet and our allies from Hagrol to focus all of their fire on the *Harbinger.*"

"Yes, My Lord."

"No!" Darius screamed. He shoved back against Kovar with every ounce of strength he had. The Ghoul went flying into the opposite wall of the bridge. Holo panels shattered with a noisy crash. A cloud of jagged fragments glittered, drifting and spinning through the bridge. Kovar stepped away from the wall and shook himself, as if to recover from a daze. Darius didn't give him that chance. He launched himself across the bridge and landed just a few feet away. Unleashing a frenzied attack, he pinned Kovar to the wall. One of his swords slipped by and hit Kovar's wrist, slicing straight through. The Ghoul's hand vanished in a cloud of glowing ashes, and Kovar howled in pain.

"Catch!" Darius said while mentally sending Kovar's sword toward Dyara.

Kovar pushed Darius back physically by shoving against his swords. "Kill him!"

"Darius look out!"

The other eleven Cygnians on the bridge drew their blades as one and began advancing on him from all sides. They hammered him with kinetic assaults, staggering him first one way, then the other. While he was distracted fending off the attacks, Kovar reached for Darius's swords and ripped them out of his hands. Both blades stopped glowing as soon as they left his control. He couldn't shield them if he wasn't touching them. Darius reached for his weapons, trying to pull them back, but Kovar ran in and shattered them with a single swipe before he could.

The kinetic attacks continued, forcing Darius back one shove at a time. After just a few seconds, he was pinned to the wall again.

Kovar walked up to him and shook his cauterized stump in Darius's face. "You took my hand. So I will take your arm."

"No!" Dyara cried. Darius saw that a pair of Cygnians had her pinned to the holo panels on the other side of the bridge.

Darius struggled to free himself, but it was no use. He watched helplessly as Kovar swept one of his swords down with agonizing slowness. The weapon passed through Darius's outstretched arm, just above the elbow.

His shield resisted for the briefest instant, flashing brightly and roaring with a violent exchange of energy; then a searing heat tore through Darius's arm, and the smell of charred flesh filled his nostrils. When his eyes recovered from the blinding glare, he realized that his right arm was missing all the way up to the shoulder, vaporized in a cloud of fading orange embers.

Agony and rage hit him at the same time, drawing streams of tears from his eyes. "There," Kovar said, his mouth gaping open in another grin. Hot, fetid breath piled on Darius's face. "But we're not even yet. Elder Tokara? What is the status of the *Harbinger?*"

"They are taking heavy fire, my lord. They've turned to flee, but they will not escape."

"Magnify the ship on the forward screens."

"Yes, master."

"Look," Kovar intoned in a throaty whisper, as

he pointed to the forward holo panels with his severed stump. "There it is—your daughter's tomb. Say goodbye, Darius."

Darius's eyes blurred with tears to the point that he could barely see. He blinked rapidly to clear them and watched in horror as thousands of red and golden lasers stabbed the Harbinger from all sides. Fiery explosions roiled along its length, and the light of its shields faded steadily. Just then, hundreds of tiny silver specks jetted out from the ship, riding on long blue tongues of fire. Escape pods. The crew was abandoning ship. They were abandoning Cass.

"No!" Darius screamed.

The shields failed with a spectacular burst of light, and a massive explosion consumed the carrier. By the time the light faded, there was nothing left. The *Harbinger* had been utterly vaporized, just like Darius's arm.

"The *Harbinger* is destroyed, my lord. One of our ZPF warheads got through."

"Good," Kovar said, his mouth gaping so wide that he could have swallowed Darius whole. "*Now* we're even."

Darius's entire being burned with a fury that he couldn't contain. It surged from deep inside of him like a living thing, and burst from his lips with an inarticulate roar. The deck and the holo panels shook violently, and a blinding light filled the entire bridge. Kovar hissed and covered his sensitive eyes with one arm, staggering away. Darius brushed aside the invisible forces holding him against the wall as if they were nothing more than cobwebs and advanced on Kovar.

He took advantage of Kovar's temporary blindness to snatch away the Ghoul's swords. They remained glowing and shielded even as they flew out of Kovar's hands. Somehow Darius was shielding them without physically touching them.

"What is this?" Kovar asked, squinting at his floating swords. The other Cygnians began stalking toward Darius with their weapons raised. Darius sent Kovar's swords sailing toward them at a high speed. All three of the blades were still inexplicably shielded, and impossible to stop. Darius ran the Cygnians through, one after another, burning gaping holes in their chests. Some tried to dodge or swat the weapons out of the air, but they were moving too fast. All eleven Cygnians died in seconds, leaving Kovar alone to face Darius's wrath.

The Ghoul's eyes darted around the bridge, finding the severed torsos and hollowed out chests of his crew. "No one is that powerful," he whispered; then he turned and ran.

Too angry to be smug, Darius sent Kovar's own swords chasing after him and used them to lash the Ghoul like whips. Kovar cried out as each impact left a patch of char-blackened skin in its wake. Darius was determined to make him suffer.

Kovar waved the doors of the bridge open and ran through. The Cygnians standing guard outside the doors turned to face Darius, and he sent two of Kovar's three swords flying through their necks, vaporizing their heads in a fiery burst of ashes.

"Where are you going, Kovar?" Darius bellowed as he ran out after the Cygnian.

Dyara ran up beside Darius, wincing from the blinding light radiating from him. "Just kill him already!" she said.

"Not yet," Darius growled. Up ahead, Kovar disappeared into an elevator. Reaching out with his Awareness to get a sense of where the Ghoul was going, Darius caught a glimpse of the inside of the elevator. Deck *F05* was lit up on the panel. The flight deck. Kovar was trying to escape.

Darius left his stolen swords floating in front of the elevators, waved open the nearest one, and physically snatched one of the three blades from the air with his left hand, leaving the other two floating in the corridor for Dyara to grab. Not waiting to see if she followed him into the elevator, he telekinetically punched *F05* on the control panel. Just as the doors were sliding shut, Dyara careened in with the other swords.

"You need to stop and think," she said. "Kovar could be leading us into a trap. There are four thousand more Cygnians on this ship."

"Let them come," Darius said.

Their elevator opened into a dimly-lit corridor, flashing red with emergency lights. Kovar was nowhere to be seen. He'd camouflaged himself, using his species' innate ability to blend with their surroundings. Darius could still sense a faint presence, though, as the Ghoul ran down the corridor some twenty meters away. Reaching into the ZPF, he pulled Kovar back. The Ghoul's mag boots lost their lock, and he came sailing down the corridor. Darius held Kovar in mid-air and turned the Ghoul to face him.

"You killed my daughter," Darius said slowly.

Kovar bared his jagged gray teeth in a snarl. "I only regret that I couldn't kill her myself!"

Darius stepped up to the Ghoul. Holding him paralyzed in mid-air, he sliced off Kovar's remaining arms, one after another. The Ghoul screamed and hissed, baring and snapping his teeth in defiance. "You are a fool! The Keth will find you and kill you!"

Darius nodded agreeably and sliced off Kovar's legs, leaving nothing but a floating torso and a gaping mouth full of snapping gray teeth. Kovar let out a long, chilling scream.

"I should leave you like this," Darius said once Kovar's energy was spent from screaming. "To die slowly from sheer agony." The stumps of his severed limbs were cauterized from the heat of Darius's blade, so there was no chance of the Ghoul dying from blood loss.

Kovar was in too much pain to reply. Darius released him and watched as he thrashed in agony.

"Just fekking kill him and let's get out of here!" Dyara screamed. "His fleet is busy slaughtering ours! Every second you delay is another second that our people are out there dying!"

Darius scowled at her, but she was right. Gripping his sword in a tight fist, he walked up to Kovar. The Ghoul was sobbing, his shoulder stumps shaking violently. But as he drew near, Darius realized that Kovar wasn't crying at all—he was *laughing.*

A frown wrinkled Darius's brow as Kovar spun back to face him. The Ghoul's eyes were wide and dancing with glee. "You're dead!" he crowed, spraying glittering globules of black blood into the air.

Before Darius could decide what Kovar meant by that, he felt the hairs on the back of his neck rise in warning, a premonition from the Sprites racing through his veins. In the next instant, the muffled boom of an explosion rumbled through the ship, and the deck jumped beneath their feet.

"What was that?" Dyara asked in a quavering voice.

Another explosion followed the first, this one much louder than the last. A wall of fire appeared, racing toward them from the end of the corridor. In that instant, Darius realized what had happened: Kovar had initiated the ship's self-destruct sequence. Turning to Dyara, he lunged to reach her and wrapped his arms around her. He poured all of his strength into shielding them as the ship cracked apart in a roiling sea of fire.

CHAPTER 11

Cassandra's rose petal lips were turned down in a frown, her bright blue eyes pinched with concern. "What... what's going on?" She stood on a flowing green field that glistened with fresh drops of rain. A huddled group of hairless white humanoids with elongated skulls and fierce, glowing eyes stood behind her. Tanik was there with them, standing between them and Cassandra.

Cassandra glanced behind her to find Tanik standing in front of the Keth. She jumped with shock. "Tanik?" She started toward him, but Darius grabbed her arm to stop her, his own arm whirring with a mechanical noise as he did so.

She rounded on him and glared at his hand. "Ouch! That hurts."

"Sorry." He'd obviously grabbed her too roughly in his hurry to keep her away from Tanik.

"I had an accident and lost my arm," he explained, flexing his hand with another mechanical noise. "I'm still getting used to the replacement. Is it really you?"

Cassandra nodded slowly, uncertainly. "Is it really *you*?" she countered.

Darius's brow furrowed. "Don't you recognize me?"

"No." She began backing away from him.

With her admission, his heart felt like it might shatter into a thousand pieces. He knew the Sprites had taken a toll on him physically, but somehow he hadn't noticed the changes in his appearance from one day to the next. Cassandra saw four accumulated months of physical deterioration all at once. "It's me," he insisted.

But she just kept backing away, unwilling or unable to believe it.

Darius woke up with a painful knot in his throat. He forced his eyes open and drew in a deep breath. A slow rhythmic beeping gave a clue to his surroundings. Glancing around, he saw that he lay strapped to a bed. The room was empty, but he recognized it well enough. He was in the med bay of a Colossus-class carrier.

"Hello?" he called out. His voice sounded scratchy and raw. How had he ended up here? The last thing he remembered was... *dying* in an explosion aboard the *Nemesis*.

Except he wasn't dead. Somehow he'd survived long enough for someone to recover him. Did that mean Dyara was alive, too? He hoped so.

Memories of the battle aboard the *Nemesis* came back to him in flashes and snippets. He remembered losing his arm. He glanced to his right and found his arm lying flat beside him, miraculously restored. He raised it with an accompanying *whirr* of servomotors. That explained the miracle. Medics had replaced his missing limb with a prosthetic covered in synthetic skin.

Darius struggled to rise against his restraints. They were unyielding, but after a moment, he figured out how to release them. Sitting on the edge of the bed, he aimed himself toward the door and pushed off, drifting through the room to reach it. Just then, the door swished open, and a familiar man walked in.

"Hello, Darius."

"Tanik?" Darius used the ZPF to stop himself in mid-air. "How did you... where did you go?" he demanded. "After starting this war, you went AWOL and left us to fight on our own!"

Tanik slowly shook his head. "You can thank

Admiral Ventaris for that. He didn't want you and I to take over his fleet and cut him out of the loop, so he made me disappear. He locked me away in a cryo tank below decks. The recent battle damaged the cryo room enough to wake me. I was lucky to escape before the *Harbinger* was destroyed."

"The *Harbinger* was..." Darius trailed off, only now remembering how Kovar had deliberately targeted the ship in order to kill his daughter. Tears welled in Darius's eyes, and he slowly shook his head. "She *can't* be dead!" he screamed.

"I'm sorry," Tanik said. "But her death was not in vain. You succeeded. We now have control of both Revenant fleets. I convinced Kovar's captains to join our cause after he died, and we overwhelmed Hagrol's defenses together. The planet is gone. Now, with so many ships under your command, it should be easy to destroy the remaining Cygnian worlds and hunt down the other Luminaries."

"They're already dead," Darius murmured. "Kovar killed them and consolidated their fleets into his."

Tanik did a double-take. "Are you certain?"

Darius shook his head. "Who knows. That's what Kovar said. I don't know why he'd lie."

Tanik nodded slowly. "Then all that's left is to

defeat the Cygnians. The war is almost over. Congratulations, Darius."

Victory felt empty without Cassandra. Every ounce of his being felt hollow and weak. He couldn't even think straight. Now he had nothing and no one. Almost.

"Did Dyara..."

"She's fine. You saved her. I picked you both up at the same time. She's in the room next to yours, recovering from her injuries."

Darius nodded. That was something at least, but not enough to diminish the suffocating horror and despair burning in his chest. The Cygnians would pay. Darius tried to picture Cassandra's face, and an image from his dream flashed through his mind's eye. He started at that. He'd been dreaming about her just before he woke up. But was it a dream, or a vision? And who were those strange beings standing in the background behind her?

"What if she's alive?" Darius asked suddenly. "I saw escape pods fleeing the ship before it was destroyed. Maybe someone rescued her."

"Darius..." Tanik trailed off, shaking his head. "None of the pods made it. The *Harbinger* was destroyed by a ZPF warhead. The blast vaporized everything within a two hundred klick radius."

"Then why did I dream about her?" Darius demanded. "I saw her, right there in front of me. You were there, too. And some... some species of people I've never seen before."

Tanik's eyes widened. "That's an odd dream."

"A vision," Darius insisted. "It wasn't a dream. She's alive, Tanik. I can *feel* it. I can feel..."

"She's *dead*. You need to accept that and move on. All you can do now is punish the ones who killed her. Wipe out the Cygnians. Finish what you started."

As Tanik spoke, Darius could tell he was lying, he could sense it and see it in his yellow-green eyes. He was hiding something, a terrible secret.

A doctor walked in behind Tanik. "I see that you're finally awake. Good. You suffered some serious injuries from exposure to vacuum, not to mention your missing arm. It's incredible you were able to survive at all, considering your ruptured suit. You're very lucky that Mr. Gurhain was there to pick you up before you could sustain any..." The doctor trailed off as he noticed the deadly look Darius was giving Tanik. The doctor's eyes darted to Tanik. "Is everything okay in here?"

"Darius?" Tanik asked, deferring the question.

"You're lying," Darius spat.

"What are you talking about?"

"I can *sense* it," Darius went on. As he said that, he probed Tanik's mind, sifting through his thoughts to find the truth. Tanik slammed a mental door in his face, but not before Darius found what he was looking for: he saw Tanik rescue Cassandra's cryo pod from the *Harbinger* and send it floating through a shimmering portal to a grassy green field, surrounded by familiar-looking trees with spiky, cone-shaped leaves. The dark blue sky and the glaring blue sun confirmed it. Cassandra was alive, and she was on *Ouroboros.*

Darius leveled an accusing finger at Tanik. "She's alive! You opened a wormhole and took her to Ouroboros."

Tanik took a quick step back. "What? How did you... Someone has been getting much stronger," Tanik replied, his voice all but purring with smug amusement. "That's unfortunate."

Darius reached for Tanik's mind again, trying to take control of him directly so that he could sift through the man's thoughts and memories at will, but it was impossible. Tanik's thoughts were reachable, albeit vague and shielded by a psychic wall. His will, however, was untouchable.

"Is something wrong, Darius?"

"You're immune.... you're a Luminary, too."

The doctor's eyes darted from Tanik to Darius

and back again. "I think... I'll come back later," he said, and fled the room.

Tanik drew his sword, and it immediately began to glow in the light of a shield.

Darius had no weapons of his own, not even a pair of mag boots to keep his feet rooted to the deck, but he didn't need either. He used the ZPF to pin his feet to the deck.

"Your usefulness has come to an end," Tanik said. "I had hoped you would find a way to kill the other Luminaries. Unfortunately, I was also counting on you to get most of the other Revenants killed in the process. Now the easiest way to exterminate them is to take control of them and make them all fly into a sun... or something more creative, perhaps."

Darius couldn't believe what he was hearing. None of this made any sense. "You want to kill them? Why?"

"Because they slaughtered my people!" Tanik roared.

"Your people?" Darius echoed. "The Cygnians attacked Earth, not the Revenants."

"No, not humans—the Keth," Tanik said. He went on to explain that he wasn't the real Tanik Gurhain, but rather an orphan of the war, raised by the Keth, and steeped in their culture. He

— 120 —

explained how he'd killed the Augur personally, and how he'd manipulated Darius to destabilize the Union from within.

"It worked," Tanik said. "And it would have worked for a lot longer if you hadn't gone poking around inside my head."

"But what about Cass? You saved her. Twice! Why would you do that if you're working for the Keth?"

Tanik smiled slowly. "I didn't save her twice. I was the one who convinced her to negotiate with the Cygnians. I allowed her to become poisoned by one of them, and *I* made sure that the only possible antidote was destroyed with the *Nomad*—but not before I took a sample of it for myself."

"You *have* the antivenin?" Darius's outrage momentarily disappeared in a flash of hope.

"Yes, but I won't need it anymore. It was a contingency, in case you got out of hand and became a threat. Don't worry, I won't let her suffer. I'll pull the plug and let her fade away quietly. I'd give you a quiet death of your own, but something tells me that you'd rather fight."

Darius gaped at Tanik. Something dark and terrible was surging inside of him again. "Take me to her."

"You seem to be confused about who's in

charge here."

Darius let the monster out, and the room swelled with a blinding flash of light. Tanik staggered back a few steps in spite of himself, wincing against the glare. "What..."

Reaching out with his mind, Darius wrenched the sword out of Tanik's hand as if the man had the grip strength of a child. "Take me to her," he ground out. *"Now."*

CHAPTER 12

"**I**mpressive," Tanik said, while shielding his eyes with his hands. "You've been *using,* haven't you? Admiral Ventaris obviously didn't warn you about the risks."

"He did."

"I'm surprised you haven't killed everyone around you in a homicidal rage." Tanik's voice was laced with derision, and something else... jealousy?

Darius shook his head. The only thing that mattered now was finding his daughter and saving her. "If you don't take me to Cass, I'll do to you what I did to Kovar. I'll cut off your limbs one by one until you're nothing but a pod." Darius shook Tanik's sword in his face to emphasize his point.

Tanik crossed his arms over his chest, unimpressed by the threat. "And then what? You'll kill me? Go ahead. Do that, and you'll never see your daughter again."

Darius almost removed Tanik's head right then, but he managed to restrain himself. Barely.

"Here's what we're going to do," Tanik said. "I'll cure your daughter and reunite you with her, but first you need to surrender the Revenants to me."

"So you can fly them all into a sun?" Darius demanded. "I don't think so."

Tanik shrugged. "Then your daughter dies. Even if I don't kill her myself, her cryo pod won't keep her frozen forever now that it's cut off from the *Harbinger's* power grid. She's going to wake up soon, and when she does, she'll need the antivenin or else she'll die. It's up to you, Darius. Save twenty thousand strangers who've all done their fair share of killing, or save your innocent daughter and go live out your lives in peace. This isn't your war."

That resonated with Darius. He wasn't even from this time. He shouldn't even be in this position! Except that he was. "I won't trade one life for twenty thousand, not even Cassandra's."

"I'm surprised at you, Darius. I was certain that you would want to save your daughter, no matter the cost. I'll be sure to wake her and tell her why she has to die. But first—"

Tanik unleashed a powerful kinetic attack that sent Darius flying across the room. He resisted, cushioning his impact with the far wall. Then he poured out all of his rage and pain and grabbed Tanik in an invisible vice, squeezing as hard as he could. The man's eyes flew wide, and fat purple veins appeared like worms crawling just beneath the skin on his forehead and temples. All of Tanik's muscles tensed and stood out like cords as he resisted both physically and mentally. It wasn't nearly enough. Darius felt Tanik's ribs crack, then break. A strangled cry escaped the man's lips, but Darius wasn't done. Not even close.

He folded Tanik's legs the wrong way, popping both knees and ruining the joints. The man screamed with thunderous volume, while rivers of blood streamed from his ruined legs like party streamers.

"You fekking fool!" Tanik roared. "She's dead! You've just killed her!"

A shimmering portal appeared between them, along with a familiar green field beneath a dark blue sky. Ouroboros. Darius's eyes flew wide, and he lunged toward the portal, propelling himself toward it as fast as his legs and the ZPF could carry him.

But Tanik made it through first, and the portal

— 125 —

vanished just as soon as he crossed it, leaving Darius to sail through open air and slam into the door to his room. He hit with bone-cracking force and bounced off, drifting away stunned and shivering with horror and rage.

The door slid open a moment later, and Dyara stumbled in, looking pale and weak. "Darius? Is everything... what's wrong?"

"It's Cass. Tanik has her."

* * *

"Think, My Love! You can't kill her. Not yet."

"I will!" Tanik screamed, spitting a fat gob of blood on the glass cover of Cassandra's cryo pod. It took all of his strength just to hold himself up on his useless legs and to numb the pain from his shattered ribs. He stabbed at the cryo pod's control panel, paging through holographic displays to find some way to shut off the power and kill the pod's occupant.

"There's a better way." Feyra insisted. Her nettlesome voice was not helping him to concentrate.

"It's too late," he replied in a hoarse whisper.

Smack! Tanik's cheek erupted in fire, and suddenly he was lying in the field, staring up at the colari trees.

Feyra loomed into view. "I am sorry for that,

but your anger has blinded you. You *must* listen to me. Darius will come to his senses and do exactly as we ask, but first, you need to *show* him what he stands to lose. Wake her, cure her, and let him see her."

"It's too dangerous," Tanik replied. "He's become too powerful. He's been using the Sprites. I don't know how he's still alive, but he's too powerful to meet in person now."

Feyra was nonplussed by that. "I assumed that he must have somehow surprised you..."

Tanik barked a laugh that ended in a wet cough that drew blinding agony from his ribs. "I surprised *him*," Tanik groaned. Tears leaked from the corners of his eyes and soaked the bed of grass where he lay. "He wasn't even armed! He stole my sword like it was nothing, and snapped my bones like twigs."

Feyra's expression grew troubled, and she looked away from him to glance around the field. "Does he know how to manipulate wormholes?"

"If he did, we'd be dead already. It would take all of our surviving warriors to defeat him, and even then..." Tanik rocked his head from side to side.

"Then don't face him. Use his daughter to manipulate him from a safe distance. This is why you saved her. Somehow you knew this was coming."

Tanik lay there, gasping in agony with thoughts of vengeance burning in his brain. As much as he hated to admit it, Feyra was right. He couldn't afford to give up the only advantage they had. Once Darius's own anger cooled enough for him to think clearly, he'd regret his decision. For all Darius knew, Tanik was pulling the plug on Cassandra's pod right now.

Tanik smiled and licked the blood from his teeth, wincing as he did so. He'd bitten straight through his tongue when Darius had popped his knee caps. "You're right," he said.

Feyra favored him with a wan smile and bent to pick him up. "I'm going to take good care of you, darling. Be happy that things turned out the way they did. This way you get your wish. You can stay here and pull Darius's strings from a distance. You won't have to risk your own life in the fighting."

"Y-es," Tanik said, his breath hitching in his throat as he began to shiver. He was going into shock. "B-ut, there is one o-other thing we c-can try."

"Shhh, save your strength, my love," Feyra cooed as she carried him through the doors to their cabin. "There will be time enough to tell me after you have rested."

CHAPTER 13

"He's going to kill her!" Darius screamed.

"Slow down, Darius," Dyara replied. "Who's going to kill who?"

"Tanik is going to kill Cass! He's probably shutting down her pod as we speak!" Darius's chest rose and fell quickly as he began to hyperventilate. Panic gripped him, and his thoughts turned to mud.

Dyara's brow wrinkled. "Cass? I thought she died on the *Harbinger?*" When Darius failed to respond, Dyara grabbed his hands in each of hers and forced him to look her in the eye. "Calm down. Start from the beginning. What's going on?"

He took a deep breath and told her how Tanik had been lying to them since the very beginning, and why.

"But that doesn't make any sense. He led the

Coalition Fleet against the Union for twelve years. You're telling me all that time he was part of some plot to undermine the Revenants and get revenge on them for killing Tanik's... foster people?"

"The Keth," Darius supplied in a cold whisper. "Yes, that's exactly what he's been doing. He obviously found a way to accelerate his plans when he met me."

"But why you? Why not go after the Revenants directly from the start?"

"Because he needed me to defeat the Luminaries first, and I did—starting with Nova, and then Kovar. He would have had me hunt down the others, too, but Kovar already did that. When Tanik found out, he tried to get me to surrender control of the Revenants to him so that he could wipe them out, and when I refused, he tried to kill me."

Dyara glanced over her shoulder to the open door of Darius's recovery room. "So... where is he now?"

"On Ouroboros, with Cassandra."

"Ouroboros?" Dyara echoed. "That's on the other side of the Eye. How did they get all the way over there?"

"He opened a wormhole to get there."

"I thought he said he couldn't open traversable

wormholes?"

Darius took another deep breath and let it out in a brittle whisper, "Another lie."

"Okay... and you said he has Cass. Are you sure? He would have had to rescue her before the *Harbinger* was destroyed."

Darius hesitated. "I don't know. I guess."

"Assuming that's true, why would he save her just so that he could kill her himself?"

"He planned to use her to blackmail me." Darius went on to explain how Tanik was to blame for her getting poisoned in the first place, and how he had supposedly saved a sample of the venom from the Cygnian who had stung her so that only he could cure her.

"Okay..." Dyara said slowly. "But then he still doesn't have what he wants. He wants the Revenants dead, right? And in order to kill them, he needs you to cede control of the fleet to him. That means he still needs her alive."

"You didn't see what I did to him," Darius groaned.

A wary look crept into Dyara's brown eyes. "What did you do to him?" She'd witnessed what he'd done to Kovar.

"I crushed his ribs and snapped both of his legs. He managed to escape before I could do anything else. If he hadn't, I probably would have killed him."

"Did you catch him by surprise?"

Darius shook his head. "He wasn't strong enough to face me. It's a good thing I've been dosing with Sprites."

"That's debatable, but regardless, we need to wait before we do anything."

"Wait? We can't wait! We need to get to the Eye and rescue Cass before it's too late!"

"Don't you think they'll have thought of that? Tanik already proved he can shut that wormhole, so unless you know how to open it again, going there won't help us. We need to wait for Tanik to make contact and reiterate his demands."

"What makes you think he will? He might have killed her already."

"If he has, then he's going to have to find a way to kill you, too," Dyara pointed out. "And by the sounds of it, you're not that easy to kill. Let's not assume the worst yet."

Darius nodded slowly, his eyes welling with tears and swimming out of focus.

Dyara pulled him into a hug and whispered in his ear. "Thank you."

"For what?" he mumbled.

"For not giving Tanik what he wanted."

Darius nodded wordlessly against Dyara's shoulder. If she knew how much he regretted that decision now, she wouldn't be thanking him. Faced with the same choice again, he wasn't sure what he would do. Cassandra's life versus the lives of twenty thousand Revenants. There had to be a way to rescue her without killing anyone.

PART 2 - THE EVIL WITHIN

CHAPTER 14

Trista Leandra stood inside the cockpit of her Archer-class MRV—Mechanized Robotic Vehicle, or mech, for short—striding down a broken street lined with cracked and crumbling skyscrapers in what used to be Atlanta. The rest of her squad trailed behind her single file in three more Archer mechs. Moonlight shivered in flooded potholes with every fifty-ton step, and rubble crunched loudly underfoot.

Trista rolled her shoulders and stretched her arms inside the control sleeves that corresponded to the arms of the mech. Inside the cockpit, a dead weight landed on her shoulder and sharp claws bit through her pilot's suit.

"Where did they all go?" Buddy whispered.

She shot the Togra a frown. At first glance he could pass for a sentient squirrel: round, stubby-legged, covered in short brown fur with white belly fur.

"What?" Buddy asked, blinking his big brown eyes at her.

"You're heavy."

"You're heavier," he replied. He nodded out the cockpit. "Better keep your eyes on the road."

Trista looked away with a grimace. *Where* had *they all gone?* After invading Earth and turning it into a designated hunting ground, the Cygnians had suddenly evacuated the planet and withdrawn their fleet, leaving only token forces on the ground.

As soon as news of that withdrawal reached the Coalition, Trista had gone to its leader, Yuri Mathos, and insisted that he send a task force to investigate. Naturally, he assumed that meant she was volunteering for the mission.

The comms roared to life. "Saber Four here—scanner drones are picking possible hostiles inside the ruins at bearing one three niner, over."

Trista checked her scanners. The bee-like scanner drones had left a red marker on the map at a point behind them and to their right. Trista stopped and turned to get a visual on the location. Her mech's spotlights revealed nothing. The suspected enemy contacts had to be lurking deep inside the ruins. Their mechs were too big to investigate inside the ruined buildings, and getting out to clear them on foot was out of the question.

Trista frowned. Their mission was to make contact with human survivors, not eliminate all the straggling Cygnians they could find, but given the close proximity of these potential enemies, it was possible they were trying to ambush Trista's squad. *The best defense is offense.* "Light 'em up, Four," she said. "Cannons only. Maybe we can spook them out."

"Roger that, Sarge."

The arms of Saber Four's mech flashed with the thumping reports of its fifty cal. Gatling guns. Crumbling concrete walls exploded in a hail of debris that plinked off their mechs' armor. Shifting clouds of gray dust drifted out, bright and shining in the beams of their spotlights. Gatling guns were ancient weapons, but ancient was easier to build and maintain, which made them perfect for the resource-strapped Coalition.

After a few seconds of sustained fire, Trista thought she saw something—shadows creeping through the clouds of gunsmoke and dust. "Hold fire!" she called over the comms. "I thought I saw something."

Four belatedly stopped firing. "You sure 'bout that, Sarge? I've got nothing on thermal or motion sensors."

Trista swept her mech first one way, then the other, checking the street. Whatever she'd seen it was gone now.

"Never mind. It's gone now. Probably just wind stirring the dust."

"Permission to resume fire?"

"Granted."

Four went back to firing into the ruins. Just as he did so, a shower of sparks leapt up from the back of his mech.

"What the fek...?" he trailed off.

Trista swept her spotlights over him and caught a glimpse of a gunmetal gray mass clinging to his back. "Hang on, you've got one on you!" she said, already running toward him.

"Get it off!" Four danced on the spot, trying to reach his back with his mech's arms, a dire parody of a human trying to scratch his own back.

As Trista ran, another wave of sparks leapt off Four's armor, and this time he screamed. A moment later, his mech stopped moving.

"Four!"

Trista reached his mech and grabbed the shadowy mound off his back in a giant metal fist. The mech's haptic feedback system kicked against her palm as the Cygnian struggled to free itself.

Four arms with wicked gray claws swiped the air mere inches from the reinforced glass of her cockpit.

Buddy whimpered beside her ear, his claws biting deeper into her shoulder as he cowered.

Trista squeezed as hard as she could, and felt bones crunching. A blood-curdling scream burst from the Cygnian's lips along with a gleaming black gout of blood, and then the monster went limp and silent. Trista threw it aside and passed her spotlights over Saber Four's mech to check his status. His cockpit had been ripped open from behind, the reinforced armor of his mech peeled open in curling sheets. The inside of his cockpit was sprayed and dripping with blood, and he was hanging halfway out of his mech in an impossible limbo that implied a broken spine.

"Four! Come in, over." Trista checked her sensors while she waited for a response. No life signs. "Fek it!" Trista roared.

"Sarge! We've got incoming," Three said.

The rest of Saber squad whirled around, their cannons thumping indiscriminately into the night before she could even respond. Trista spun away from Four to see more chameleon-skinned Cygnians streaking wraith-like from the broken windows of ruined buildings, converging from all sides. Trista's sensors lit up with no less than seven contacts.

Targeting the nearest one, she opened fire. Fity cal. rounds ripped her target open with an explosion of black blood and glistening guts. Just as she targeted the next one, she heard and felt a heavy *thud* as something landed on her back, followed by the teeth-gritting *screech* of alien claws cleaving through her armor.

CHAPTER 15

Darius stared into the shimmering portal, blinking in shock as a bipedal alien stepped through. The alien's features were bony, but its frame and musculature were distinctly feminine. Her translucent white skin sparkled and her pale blue eyes danced with bright specks of light. A high brow rose over eyebrow-less eyes to an equally hairless scalp. Darius recognized her as one of the same aliens he'd seen standing behind Cassandra in his vision of her on Ouroboros.

"Hey!" Darius said as the alien cleared the portal. It vanished behind her.

When the alien didn't react to the sound of his voice, he walked in front of her to force a confrontation, but she passed straight through him as if he were a ghost.

Staring in horror and slowly shaking his head,

Darius watching the alien go walking down long aisles of mag-locked rectangular crates.

Darius recognized where they were. They were inside the *Deliverance's* munitions storage room. All kinds and classes of missiles and ammo were stored in here in shock-proof armored crates.

As he watched, she stopped beside a particular crate. Reaching into her loose-fitting brown tunic, she produced a luminous knife and used it to slice the lid of the crate open. Raising her free hand toward the crate, she sent the lid drifting away, and a familiar-looking missile drifted out. It was one of the planet-busting ZPFs. Using her knife to open a panel on the missile, the alien spent a moment fiddling with wires inside of it, and then left it there, unsecured and floating inside the munitions room.

Just then, another portal appeared, shimmering in the air where the first had been. Peering through that portal, Darius glimpsed a familiar man standing on the other side, leaning on a pair of rough-hewn wooden crutches. *Tanik.*

Darius ran toward the portal, but his legs refused to obey. It was as if they were stuck in tar. He watched helplessly as the alien disappeared through the portal. Once again it vanished in her wake, leaving Darius alone with what was almost certainly a ticking bomb.

He tried walking over to the weapon. This time his legs responded, and he made it there in a matter of seconds. He didn't know much about how ZPF warheads worked, but it was obvious that some of the wires had been crossed, and the intention behind that was obvious enough. *Tanik can't kill me face to face, so now he's trying to assassinate me with a bomb.*

Darius tried sending a message to the bridge via his extra-sensory chip, but his chip was not responding. His heart thudding in his chest, Darius studied the inside of the missile, trying to figure out how to defuse the warhead. He reached in with a shaking hand....

Only to be hit by a searing blast of heat that washed him into a blinding sea of agony.

Darius awoke with a start, blinking his eyes rapidly to clear away the bleary film of sleep. His quarters snapped into gloomy, starlit focus.

"Lights, twenty percent," Darius said, and a pale golden light filled the room. A wall of holo panels opposite the wall where he'd anchored his sleeping bag conveyed the star-studded darkness of the Hagrol System.

It was just a dream.... or a vision? Darius used his

ESC to activate his quarter's comm system and contact the bridge.

"Lieutenant Commander Rowles here, what can I do for you, Admiral Drake?"

Darius considered that. "Get a squad of Marines to sweep and guard each and every store of munitions on this ship."

"Yes, sir... may I ask the reason for your orders?"

"It would take too long to explain," Darius said. "Just get it done, Commander."

"Yes, sir."

Darius's mind raced, trying to come up with additional countermeasures. How could he defend against an enemy that could appear anywhere, with no warning? If the goal was to assassinate Darius and take over his fleet, then why bother to sabotage a ZPF missile? Why not simply plant a lesser explosive device in Darius's room while he was sleeping? *Maybe the Keth don't have any explosives of their own.*

Darius ran through a list of possible assassination attempts in his head, and the ways to defeat them. They could steal a bomb or other explosive device, as he'd seen in his vision. The counter to that was to make sure that all of their munitions were secured and guarded at all times.

But keeping track of everything from grenades to missiles was not a realistic solution. It would be safer and easier to simply remove himself from the *Deliverance.* He could hide aboard a smaller vessel with no explosives on board. As an added benefit Tanik wouldn't know where to find him, at least not immediately. As an added precaution, Darius would assign a few Revenants to his ship to watch over him while he slept.

Unzipping himself from his sleeping bag, Darius went to pack a bag of supplies from the storage lockers in his room. Soon after he finished packing, the speakers in his room crackled to life.

"Admiral, Commander Rowles here. One of the squads just reported an intruder in the aft munitions bay. They managed to disarm her, and take her into custody."

Darius breathed out a sigh. "Good work, Commander. Tell them I'll be right down to interrogate her."

"Yes, sir. There's one more thing. She appears to be a Keth, sir, and she came aboard via a wormhole."

"I already know that."

"You know, sir?"

"I had a vision," Darius explained.

"I see. Permission to make an observation,

sir?"

"Granted."

"If the Keth are once again capable of transporting themselves via wormholes, we could be in a lot of danger."

"I was just thinking about that myself," Darius replied. "but if they can do that, why haven't they sent saboteurs aboard our other ships? Their goal is to kill the Revenants. The surest way to do that would be to sabotage all of our ships at once."

"Perhaps only a few of them are strong enough to open wormholes," Commander Rowles replied.

"Or just one," Darius mused.

"Such as?"

"Tanik Gurhain."

"Gurhain? Isn't he..."

"A Revenant?" Darius supplied. "No, he's with them. It's a long story, Commander. I'll tell you later. Right now, we need to get as much information as we can from our uninvited guest before the Keth send someone else. If we're lucky, they haven't realized yet that her mission failed. I'm on my way to the aft munitions bay. Tell the Marines to watch that Keth like their lives depend on it."

"Yes, sir."

CHAPTER 16

"Get him off!" Trista screamed.

"Hang on, Sarge!" Saber Two replied.

Trista heard another shriek of claws raking on her mech's armor, she glanced behind her to see dark slashes peeking between strips of gray metal. She was out of time.

"Hang on, Buddy," she said, just before she threw her mech backward. It fell over with a ground-shaking *boom*. After waiting for half a second, Trista struggled to right her mech, using its arms to push off the ground.

The rest of her squad was still firing their cannons into the night. "They're scattering, Sarge!" Two said.

"Good," Trista replied. She spun around to check the status of the Cygnian that had been clinging to her back. It was lying there in a dull gray heap, unmoving. Despite that, her sensors indicated that it was still alive and breathing. She'd knocked it unconscious by landing on top of it.

Trista armed her 50 cal. cannons and aimed them both at the alien monster. But she hesitated. If they could take this Cygnian back to the fleet and interrogate it, they might be able to find out why the Cygnians were withdrawing from Earth.

Heavy footsteps boomed, and a pair of mechs came into view. "Want me to do the honors, Sarge?" Saber Two asked.

"No," Trista replied. "We're taking this one as a hostage."

"A hostage? What for?"

Trista shrugged inside her mech, and her control sleeves conveyed the movement to the machine. "See what it knows about the Cygnians' recent withdrawal. Pick it up, Two, and try not to kill it. If it wakes up, hit it with stun bolts."

"Roger..." Two went stomping out and picked up the monster with giant metal hands.

"Let's move out," Trista said.

"What about looking for survivors?" Three asked.

"Keep looking on our way back to the transport," Trista replied. "The mission priorities have changed."

"Yes, Ma'am."

* * *

"What if he lies to us?" Buddy asked, as he peered through the window into the interrogation room.

"He can't," Yuri Mathos growled. "Neural probes never fail."

Trista nodded along with that, watching as medics prepared various syringes for the Ghoul they'd captured. The ghoul was heavily sedated and strapped to an examination table, but the doctors weren't taking any chances. One of the syringes they were preparing contained an additional sedative, while the other contained a colony of nanites. The nanites were similar to those used to inject the self-assembling extra-sensory chips (ESCs) that acted as neural interfaces for computer systems and networks, except that these would travel to the host's brain and go digging around for information.

One of the doctors in the interrogation room turned to the window and gave a thumbs-up gesture.

Yuri reached for the intercom beside the observation window with one black-furred hand. "Proceed," he said.

Wasting no time, one of the medics injected the syringes one after another. After that, both medics left the room and came into the observation room. One of them strapped in at a nearby control station to make contact with the nanites they'd injected. Trista walked over with Yuri Mathos to take a look.

"Well?" Yuri asked.

"We're inside the host's brain," the medic said. "What would you like to ask first?"

"Ask him—"

"Her," the medic corrected.

Yuri glared at the man with sharp blue eyes. "Ask *her,* why the Cygnians retreated from Earth."

"Yes, sir. One moment..." The medic typed out the necessary parameters to direct that question to the Cygnian's brain. The reply came back a moment later—written in Cygnian.

"The fleet has withdrawn to join the defense of our worlds."

"The defense of...?" Trista trailed off shaking her head.

"Defense from what?" Buddy chimed in. "What do they have to fear?"

"Quiet," Yuri hissed. "Ask what they are defending themselves from."

The medic input that query into the computer next. A moment later the reply appeared on his screen.

Trista read it before he could. "From the Revenants. They're real? I thought that's just something people believe in to make themselves feel better about the children who don't come back from the Crucible."

Yuri stroked the tuft of white fur on his chin. "Perhaps they are mistaken about the identity of their attackers. Or perhaps not. Whatever the case, any enemy of the Cygnians is a friend of ours. This is very good news. I suggest you get some rest while you can, Sergeant. We're headed for Cygnus Prime in the morning."

Trista nodded slowly. "Yes, sir."

CHAPTER 17

Darius stood in the brig with their unconscious prisoner and the four Revenant Marines who had captured her. "Are you certain she's a Keth?" Darius asked.

"Yes, sir," the Marine Corporal replied.

Darius scowled as he studied her face. The Marines had strapped her into an acceleration harness in one of the brig's cells. She was bony and thin with shimmering white skin, an elongated skull, and three-fingered hands.

"What should we do with her?" the corporal asked.

The Keth and Tanik had Darius's daughter, but now he had one of theirs. There might be a way to make some kind of a trade. Then again, even if he could, as long as they could teleport themselves in and out of secure areas without warning, no one

— 153 —

would be safe. Darius needed to learn how they did that, and if there was some way to defend against the ability.

"We need to interrogate her," Darius said.

"You want us to escort her to Med Bay for you, sir?"

Darius waved a hand in the Marine's direction. "No need for that, Corporal. I can handle the interrogation from here."

"Yes, sir."

Darius reached out for the Keth prisoner's mind. She was unconscious, which made it impossible for him to assume control of her. Rather than request a stimulant to wake her up, Darius used the ZPF to clear away the effects of the stun blasts she'd sustained. She woke with a start, ice-blue eyes flashing wide open. Darius zipped into her mind and brushed past her defenses before she could even figure out where she was. Rifling roughly through her memories, he saw her together with Tanik—in a *romantic* context. Her name was... *Feyra*. This wasn't just any Keth. She was Tanik's partner. Darius saw more memories flashing before his mind's eye, Feyra's and Tanik's childhood growing up on Ouroboros in a violent, ruthless alien culture. He searched for more recent memories and saw the Keth returning to

Ouroboros to rebuild. He saw how few of them were left, and how in spite of that, their barbaric training practices continued—children killing each other in coming of age duels to see who was worthy of adulthood. Darius inwardly cringed at the thought. Moving on, he probed for any memories relating to his daughter, Cassandra.

That was when he saw Feyra and Tanik standing around Cassandra's cryo pod. Tanik was determined to kill her, but Feyra argued for Tanik to spare her life. She convinced him to keep Cass alive so that they could use her to blackmail him again later on. She was certain that he'd give up the Revenants in order to save her.

Darius felt anger churning inside of him like a raging inferno, making it hard to think straight. He forced himself to focus, to find the information he needed. Delving deeper into Feyra's mind, he searched for anything related to wormholes, the ability itself, and ways to protect against it.

After just a few moments, he had what he needed. He withdrew from Feyra's mind and returned to his senses with a physical jolt.

"I have what I need, Corporal. Guard this prisoner with your lives."

"Yes, sir..." the corporal trailed off, obviously curious about whatever Darius had learned.

Darius glanced at the Keth. She was watching him with her dazzling, blue-white eyes.

"Tanik will kill you for this," she said, speaking in a halting version of Primary.

Darius favored her with a grim smile. "Not if I kill him first."

Darius used his extra-sensory chip to contact Dyara, who he'd summarily promoted and left in charge as his second-in-command of the *Deliverance* and the fleet itself.

"Darius?" she asked.

"Plot a jump to the Eye and coordinate it with the rest of the fleet. Once you've plotted the jump and warmed up the Alckam drive, wait for me to give the order for us to jump."

"The Eye? Why are we going there?"

"I'll explain when I arrive on deck. Just trust me. We need to go there *now*, or we're all going to die."

"Okay."

Darius thought about what he'd learned from Feyra on his way up to the bridge. In order to open a wormhole all he had to do was visualize the person or thing he wanted to reach, and then imagine opening a physical portal in order to get there. The limiting factor was having enough raw power to do such a thing, and very few Revenants did—Feyra couldn't. He'd learned that much from searching her mind. She'd needed Tanik's help to open the wormhole she'd used to board his ship. The defense against wormholes was equally simple. Two wormholes couldn't exist in close proximity to each other, so the creation of one would block the creation of another within a radius of at least a few hundred thousand kilometers. That would be enough to protect a planet or a fleet, or both, but creating a stable wormhole that could sustain itself without a constant effort from him was not so simple. The Eye of Thanatos was one such portal, but Tanik had almost certainly shut it to keep the Revenants out after they'd left Keth space. Which was why Darius was taking the fleet there now. The Eye would be as good a place as any to practice using the ZPF to create wormholes. Fortunately, warp bubbles were a secondary level of protection. It wasn't realistic to travel at warp speeds indefinitely, but at least they'd be safe from incursions by Tanik and his Keth brethren over the course of the month it was going to take them to reach the Eye. A *month.* Darius grimaced, and his brisk stride faltered at the thought of waiting that long to organize a rescue for his daughter. Could she afford to wait for a whole month? There had to be a better way. Some way to get to her sooner.

He considered opening a portal to Ouroboros now, but how many Keth would he have to fight through on the other side in order to reach her? He couldn't hope to defeat them all by himself, and if he brought an army with him, they'd probably just spook the Keth into fleeing.

Darius weighed his options. Tanik didn't know that he'd learned how to open wormholes from Feyra, so that gave Darius the advantage of surprise. If he could figure out how to create a wormhole to reach Ouroboros, and sustain it while his soldiers executed an attack on the Keth, he would be simultaneously protecting his fleet and bottling up the Keth at the same time. At the very least he'd be forcing them to escape by conventional means, aboard whatever starships they had at their disposal.

Yes... Darius nodded to himself. That would be the fastest way to get Cassandra back. The question was, could he master the necessary skills in time to save her?

Darius shut his eyes and took a deep breath. Reaching out with his awareness, beyond his fleet, beyond the Hagrol System and neighboring stars... he cast his mind far beyond that, imagining he could see the entire galaxy in his mind's eye. With that godlike view, he fixed Cassandra's face in his mind's eye and tried to find the familiar tone and texture of her presence....

It didn't work—either because she was still in cryo, or because she was dead. Darius chose to believe the former. Reaching out once more, he tried to find Tanik this time. His presence was faint but detectable. Darius honed in on it, racing past countless stars and their planets until he saw a familiar green and gray world pocked with blue lakes and rivers that meandered across the surface like the veins in the whites of an eye. Darius cast himself down, racing past clouds in the atmosphere of the planet, until he was standing on a grassy green field, staring into a dark, brooding forest not far from Tanik's location.

There he tried to follow the vague ideas he'd plucked from Feyra's mind and imagined himself peeling back the fabric of space-time to physically reach the location where he'd mentally pictured himself.

Hearing a gentle humming noise, Darius risked cracking his eyes to slits to see the result.

A shimmering portal had appeared there in the middle of the corridor with a grassy green field and a brooding forest on the other side.

Darius couldn't believe it. His excitement and anticipation soared, interrupting his concentration, and the portal vanished. He felt tired and energized at the same time. Opening a portal was not easy, but at least it was possible, and now that he knew what to do, he could do it again.

Darius used his ESC to comm the bridge once more. "Dyara," he said. "There's been a change of plans."

"I'm listening," Dyara replied.

"Have the fleet move into a tight formation with the *Deliverance*. Pack our ships in as close as possible. Meanwhile, I need you to mobilize every able-bodied soldier on the *Deliverance* and have them all join me in the aft hangar. That includes you."

"Packing our fleet together would leave us vulnerable to another attack," Dyara pointed out. "If the Keth or Tanik manage to board one of our ships and steal a ZPF bomb, they could take out the entire fleet in the same blast," Dyara said.

"They'll be too busy defending themselves to worry about attacking us," Darius replied. "And I know how to defend us from their wormhole-attacks now. Gather the fleet around us and meet me in the aft hangar."

"How can you defend us?"

Darius took a moment to explain what he'd learned from Feyra, how to create wormholes, and how to defend against them.

"Jumping to warp prevents them from using wormholes to reach us? Then why don't we just do that?"

"Because we can't stay in warp forever," Darius explained. "It'll be safer to kill Tanik and the Keth."

"If we can, you mean," Dyara replied.

"We can. We outnumber them. Meet me in the aft hangar bay, and I'll explain everything."

"All right..."

Darius shut down the connection and turned and ran for the aft hangar bay. He needed to open another portal *soon*, before Tanik tried to open one of his own to get Feyra back.

CHAPTER 18

"It's that easy to open wormholes?" Dyara asked, while gazing into the shimmering portal that Darius had summoned.

"It is for me," Darius replied, and turned from her to watch as soldiers streamed into the hangar by the hundreds. Before long several thousand were gathered around them, all staring at Darius's wormhole with wary awe.

He turned in a circle to address everyone in the hangar. Using his ESC to access the ship's intercom system, he configured it to amplify his voice through overhead speakers. "As you may know, we've recently encountered your old enemy. It seems that the Keth manipulated us into starting a war with the Cygnians in the hopes of weakening us. They used an undercover agent by the name of Tanik Gurhain."

Shock and outrage rippled through the group as they processed that news. Many of these Revenants had met Tanik.

"Tanik hid his true intentions from us, just as he hid his true nature. Not long after he learned that I killed the last Luminary, he revealed to me that *he* is another one, and he tried to kill me so that he would be free to take control of the Revenants himself, *and* lead you all to your deaths! I defeated him and chased him back through a wormhole to Ouroboros."

Darius went on, "Tanik manipulated us into a war with the Cygnians in order to destabilize the Union. He and his Keth allies hoped that war with the Cygnians and with each other would get most of us killed without them ever having to fight us themselves.

"As I speak, Tanik and the Keth are on the other side of this portal, laughing at us as they rebuild their home! They think that their plan has worked, but I'm living proof that it has failed. They never expected any of us to be able to open a wormhole back to their corner of the galaxy. Now that we have, we have an opportunity to launch a surprise attack and finish what the Augur started all those years ago. It's time to wipe out what's left of the Keth. Only then will we be free to establish a lasting peace throughout the Union."

A rumble of disagreement spread through the crowd, and a nearby Revenant raised his voice to express his objections: "We followed you against the Cygnians because we disagreed with the Augur's war against the Keth, and now you want us to take up that same cause again?"

Darius shook his head. "Don't think about the Augur who enslaved you to fight in a war that you never really understood. Think about all of your friends and relatives who died fighting the Keth! Think about the Keth agent who we recently captured aboard this ship, who was trying to sabotage our munitions store and kill us all. Don't fight for me, or for the Augur's enigmatic reasons, fight for your own survival. The Keth won't stop plotting against us until all of us are dead. It's kill or be killed, and right now we have the element of surprise. That won't last forever. As long as I'm holding this portal open, Tanik won't be able to open a wormhole to help the Keth escape."

"How do you know that?"

Darius explained what he'd learned from interrogating the Keth agent they'd captured, and silence rang in the wake of those reassurances.

"They could still escape aboard their starships," Dyara said from beside him.

Before Darius could come up with a reply for that, someone else answered: "They don't have any. Until we came along and diluted their power base, they used to travel between their worlds via portals just like this one. They had no need to build interstellar vehicles, and their empire was never very large to begin with."

That news took Darius by surprise, but it was a welcome surprise. A small smile graced his lips and he nodded. "There you have it," he said. "So it seems we are poised to wipe out the Keth once and for all. Let's make it happen."

Heads began bobbing around the hangar. It was obvious that he'd convinced these soldiers to fight for him. He could have forced them all to follow him into battle, but keeping the portal open to Ouroboros was hard enough without having to expend additional energy to subdue the wills of several thousand soldiers at the same time.

Darius drew his sword with a metallic shriek and held it high. Sucking in a quick breath, he let it out in a roar: "Death to the Keth!"

"Death to the Keth!" the assembled Revenants thundered.

"Death to the Keth!" Darius said again, pumping his sword in the air like a fist.

The Revenants took up that cry once more, and

then Darius turned and led the charge through the wormhole.

CHAPTER 19

It was disconcerting to go from standing in the hangar one minute, to a rippling green field the next. A gust of wind blew Darius's overgrown hair into his eyes and swayed the umbrella-shaped tops of nearby trees. A rumble of thunder sounded, and fat rain drops began pelting down.

Booted feet came thudding out of the portal behind him in a never-ending stampede. Darius turned to watch his army assemble in the field. Before long people were forced to elbow each other out of the way as they crowded through, and Darius had to back up to make room for all of them. Dyara appeared, picking her way through the crowd to reach his side.

In a matter of minutes, all two thousand Revenants from the *Deliverance* had assembled on the field, and they were all looking to him for orders. Their gazes were fraught with suspicion and resentment. Darius wasn't the leader they would have chosen. He wasn't the most experienced in battle, or even the most competent when it came to tactics or strategy, but sticking close to him was the only chance any of them had to protect themselves from falling under the sway of other luminaries—luminaries like Tanik, who would like nothing more than to get them all killed.

"By now the Keth must have sensed us coming," Dyara said, glancing behind them to the shadowy forest.

"Maybe," Darius agreed. "Even if they have, it's too late to stop us now." Raindrops seeped into his jumpsuit, chilling him despite the warm air. Another peal of thunder boomed. Darius waited for it to die down before addressing his army. Even so, he had to raise his voice to be heard over the rain. "If you're standing directly beside the portal, you get to stay here and guard it. Everyone else, summon your shields and follow me!" Darius pumped his sword in the air and cried, "Death to the Keth!"

A scattered echo of that cry reached his ears, taken up by a few of the Revenants, as he turned and ran for the tree line. Dyara kept pace beside him.

"Can you sense Cassandra from here?" she asked. They entered the forest and what little light was filtering through the storm clouds disappeared, filtered out by the dense canopy above.

Darius reached out with his awareness and immediately found a group of about thirty alien presences and one human further up ahead. The human was Tanik, if the familiar darkness of his presence and thoughts was anything to go by. But Darius couldn't sense Cassandra anywhere. "No, I can't," he said as he leapt over a fallen log and then ducked under a low-hanging branch. "It's probably because she's in cryo."

Dyara nodded but said nothing. She didn't need to say it. Cryo could be the reason they couldn't sense her. Or else it was because she was already dead.

"When we find Tanik, we'll find her," Darius said, more to reassure himself than Dyara.

Footsteps thudded along behind them in a steady rumble that competed with the thunder. Tree trunks blurred past them as they ran. Within just a few minutes, another grassy clearing came peeking through the trees—along with something else, a log cabin.

Darius could sense and vaguely see, aliens gathered together in the field up ahead. The Keth weren't running. They'd decided to stand and fight.

That gave Darius pause, but it was too late to stop and come up with some cunning strategy now. He barreled out of the forest and into the clearing with Dyara. Revenants poured out of the forest on all sides, encircling the huddled group of ghostly-white aliens in the center of the field. Tanik was nowhere to be seen, but Darius could sense him. He gripped his sword in a tight fist and started toward the Keth. Dyara kept pace beside him as he went. Meanwhile, the Revenant army was busy circling around through the trees to cut off any possible retreat.

Darius stopped walking once he came within a dozen meters of the Keth. "Where is Tanik?" he asked.

The group of aliens parted, revealing a knot of huddled children in the center of their circle, along with something else—a glass and metal cylinder gleaming with raindrops. Cassandra's cryo pod. Tanik Gurhain stood beside it, leaning heavily on a pair of wooden crutches.

Darius's heart leapt into his throat at the sight of the cryo pod. He reached for it with his mind, trying to carry Cassandra safely out of the Keth's midst, but they resisted him, collectively holding her in place.

A *boom* of thunder split the air, and a jagged fork of lightning flashed down between the trees not far from the clearing.

"Give me my daughter, Tanik!" Darius demanded.

Tanik dropped his crutches and came *floating* out to greet him, his feet hovering a full foot above the ground. Both of his legs were encased in crude-looking splints.

"Why would I do that?" Tanik replied. "As soon as you have what you want, you'll kill us. Besides, you have someone that we want, too. Return the Keth woman you captured, and we will return your daughter to you. That's a fair trade."

Darius snorted. "You're outnumbered and surrounded. We could simply kill you all and take Cassandra back by force."

"Not before we could kill her," Tanik replied, and gestured to the aliens gathered behind him. The crowd of Keth parted just a little more to reveal an adult Keth holding a glowing sword poised above Cassandra's cryo pod, ready to plunge it through the fragile glass cover and into her chest.

A rising murmur sounded from the soldiers gathered behind Darius. One of them shouted out, "Darius doesn't speak for all of us! Let's just kill them all before it's too late! Death to the Keth!"

"Death to the Keth!" the others shouted. Before their collective voices even died away, Revenants came pouring into the clearing on all sides. Their footsteps made the ground tremble, while their glowing swords and shields peeled back the gloomy twilight of the storm.

Tanik gave a twisted smile and called out. "Amara! Kill the girl if even one of them engages us in combat!"

"No!" Darius shouted, and simultaneously reached out to subdue the minds and wills of every single soldier he'd brought with him. He forced them all to freeze right where they were. Suddenly the thunder of footfalls ceased, and all was quiet but for the actual thunder, and the rain slanting down in a steady roar. Darius listened to raindrops hissing as they hit his shielded sword and those of the soldiers in the field.

"Well?" Tanik demanded. "Are you ready to talk terms?"

"Darius..." Dyara whispered in a warning tone.

He hadn't bothered to suppress her will, since she hadn't joined the charge against the Keth. He shot her a dark look and shook his head. "Not now, Dya." Turning back to the fore, he started toward Tanik, covering some of the distance between them to make it easier to talk over the rain.

"I have your wife," Darius said. "If you kill Cassandra, I'll kill her."

"My *wife?*" Tanik laughed, and a ripple of alien warbling rumbled through the Keth. "She's hardly that, Darius. And not irreplaceable. My people aren't nearly as sentimental as yours. Why do you think we sent her in the first place? Because we could afford to lose her."

Darius peered at Tanik through heavy curtains of rain. The field was turning to mud and puddles, washing away under the assault. He struggled to decide if Tanik was bluffing. He remembered what he'd seen in Feyra's mind. She and Tanik had grown up together, and as adults they'd certainly become more than friends, but there was no way for him to know just how deep their bond was without going back to take another look inside her head. He reached out for a glimpse of Tanik's thoughts, but the man was shielding them too effectively.

"You're bluffing," Darius said.

"No, I'm not, but we're not entirely without

sentiment," Tanik replied. "We're willing to agree to a trade: your daughter for Feyra, and the guarantee that we will be allowed to leave Ouroboros in peace."

Darius shook his head. "I don't think so."

"Then we're at an impasse. You can kill us all here and now, but you'll lose Cassandra in the process. You have to decide what's more important to you. This victory, or her life."

Darius ground his teeth together. "If I let you go, you'll only try to kill us again later."

Tanik shrugged, and his smile grew. "Try? Yes. Succeed? That's up to you. At least now you know how to prevent us from transporting ourselves directly onto your fleet. You also know that our numbers are few and that we have no advanced technology to use against you. It's thirty of us against twenty thousand of you. The odds are in your favor, and you've already proven that you can defeat me all by yourself. I'm the best that my side has to offer, so what do you have to fear?"

Darius felt like he was being manipulated again. Tanik was too smug, too confident. He had something in mind, some yet-to-be-revealed new plan or avenue of attack that was sure to take Darius by surprise.

He took a stab at what that plan might be. "The

only way I can protect everyone is to keep them close and to keep a wormhole open somewhere nearby, indefinitely. I'll grow tired and weak eventually. When I do, you'll come and assassinate me, and then you'll kill everyone else."

An ominous rumble of thunder rolled overhead to punctuate Darius's concerns.

"I'm feeling magnanimous, so I'll give you a tip: opening a wormhole into a warp bubble is impossible."

"I already knew that," Darius replied.

"Then you know that you can rest while you're traveling between the stars. If you don't stop in any one place for too long, you should be able to protect your fleet without any difficulty at all." Tanik's yellow-green eyes glittered in the light of his ZPF shield. "Now, what do you say? Do we have a deal?"

"I want to see Cassandra, alive and well. You said you have the antivenin. Wake her up and administer it. I'm not agreeing to anything until I see that you've held up your end of the deal."

"I had a feeling you might say that." Tanik reached into the dark cloak he wore and produced a syringe full of a clear fluid. Turning on the spot, he floated back into the huddled group of Keth and stopped beside Cassandra's cryo pod.

Darius wanted desperately to be there by her side when she woke up, but he couldn't risk allowing himself to be surrounded by the enemy. Darius ground his teeth and repeatedly curled his free hand into a fist while he waited. After just a few seconds, the lid of Cassandra's pod swung open, and Tanik reached in with the syringe to administer the antivenin.

"Bring her to me!" Darius demanded, screaming to be heard over the pouring rain. But the rain was lighter now. The storm was passing.

Tanik bent over Cassandra's pod and lifted her out. Turning on the spot, he floated back to Darius with Cassandra draped over his arms. Darius's heart fluttered at the sight of her, and his palms began to sweat. He held his breath, waiting to see her eyelids flutter open...

But nothing happened.

"What's wrong?" Darius demanded.

Tanik's smug demeanor vanished. He laid Cassandra in the grass at his feet and nodded to Darius. "Her heart has stopped. You need to administer CPR."

Darius stared in shock, watching as raindrops fell and ran down Cassandra's pale cheeks, soaking through her clothes and hair.

"Quickly!" Tanik urged.

CHAPTER 20

Darius dropped his sword and rushed forward to administer CPR on Cassandra. He almost forgot to watch his back in the process, but when Tanik began crowding suspiciously close, he gave the man a telekinetic shove and sent him flying away.

"If she dies, then so will all of you!" Darius shouted between chest compressions.

"She won't die," Tanik assured as he floated back over, keeping a respectful distance this time.

Darius opened Cassandra's mouth and held her nose shut. Her skin was ice cold. He breathed hard into her lungs. Her chest rose, but nothing else happened, so he went back to chest compressions. After performing an indeterminate number of them, he tried the kiss of life for the second time.

This time she stirred. A second later, her eyes flew open, and she saw him. She screamed with fright, and her eyes darted around with alarm. "Where..."

He crushed her into a fierce hug. "You're alive!"

"I was dead?" Cassandra pushed him away. She glanced around at the Revenant army standing frozen in the field, and started to get up for a better look.

"Let me help you," Darius said, and yanked her to her feet by one arm.

Cassandra's rose petal lips were turned down in a frown, her bright blue eyes pinched with concern. "What... what's going on?" She glanced behind her to see Tanik and the Keth standing there. "Tanik?" She started toward him, but Darius grabbed her arm to stop her, his own arm whirring with a mechanical noise as he did so.

She rounded on him and glared at his hand. "Ouch! That hurts!"

"Sorry." He'd obviously grabbed her too hard in his hurry to keep her away from Tanik. "I had an accident and lost my arm," he explained, flexing his hand with another mechanical noise. "I'm still getting used to the replacement." He looked up and studied her face. "Is it really you?"

Cassandra nodded slowly, uncertainly. "Is it really *you*?" she countered.

Darius's brow furrowed. "Don't you recognize me?"

"No." She began backing away from him.

A painful lump rose in Darius's throat, followed by a brief, piercing sense of deja vu. He'd been here before, said and done all of this before... but when?

His dream. Right before his confrontation with Tanik.

"It's me," Darius insisted, and deja vu struck him again.

Cassandra kept backing away until she came within Tanik's reach. He reached out and placed a hand on each of her shoulders in an almost paternal way. "Your turn, Darius."

Cassandra glanced up at Tanik with wide eyes. "What..."

"Cass! Get away from him!" Darius shouted.

But it was too late. Tanik produced a glowing dagger from his robes and held it to Cassandra's throat.

"Dad..." Cassandra trailed off in alarm. She peered down her nose at the dagger, not daring to move her head for a better look.

"Don't move," Darius said. "You'll be free in a

— 179 —

minute."

"What's going on!? What are all of those soldiers doing here?"

"It's okay, Cass," Dyara said, passing into view as she crossed the odd half a dozen paces between Darius and Tanik. She had her hands raised to show she was unarmed, but Tanik wasn't satisfied by that. He pulled Cassandra back a step and inched the dagger closer to her throat.

"Not another step," he warned.

The Keth shuffled their feet restlessly, their eyes flicking around the clearing to the encircling Revenants. All of them were frozen on the spot, staring dead ahead with glazed and sightless eyes, like a living terracotta army.

"Well?" Tanik prompted. "I'm waiting. Where's Feyra?"

Darius smirked. "I thought you didn't care about her?"

Tanik shrugged. "A trade is a trade. If you don't hold up your end of it, then neither will I. Consider Feyra's safe return a show of good faith. After that, we can discuss how you're going to let us all leave here unharmed."

"Dyara," Darius said.

She turned to him with eyebrows raised.

"Go back through the portal and get Feyra.

Bring as many guards as you think you need."

Dyara nodded slowly and walked by him, heading back the way they'd come. He could feel the indecision radiating from her thoughts. She didn't approve of this trade, but she also couldn't bring herself to give up Cassandra for dead. She'd grown too close to Cass.

"Hurry!" Darius called after her.

Dyara broke into a run and disappeared between the trees, leaving Darius alone to face Tanik and the Keth with his army of mindless soldiers.

Tanik smirked infuriatingly. He knew he'd won. Filled with nervous energy, Darius began pacing back and forth in front of Tanik. He summoned his sword back to his hand from where he'd dropped it in the field.

Tanik arched an eyebrow at that. "Don't get any stupid ideas."

Darius aimed the glowing tip of the blade at him. "Shut up."

Tanik's grin spread, but the scars running across his face twisted it into a sneer.

"Dad..." Cassandra gulped. "What happened? Why are we fighting Tanik? He saved my life."

Darius nodded agreeably. "And now he's threatening it. Ironic, isn't it? He saved my life, too."

"And then you broke my legs," Tanik said. "Some gratitude."

"Did I tell you to talk?" Darius demanded.

Tanik's eyes glittered darkly. "You seem to have forgotten that I'm holding a blade to your daughter's throat."

Darius ignored him and stopped pacing to look Cassandra in the eye. "He was with the Keth from the start. He lured you away from the fleet to negotiate with the Cygnians so that you would get poisoned. Then he took a sample of the venom from the Cygnian that stung you so that only he could bring you out of cryo safely."

"But why would he do that?"

"To get leverage over me, which he's now using to save himself and the Keth survivors."

"I don't get it," Cassandra said.

Darius shook his head. "Don't worry about it." He went back to pacing. "Right now let's just focus on getting you out of this alive."

"Good thinking," Tanik put in. "But if I may, I believe I can clarify some of your daughter's confusion—you see, Cassandra, when your people, your friends, your neighbors, and their children are all slaughtered in front of your eyes and hunted to the brink of extinction with utterly no provocation, it makes you realize that there are only two kinds of people in war: the winners, and the corpses."

"*Your* people? The Keth are your people?" Cassandra asked. "You're a human!"

"They adopted him," Darius explained. "He was orphaned during the Revenants' war."

Cassandra said nothing to that, and a heavy silence fell. The air grew thick with it until Darius could hardly breath. He struggled to control his breathing as he paced back and forth. Fatigue was creeping in, weighing him down in ways that went beyond the physical. He was struggling to maintain the wormhole and his grip on all of the soldiers in the field at the same time.

"Getting tired, Darius?" Tanik taunted.

Before Darius could think of a fitting retort, he heard the steady pounding of footsteps and turned to see Dyara running back into the clearing with four Marines and their Keth prisoner in tow. As they elbowed past the frozen army of Revenants, the Marines' helmets turned every which way, taking in the scene around them. Their expressions were hidden, but their body language was clear: they were afraid to become frozen like the others.

Darius stopped pacing and nodded to Dyara. "Make the trade," he said in a hoarse whisper of a voice. Sweat was pouring from his brow and running in rivers down his back. He felt hot and cold all over, and his eyes were threatening to slam shut of their own accord. He swayed on his feet as he turned back to Tanik.

Dyara and the Marines walked into view, escorting Feyra to the Keth. They stopped a few paces away, and Feyra continued on alone. Her hands were unbound. As soon as she reached Tanik, she stood on her toes and kissed him on the cheek, and then turned to take her place beside him.

"Now send Cassandra over," Darius ordered.

"Not yet," Tanik replied, smiling smugly once more. That expression spread to Feyra's face with a flash of her pointy white teeth.

"We had a deal!" Darius exploded, and aimed his sword at Tanik's chest once more. "Release her!"

"First, allow your wormhole to collapse so that we can summon one of our own and leave."

"How do I know you won't drag Cassandra through with you?"

"You're just going to have to trust me," Tanik said.

Darius barked a laugh. "Not happening."

"Then we can stand around here and wait until you become too exhausted to sustain your wormhole. At that point, I *will* take Cassandra with me." Tanik chuckled darkly at that.

Darius scowled. He was through negotiating. He reached for Tanik's arm with all of his remaining strength to force the dagger away from Cassandra's throat.

Tanik's dagger began inching away from Cassandra's throat.

"Run!" Darius gritted out.

"Let me help you, my love," Feyra said. She held out an empty hand, and a sword leapt from the scabbard of the nearest Keth. It immediately began glowing with a shield, and she held the blade in front of Cassandra's abdomen, ready to slice her in half if she tried to escape.

Darius directed some of his energy to pull Feyra's weapon away, too.

It didn't work. He wasn't strong enough to fight them both. "Dyara!" he said. "Help me!" He could feel her adding her strength to his, but then the Keth began helping Tanik. It was a telekinetic tug-o-war with just two against more than thirty.

"You're juggling too many balls, Darius," Tanik chided. "You've got to let one of them drop. I suggest you let us go before one of us overcompensates and there's a terrible accident." To emphasize his point he tugged his blade suddenly closer to Cassandra's throat, and it began smoking with a horrid stench. Cassandra cried out in pain as the glowing blade burned a black line around her neck.

Darius gritted his teeth and pulled harder. Darkness crowded at the edges of his vision. He could feel himself fading. If he kept this up, pretty soon he'd pass out, and then they'd all be dead. Tanik was right.

Darius dropped his hold on the Revenants first, and they snapped out of it with an indignant roar.

"Darius!" Tanik said, his voice rising in warning as hundreds of Revenants began advancing on him and the Keth once more.

Darius allowed the wormhole back to the *Deliverance* to collapse, and in that same instant, used all of his now undivided strength to yank both Tanik and Feyra away from Cassandra as hard as he could.

They went flying in opposite directions and landed in the midst of startled Revenants. Before any of the other Keth could react, Cassandra made a run for it. Darius grabbed her in a telekinetic vice and brought her sailing through the air to meet him.

Just as she reached him, the Revenant army

parted around them like a rushing river around a rock and began attacking the Keth on all sides. The Keth all drew their swords in unison, and blades clashed with a hissing roar of shielded metal.

Darius caught Cassandra's eye and said, "I'll be back!"

With that, he drew on the ZPF and leapt over the heads of the Revenants to land in the middle of the Keth formation. He was just about to cut down the nearest Keth, when he noticed that he was surrounded by children. That gave him pause.

Then the older ones drew shimmering blades of their own, and Darius realized he was in danger. He parried the first blow and leapt away before any of the others could land. As he sailed above the Keth formation once more, he saw Revenants flying high into the air from two disparate points as both Tanik and Feyra floated up and away, defying gravity in a way that Darius hadn't known was possible.

Darius soared down just behind the Revenants' lines, pushing the nearest ones out of the way to avoid spearing himself on their swords. Recovering from his landing, Darius elbowed through his army to join the attack on the Keth. Just as he reached the front line, a shimmering portal appeared in the middle of the Keth's formation. Tanik and Feyra both floated straight through, and the Keth backpedaled toward it, furiously parrying swords from all sides in a desperate retreat. Darius jumped out and thrust his sword at one of the fleeing aliens, slipping past the Keth's guard to burn a blackened hole in his chest. The alien collapsed in a heap at Darius's feet. One after another, more Keth fell and were promptly trampled underfoot as the Revenants pressed forward. Darius sensed alien minds sliding into darkness as they died.

The last three surviving Keth backed through the portal together, and it vanished, taking a few over-eager Revenants with it.

Silence fell over the battlefield, and a feeble rumble of thunder sounded in the distance. Booted feet shuffled as the soldiers' attention shifted. Accusing eyes stabbed Darius from all sides.

"You!" a nearby woman said, and pointed her sword at him. "It's your fault they got away!"

CHAPTER 21

Tanik dispatched the final Revenant himself, running the woman through with his sword. As she collapsed on the rocky ground, he surveyed the barren moonscape of gray dust and craters that he'd brought his people to. This world had a breathable atmosphere, but not much else to recommend it. The Keth huddled together in a small group, looking around with wide eyes and concerned expressions. Fully half of them were missing. Counting the children, there couldn't have been more than twenty of them left. It was going to take a miracle of genetic engineering for them to survive as a species with such a limited gene pool, but they could worry about that later.

"Gurhain! Where have you brought us?" Vartok demanded, his voice sounding close behind Tanik.

Tanik rolled his eyes, *of course*, Feyra's father would be among the survivors. Pasting a smile on his face, he turned to face the man. Feyra walked over to stand beside him as he faced her father.

"Does it matter?" Feyra asked. "He just saved all of our lives!"

"Yes, it matters, Daughter." Vartok stopped uncomfortably close to them and glared at Tanik. "If this planet kills us all with unknown toxins, he won't have saved anyone." Vartok made a show of looking around. "It doesn't appear to be very habitable. There's no food or water in sight! And it's freezing."

Tanik endured those complaints without comment. When Vartok finished speaking, he said, "I've been here before. It's an abandoned staging ground that was used by the Revenants during the war." Tanik pointed to the rim of the crater they were standing in. "Just over that rise is an abandoned facility with more than enough food and water to sustain us."

"For how long?" Vartok demanded. "We can't hide here forever. You were supposed to be able to control your human puppet. Now he's run amok and almost wiped us out! You were supposed to use him to get rid of the Revenants, not lead them to victory against us! It's clear that he's become even more powerful than you, and your plan has failed. We should execute you and be rid of your incompetence."

I'd like to see you try, Tanik thought. But they both knew it was an empty threat. He was the only one among them strong enough to open a wormhole to get them out of here. Not letting his contempt show, Tanik bowed his head, and said, "I will take care of him, master."

"How?" Vartok demanded. "It's clear that you cannot defeat him yourself."

"I could if I were to fill myself with Sprites as he has done," Tanik replied.

Feyra clutched his arm, her nails digging into his skin. "It's too dangerous," she whispered.

Vartok nodded along with that. "You've already filled yourself as much as you can. Unless you want to sacrifice yourself in the process, I suggest you come up with a better plan than that."

Tanik grimaced. Vartok was right. He had tried dosing with living water during the battle for Ouroboros, and he'd nearly killed himself in the process. Some people were more resistant to the detrimental effects of the Sprites than others. Most couldn't survive more than the initial activation, and some didn't. Darius was unusually resistant to be able to imbibe as many of them as he had.

"There's another option," Tanik said.

"And that is?"

"We engineer a virus to target and kill the Sprites. We can infect Darius and all of the other Revenants without their knowledge. They'll be stripped of their powers before they even realize what's happening. Once Darius is too weak to defend himself, I'll find him and kill him. After he's gone, hunting the others down will be easy."

"And what if your virus infects us, too?" Vartok asked.

"We'll inoculate ourselves against it," Tanik suggested. "Besides, staying here will be an effective quarantine."

"Until Darius comes here looking for us," Vartok pointed out.

"Hide your presences and don't draw on the source field for any reason. He won't find you if he can't sense you."

"What if you get yourself killed and leave us all stranded here?" Vartok asked.

"The Revenants left behind transports at the facility I told you about. If the need arises, you can use one of them to fly away to a more habitable world."

Vartok's eyes pinched into baleful slits. "Show me."

"Of course," Tanik said, and sent himself floating up the rise to the rim of the crater. The effort of doing so nearly exhausted him. Between the recent battle and the constant drain of hovering above the ground to keep weight off his broken legs, he was in desperate need of rest. Once he returned to Union space, he'd get a nanite injection to knit his bones together faster. He didn't share the Keth's disdain for technology. There were some things they could learn from their enemy.

As soon as they reached the rim of the crater, the abandoned facility came into view—a sprawling complex of blocky modules and transparent hydroponic domes, all connected by narrow tunnels. Landing pads stood around the perimeter, most of them empty. Two of the six in view had transports landed on them.

"There it is," Tanik declared.

"It will do," Vartok said.

Tanik bore his father-in-law's demanding and ungrateful behavior just as he always had—by pretending not to notice.

Feyra rubbed his arm appreciatively. "Thank you," she whispered.

He nodded but said nothing. She was the only reason he hadn't killed Vartok years ago and taken his place as the leader of the Keth. That, and because he doubted the survivors would accept a human for their new leader.

"Are you sure your virus will work?" Vartok asked, his pale forehead wrinkling with doubt. Sprites crawled in random patterns beneath his translucent skin, like an infestation of luminous ants. "You will need help to develop it."

"I will make it work," Tanik said. "And I won't have trouble convincing people to join my cause."

"Very well. You have one last chance. If you fail again, you will no longer be welcome among us."

Feyra caught Tanik's gaze, her blue-white eyes filled with concern. He could imagine what she must be thinking. What if he failed? Years ago they'd discussed the possibility of running away together, but she couldn't bring herself to leave her people. That left Tanik only one choice if he wanted to be with Feyra: he had to defeat the Revenants.

Tanik nodded to Vartok. "I will bring you Darius's head to mount on your wall."

That drew a rare smile from the Keth patriarch. "A fitting end for him."

Tanik inclined his head one last time and turned to Feyra. Kissing her goodbye, he said, "I will return as soon as I can."

She nodded. "I will be waiting, my love."

CHAPTER 22

Surrounded by an angry mob of armed soldiers, Darius saw only one way out. He subtly smoothed away their ire through the zero-point field. As the angry, accusing looks directed at him faded to confusion, Darius strode over to Cassandra.

"How are you feeling?" he asked, hoping that Tanik's antivenin hadn't been a temporary solution to the poison running through her veins.

"I feel fine," Cassandra said.

"Good."

Dyara joined them, glancing around in bemusement at the other Revenants. They weren't frozen as they had been before, but they seemed to be at a loss, as if they'd suddenly forgotten what they were doing.

"Darius, are you..." Dyara trailed off, and fixed

him with a suspicious look.

"Let's go," he said, taking Cassandra's hand and striding through the Revenants' midst until he found an area clear enough to open a portal back to the *Deliverance.*

"You can't just take control of people every time they disagree with you!" Dyara said.

Darius glanced at her. "Let's argue about it later. Right now there's no one and nothing stopping Tanik from infiltrating and taking control of our entire fleet. For all we know, that's where he is right now." He closed his eyes and used what little strength he had left to try opening a portal back to the *Deliverance.*

The air shimmered in a spherical bubble, and the *Deliverance's* aft hangar bay appeared. Darius breathed a sigh. The fact that he could open a wormhole meant Tanik hadn't infiltrated the fleet.

"Everyone, follow me!" Darius called out, while subtly nudging them to do so.

Taking Cassandra by the hand, he walked through to the *Deliverance.* Leaving the planet's gravity behind and returning to zero-G, literally felt as though a great weight had been lifted from his shoulders. Darius walked to the far end of the hangar with Cassandra and stopped beside the exit. Dyara came jogging over, emerging from the stream of returning Revenants.

"So?" she prompted. "What do you have to say for yourself?"

"What would you have done differently?" he asked. "Would you have rather sacrificed Cassandra's life?"

Cassandra looked from Dyara to him and back again.

Dyara's mouth popped open, but no sound came out. She didn't seem to have a ready answer for that.

Soldiers poured through the wormhole, flooding the hangar deck in an orderly shuffle of boots. Subduing their wills appeared to have a cohesive, calming effect on the group. Unfortunately, it was also exhausting, and Darius was fast approaching the limit of his endurance. His whole body felt like it was on fire.

"You're getting too used to this," Dyara said at last. "The power is going to your head."

"Show me someone else who can defeat the Cygnians and protect us all from Tanik and the Keth, and I'll gladly step aside to let them do it," Darius replied.

"I'm not sure the Cygnians are really the enemy," Dyara replied, shaking her head. "Getting us to go to war with them was the Keth's plan.

There's got to be a reason for that."

"She's right, Dad," Cassandra said. "Gakram was different," she insisted, her voice cracking with grief. "He sacrificed himself to save me while we were on board the *Nomad*."

Darius turned to her with eyebrows raised. "One good person isn't enough to redeem an entire species. If they're not the enemy, then why haven't they backed down? They're free of the Augur's influence, and now half of their worlds have been destroyed, yet they haven't even tried to surrender."

"They're probably too proud for that," Dyara said.

"Or too bloodthirsty," Darius countered. "Either way, it's too dangerous to turn our backs on them now that they're wounded. Either we finish them off, or they'll come back to haunt us after they're done licking their wounds."

Dyara chewed her lower lip. "Maybe we can coax them to the negotiation table. There could be a peaceful solution. If we can find one, that would free us to deal with Tanik and the Keth."

"*Negotiate?*" Darius roared. "You mean like Cassandra tried to negotiate with them?"

"It might work this time," Cassandra put in. "The Cygnians aren't all bad. They aren't evil because they're born that way. It's because of the way they're raised."

Darius looked from Dyara to Cassandra and back again. He could tell he wasn't going to win this argument, but he didn't need their support. Now that he knew how to use wormholes, he could destroy the remaining Cygnian worlds all by himself.

"All right," he said. "We'll withdraw the fleet to Union space."

Dyara smiled. "Thank you. You should also talk to the Revenants. Let them leave the fleet if they want to. Give them a choice. They've been forced to fight for long enough." Dyara reached for one of his hands and squeezed. It was all Darius could do not to yank his hand away and squeeze her throat until her lips turned blue. That impulse gave him pause. When had he become so violent?

"Tell them they're free to go if they want to."

"I'll think about it," he said, glaring at her and fuming. His chest rose and fell in a steady rhythm of short, angry breaths. How dare she tell him what to do!

"And one more thing," Dyara said. "Now that you have Cassandra back, and you don't have to fight the Cygnians anymore, stop dosing with Sprites. They've changed you, and not for the better. I can see them in your eyes, you know. Everyone can. You look like a—"

"Like a what?" Darius demanded.

"Like a Keth," Dyara finished.

Cassandra regarded him with a look of sudden understanding. "I thought it was just me!"

Darius glared at his daughter. "Now she's turning you against me?"

"What?" Cassandra blinked. "No."

Darius shook his head and looked away. He was too tired to deal with this kak. Turning back to Dyara, he said, "Plot a jump to the nearest Union planet, Commander." He nodded over her shoulder to the portal where Revenant soldiers were still streaming through. "I can't hold that wormhole open forever, and we won't be safe without it until we're in warp."

Dyara nodded but said nothing to verbally acknowledge the order. She was still waiting for him to acknowledge her concerns, but he had no intention of giving them more attention than they deserved. Dyara and Cassandra would never understand. No one would. It wasn't their job to single-handedly save the galaxy. They didn't have trillions of sentient beings counting on them.

"If anyone needs me, I'll be in my quarters meditating." Darius turned and stormed off, eager to be rid of their accusing looks and false concern. He'd stop using the Sprites when Tanik, the Cygnians, and the Keth were all dead, but not before.

Darius's thoughts drifted to the flasks of living water he'd had stashed in his quarters aboard the *Harbinger*. They'd been destroyed with the ship, and the *Deliverance* hadn't originally been a Revenant vessel, so it wouldn't have a supply of living water. He would have to get the other ships in the fleet to send some over ASAP. He needed to recover his strength, after all.

CHAPTER 23

Trista couldn't believe her eyes. She had to walk up to the holo panels for a better look—as if a few feet could bring into better focus a sight that was hundreds of thousands of kilometers away.

"Where's the planet?" Buddy asked.

"That's the question, isn't it?" Yuri Mathos growled as he joined them by the holo panels.

"Are you sure these are the right coordinates?" Trista asked.

"They are," Yuri confirmed, while stroking the tuft of white fur on his chin.

Gatticus came to join them at the wall of holo panels in Yuri's quarters. "My optical sensors are detecting a cloud of dust where Cygnus Prime used to be," he said. "Thermal and radiation readings suggest an explosion."

Trista glanced at the android. "An explosion?" she echoed. "You're telling me that something destroyed the entire planet? What could do that? Even antimatter isn't that volatile."

"I cannot say what caused it," Gatticus replied.

"No wonder the Cygnians are withdrawing from Union worlds," Yuri said. "They've met their match with these so-called Revenants."

Trista frowned, suddenly wondering whether or not that was a good thing. "What's going to happen after they're done with the Cygnians? We don't know anything about them. They could be worse than the Cygnians."

"They're lost children, coming home after a long time away," Yuri said. "I'm sure their agenda isn't to spread wanton mayhem and destruction."

"We have to meet them," Trista said. "We need to know how they're destroying planets, and what their agenda is—and if any of the rumors about them are true."

Yuri turned to her with his slitted blue eyes narrowed in thought. His triangular ears flicked restlessly on the top of his head. "I'm sure those rumors are all greatly exaggerated."

"I wouldn't be so sure about that if I were you," an unfamiliar voice said.

Trista flinched and spun around to find the speaker. An unfamiliar man in a dark, hooded robe stood in the open door to Yuri's sleeping area. It looked like he had a *sword* strapped to his side.

"Who are you and how did you get in here?" Yuri demanded.

The man reached up and pulled back the hood of his robe, revealing a bald head and bright yellow-green eyes. "My name is Tanik Gurhain. I used to lead this fleet, many years ago. As for how I got in here, I'll explain that in a moment, but first, a warning: stay away from the Revenants. The rumors are all true. They'll bend your wills to theirs without a second thought, and you and your fleet will become their unwitting slaves."

Yuri drew his sidearm and pointed it at Tanik's chest. "Whoever you are, you made a big mistake to come into my quarters uninvited," Yuri said.

Tanik didn't seem concerned by the appearance of the weapon.

Yuri promptly squeezed the trigger, and a blue stun bolt flashed out and hit Tanik square in the chest. The light of the blast somehow suffused his entire body with a lingering white glow. Trista frowned in confusion. That was a side effect she'd never seen before. Furthermore, the light didn't show signs of fading, and neither did Tanik's awareness. He gave a crooked smile and chuckled.

"To answer your prior question about how I got in here, I teleported here from a planet that's thousands of light years away, on the other side of the Eye."

Yuri stared at his sidearm in shock, as if it had somehow malfunctioned.

"You see," Tanik went on. "I'm a Revenant myself, a *rogue* Revenant, and I need your help."

"Our help?" Trista echoed. "For what?"

"To defeat the others before they enslave the entire galaxy."

Yuri recovered from his shock and aimed his weapon at Tanik once more. Trista noticed his finger dart up to flick the setting beside the trigger. "I don't know how you did that, but this time it's set to kill. Don't move or I'll shoot. A squad is on its way here to arrest you as we speak."

Tanik waved his hand at Yuri, as if he were brushing away a fly, and the weapon leapt out of his hand.

"What..." Yuri blinked in shock.

Tanik made a circle in the air with his finger, and the gun mimicked that motion, flying around Yuri's head in a circle, just out of reach, taunting him. He didn't bother trying to reach for it.

"So the rumors *are* true," Trista said, tracking

the weapon with her eyes.

"Oh yes," Tanik said. He held up his other hand and slowly made a fist.

The sidearm crumpled in on itself into a misshapen lump and then exploded with a burst of light and heat. Trista threw her arm up and stumbled away from the explosion, cringing with the anticipated blast of shrapnel.

But that blast never hit. She lowered her arm and stared into a ball of orange fire, a perfectly contained sphere of heat and kinetic energy, somehow frozen. The dazzling cloud of shrapnel slowly faded and cooled before her eyes, and Tanik opened his fist, leaving the pieces of Yuri's weapon to drift between them in a harmless cloud of debris.

"How did you..." Trista trailed off, speechless. She could feel Buddy trembling with fear where he sat perched on her shoulder.

"That was nothing," Tanik said. "But just imagine what twenty thousand people like me could do—twenty thousand people who can teleport in and out of the most secure areas imaginable: bank vaults, data centers, government buildings. There's no way to stop them from taking anything they want. No way to impose sanctions or convict them of crimes. They'll become the rulers of the galaxy by default, and soon you'll find yourselves longing for the days when the Cygnians ruled over you. Unless..." Tanik smiled. "Unless you help me."

"Help you to do what?" Yuri demanded. "You've painted a picture of an invincible army. If what you say is true, there's nothing we can possibly do to stop them."

"Not true. There is one thing you can do." Tanik reached into his robes and produced a clear glass cylinder filled with dancing white specks of light. "*This* is the source of the Revenants' power. An alien organism, a symbiont. It's a kind of fungi, actually. Find a way to target and kill it inside a host's bloodstream, and you will have found a way to strip the Revenants of their powers."

"And I suppose we're going to test this on you?" Yuri ventured.

"No, not on me. You're going to need someone with my abilities on your side." He shook his canister of glowing water by way of indication. "You can use this to test the virus."

"What if we decide not to help you?" Yuri asked.

Tanik sighed. "Something tells me you'd rather cooperate."

Trista nodded slowly, suddenly seeing the

wisdom of what this man was saying. The Revenants were the real enemy, and they had to be stopped before it was too late. "He's right. We should cooperate."

"Yes," Yuri replied slowly. "We will help you."

"Good," Tanik replied.

Gatticus was looking at Trista as if she'd just lost her mind. "It's okay," she said, and placed a hand on his arm in an attempt to reassure him. "He's on our side."

The android didn't look convinced.

"Is something wrong, Gatticus?" Tanik asked, his head cocking to one side.

Gatticus rounded on him, blinking in shock. "How did you know my name?"

CHAPTER 24

"It is a pleasure to meet you, Mr. Drake, and welcome to Tarsus," Executor Resonda said, while holding her hand out in greeting.

Darius took the android's hand with a tight smile and a shallow nod.

She went on, "The Union owes you and your fleet a great debt. Reports are just now reaching us of the devastation in Cygnian space. It's hard to believe, but certainly welcome news. The Cygnians' tyranny is finally coming to an end."

"Yes..." Darius trailed off, while making a show of looking around the Executor's palace. They were standing in the throne room, a vast hall with gleaming marble columns and floors, flanked on both sides by massive windows that afforded panoramic views of Tarsus City. Gleaming glass towers stabbed the violet sky. Streams of air traffic flowed in orderly lines between those spires. None of the buildings were collapsed or otherwise tarnished by the war.

"Your world seems remarkably unscathed," Darius said, looking back to Resonda. He remembered noting the same thing on the trip down from orbit. Instead of ruins, he'd seen vertiginous cities, orderly urban parks and lakes, along with pristine forests of blue and red trees, none of them turned to charred skeletons by the flaming ruins of crashing starships.

"We've been very fortunate," Resonda agreed, smiling tightly back at him.

Darius had seen plenty of devastation on the other planets the fleet had visited over the past two months. Unlike Tarsus, none of those worlds had been governed by androids. Androids were the Cygnians' appointed governors, or *Executors* as they were called, and they were unfailingly loyal to their programming and their Cygnian masters. Darius had met one exception to that rule—an android named Gatticus, whose memory and associated loyalties had been damaged beyond repair.

Darius absently wondered what had happened to Gatticus. Tanik had jettisoned him from the

Deliverance before the civil war had begun. It was a pity. That android had helped Darius and his daughter survive after they'd awoken from cryo. He would have liked to reward the android by giving him a position in his new government.

A prickle of warning raised the hairs on the back of Darius's neck. He could sense the Cygnians who'd been hiding along the ceiling now creeping into position above his head. This planet was crawling with them. The Tarsians had obviously made some kind of deal in order to stay out of the war.

Darius nodded to Resonda. "Excuse me for a moment." Using his ESC to activate the comm piece he wore in his ear, Darius said, "Commander, you may commence launching our troops."

"Yes, sir," came Dyara's reply.

"What?" Resonda blinked at him. "You assured us that you came in peace! We have no warships. We mean you no harm!"

Darius stabbed his index finger at her like a sword. "And you assured me that Tarsus was not under Cygnian control." Darius gestured to the ceiling and pulled the lurking Cygnians down. They shrieked and wailed, struggling to right themselves and land on their feet before they hit the floor. Darius maintained his hold on them, making sure they landed on their backs instead. The floor boomed and shook with heavy impacts. That fall wasn't enough to kill them, but it had to hurt. The Cygnians rolled over, hissing and flashing gaping mouths full of dagger-long gray teeth.

Darius drew his sword and summoned a shield. The first Cygnian drew itself up to stand on hind legs, and shook itself like a dog. Four giant black eyes rolled out from behind thick eyelids and blinked slowly at him. Practically blind in daylight, the beast cocked its head, listening to better locate him. Darius stomped one foot and grinned. "I'm over here." Two sets of thick arms rose from the monster's sides, and Darius saw its legs bend, ready to pounce. Four more Cygnians prepared to do the same on all sides of him.

Darius casually flicked his free hand at the Ghoul facing him, and it went flying into an ornate marble pillar. The pillar broke in the middle and crumbled down on top of him, crushing the alien with a sickening crunch and a thick spurt of black blood.

"Anyone else?" Darius asked, turning in a slow circle to address the others.

The remaining four appeared to hesitate. Then one of them, a Banshee, standing on six limbs rather than two, reared back and lunged into the air with a piercing shriek.

Darius seized it in midair, holding it there, and then threw his sword at it like a spear. The blade remained shielded even though he wasn't touching it—an ability that only he seemed to have. The weapon sailed right through the Banshee's chest and out the other side, and the creature's torso disappeared in a flaming cloud of ash. Darius allowed the grinning head and the lower half of its body to fall with meaty splats.

Glancing between the final three, Darius said, "Submit." The Cygnians snarled and rocked their heads, refusing the order, so Darius added the weight of his mind to the suggestion, making it an order they couldn't refuse. They bowed their heads in unison and prostrated themselves before him. "Much better."

"How did you..." Resonda trailed off, backing away quickly.

Darius rounded on her. "Where do you think you're going?"

"I-I didn't have a choice! I had to obey them!" she objected.

Darius's sword sailed back into his waiting palm, and he flourished it with a grin. "Baaad robot," he drawled. "That's a tired excuse. There's always a choice."

"You just said it!" Resonda cried. "I'm a robot! I'm *programmed* to behave, to follow commands. That's why the Cygnians put us in charge! Because they knew we'd be faithful stewards of their empire."

Darius suddenly stopped advancing on her, as if her arguments had given him pause. "So what you're saying is, you're a mindless slave?"

"Exactly!" Resonda replied.

"Then that means you're a lost cause."

"Wait, no—"

Darius threw his sword again, and it lopped off Resonda's head with a shower of molten embers. The body toppled to the floor, and Darius's sword sailed back into his hand. Darius sheathed it with a smirk and shook his head. He'd replace her with a worthy Revenant and a cadre of his *enforcers* once the planet was cleared of Cygnians.

He'd already done that on five other worlds so far—of course, on those worlds it hadn't been necessary to make a full scale invasion to root out the Cygnians. The local populations had already done a good job of that themselves. In most cases the Cygnians' withdrawal had left only skeleton forces behind, which were ill-equipped to deal with the angry mobs of citizens they faced.

Tarsus was an odd exception to the Cygnian withdrawal, but that probably had something to do with the planet's ship-building industries. It was too important for the Cygnians to abandon completely.

Darius contacted Dyara once more. "Dya, I'm going to stay down here for a while to help secure the planet. Make sure our troops understand that they're not to make a mess. We need to take planets like Tarsus intact if we're going to rebuild the Union."

"Yes, sir," Dyara said again.

Darius smiled at her respectful tone. He'd won Dyara and Cassandra over by pretending to stop using the Sprites, and by making them feel like he was actually listening to their concerns. It was easier that way. They thought he was seriously entertaining their idea of sending an envoy to negotiate with the Cygnians. They had no idea that he'd already opened portals to the Cygnians' remaining worlds and personally traveled to each of them with a ZPF bomb. These scattered enemy forces that they were rooting out in Union space were all that was left of the Cygnian people. Their species was on the brink of extinction.

As for the other Revenants, they'd been easy

enough to win over once Darius had outlined his plans to make them all wealthy and powerful rulers in his new empire. Even the lowly *enforcers* propping up each governor would be like royalty. If there was one thing the Revenants seemed to have in common, it was their thirst for power, so they were an easy sell.

Cassandra was too young for the fulfillment of such ambitions to motivate her, and Dyara seemed oddly distracted by her lingering feelings of attachment toward him. What she most wanted was for him to walk away from the war and the promised reward of power in order to live a normal domestic life with her in relative obscurity. Perhaps he could slip some Sprites into one of her drinks. That would open her eyes in a hurry. Maybe then she'd start looking forward to her true destiny—to rule the galaxy by his side.

Darius smiled at the thought and went striding through the throne room. His mindless Cygnian slaves trailed meekly behind him. Walking straight up to the golden throne, Darius climbed the dais and tried the seat on for size. It was built for an android, so the padding was lacking, but otherwise, it felt like a good fit. Tarsus was the most important world that they'd liberated thus far, so it was fitting for it to become the capital of his growing empire.

Darius allowed his eyes to drift shut, taking a moment to rest his weary mind. The need to constantly hold a wormhole open wherever he went was exhausting. It was tempting to let his guard down for a moment. He'd spent two whole months guarding himself and his fleet from Tanik's return, but how would he know if Darius dropped his guard for a moment?

He wouldn't. Darius allowed his portal to collapse and let out a deep sigh. He cracked one eye open, half-expecting Tanik to come striding out of thin air and into the throne room, but nothing happened. Darius reached out with his awareness, searching far and wide, but Tanik was nowhere to be found. His Keth allies were gone, too. Maybe Darius had gotten lucky, and Tanik had accidentally killed them all in his hasty retreat from Ouroboros. That, or they'd given up trying to defeat him.

Darius smiled at the thought. Wishful thinking. It wouldn't be a good idea to let his guard down permanently. Summoning another wormhole in front of his throne, Darius got up and walked down to the shimmering portal. A bleak, rocky landscape was visible through the center of that portal. Glancing at each of his mindless Cygnian slaves in turn, Darius gave them a mental nudge to walk through the portal. "Time to join your brothers and sisters," he said, and watched as they stepped through the portal one after another to their designated prison world.

The Cygnians were enduring symbols of fear and terror to all species throughout the Union. As such, it wasn't in Darius's best interests to completely eliminate them. Having a planet full of hungry Cygnians would be useful to motivate criminals and dissidents to change their ways. Not to mention, if Darius could find some way to reliably control them without exhausting his own personal stores of energy, they would make excellent soldiers to keep local populations in line. Perhaps he'd find a way to lobotomize them and turn them into cyborg soldiers. Failing all else, a modern version of cock fights might draw a crowd. Darius snorted with amusement at the thought. He'd certainly buy tickets to that.

CHAPTER 25

"**W**here is he sending them?" Dyara asked.

Cassandra peered down on the parade grounds around the Tarsian palace. At least a thousand Cygnians were marching like lemmings through a portal to a dark and desolate-looking world while her father and several hundred Revenant soldiers looked on. A cheering crowd of Tarsians from all different species stood safely behind the Revenants' ranks, watching them go.

"That planet doesn't look very nice," Cassandra said. "I know they're prisoners, but if they starve to death because of us, it won't help us to negotiate a peace treaty with their leaders."

Dyara caught her eye with a grimace. "I'm not sure that your father is actually planning to negotiate. He keeps making excuses."

Cassandra had heard all of those excuses a thousand times over the past few months. He kept saying he wanted to negotiate from a position of strength, and to him, that meant re-forming the Union under his command before they discussed any kind of treaty with the Cygnians. The way she saw it, his logic was flawed. If the Cygnians agreed to a surrender now, then there might be a faster and easier way to get them all out of Union space. They might agree to leave peacefully, rather than resist only to end up captured and sent to whatever prison world her father had chosen for them.

Cassandra was tired of the fighting. What was the point, anyway? It was clear that the Cygnians stood no chance against Revenant soldiers who could bend their wills and make them into mindless slaves without breaking a sweat.

If her father refused to start the negotiations, then maybe she could convince the Cygnians to take the first step. But trying to get them to negotiate had almost gotten her killed the last time. This time Cassandra would be smarter. She'd talk to them from a safe distance. With that in mind, she closed her eyes and cast her mind out into space, using her awareness to search for Cygnian space.

Stars streaked through Cassandra's mind's eye, the inhabited ones shining brighter than the rest. She recognized the collective presences of familiar species—Lassarians, Murcians, Vixxons, Korothians, Dol Walins, Sicarians, Humans... in some systems they were all mixed together, and she could sense Cygnians scattered among them, but she couldn't find a particularly strong concentration of Cygnians anywhere. Picturing the super-heated dust clouds that corresponded to Cygnus Prime, Hagrol, and the other Cygnian worlds that they'd destroyed, Cassandra managed to find the star cluster where the Cygnians should have been.

But none of the surrounding systems were inhabited by Cygnians here, either. Looking closer, she found the reason—another four super-heated dust clouds. There were nine of them in all. Miniature, planet-sized supernovae that had no place in healthy star systems.

Cassandra's eyes flew open, blazing with fury. "He lied to us! He killed them all!" she screamed.

"What? Who lied and who's them?" Dyara asked.

Cassandra explained, and Dyara's face grew ashen. "Are you sure?"

"Check for yourself," Cassandra said.

Dyara's eyes slid shut, and her breathing slowed. Cassandra looked away, back down to the parade grounds while she waited. Indignant rage roiled inside of her, growing with every passing second. This was too much. Something had to be done. People had to know what their new emperor had been doing behind their backs.

Dyara's eyes cracked open, and she nodded. "You're right."

A cold gust of wind blew over the roof of the palace, pushing Cassandra against the railing as if goading her to go down and confront her father.

"We can't let him get away with this," Cassandra said. "I'm going down there. I'm going to tell everyone what he did! We'll see if they still want to follow him when they learn that he's a mass-murderer!"

Dyara winced and placed a hand on her shoulder. "I'm sorry, Cassandra. It must hurt to see what he's become."

Cassandra shrugged off the hand. "Whatever. It's the Sprites, not him. I bet he's still using them, too."

"Probably," Dyara agreed. "But let's not do anything to confront him yet."

"Why not?" Cassandra demanded.

"Because you need to know your audience.

You and I both met Gakram, and we know what he was like. We know that the Cygnians aren't all bloodthirsty savages, but how many of the Revenants are likely to agree with you? And more importantly, how many of those citizens down there will agree with you? Listen to them—"

Cassandra strained to hear past the thudding of her own heart, and the crowds' cheering snapped into focus.

"They're happy to be rid of the Cygnians," Dyara explained. "If they find out that your father has defeated them entirely, they're not going to be horrified. They'll just cheer louder. To them he's a conquering hero, and to the Revenants, he's a ticket to power, riches, and an easy life. They're all firmly under his sway. He doesn't even have to force anyone to follow him anymore."

Cassandra's cheeks bulged with impotent fury. "So what are we supposed to do?"

"We bide our time and wait, make him think we're on his side, just like everyone else. One day, when people see the side of him that we have, and they're fed up with his tyranny, then we take advantage of the fact that we're still close enough to do something about it."

The heat of Cassandra's anger bled away into a cold suspicion. "Do something? You mean like *kill* him?"

Dyara hesitated. "If that's what it takes, maybe."

"He's my dad, Dya! He might be off his *goffity* head, but he's still my dad. It's the Sprites that are making him like this. It's not his fault. It's happened to me, too. I'm not the girl I used to be either."

"They've changed all of us," Dyara replied. "But we haven't become megalomaniacs and lost all perspective like your father."

"Megalo-what?"

"It means power-hungry. We're also not drowning ourselves in the Sprites every day. Your father is. He's an addict, Cass. And like all addicts, he's never going to get any better until he can admit that he has a problem. Until then, he's dangerous."

"To the Cygnians, sure," Cassandra agreed.

"No," Dyara shook her head. "They're just an outlet for the demons inside of him to get their exercise. What happens when the Cygnians are all gone and he needs a new outlet?"

Cassandra looked back to the parade grounds below with an uncertain frown. "He's not killing them," she said. "That means there's hope. If he were such a bad person, he'd just kill them all. Or torture them." She watched as the last of the Cygnians filed past Darius on their way to their prison world. They all passed within easy reach of him, but none of them seemed tempted to do anything about it. Of course, they no longer had minds of their own with which to resist.

Even as Cassandra was thinking about that, one of the Cygnians darted out of line and grabbed her father's arm in its massive jaws. She watched in horror as it shook its head and ripped his arm right out of its socket. A bright red spurt of blood followed, which meant that it hadn't gotten Darius's mechanical arm. He stumbled away and fell over, and the crowd erupted in chaos. They screamed, running in all directions. The Revenants were frozen in shock, and the portal had disappeared, leaving the remaining Cygnians in a stagnant line.

The one that had attacked Darius was floating helplessly in the air, swiping at him with dagger-long claws.

"Get the crowd under control!" Darius's voice boomed as he regained his footing on the podium where he stood.

Cassandra recovered from her shock and rounded on Dyara. "We have to go down and help him!"

"He doesn't look like he needs our help," Dyara pointed out.

But Cassandra wasn't listening. She was already racing across the rooftop to the stairwell.

CHAPTER 26

"**Y**our name?" Tanik asked with a furrowed brow and slowly shook his head. "One of the others must have mentioned it," he said, gesturing vaguely to Trista and Yuri.

Gatticus met Tanik's gaze unblinkingly. "They did not, and I do not remember ever meeting you, so the question remains: how do you know my name?"

"You got me," Tanik said, holding up his hands with a crooked smile. "We did meet, aboard the *Deliverance*."

"The *Deliverance*..." Gatticus said slowly. That name sparked a memory. Several months ago he'd woken up aboard an Osprey bomber/transport to find himself stranded in the middle of deep space with no fuel and no memory of how he'd gotten there. He'd checked the logs of the Osprey and found that it had been launched from a Union carrier named the *Deliverance.* The course laid into the autopilot had been designed to leave him stranded with no hope of rescue, which meant that someone on board that ship had been trying to get rid of him—permanently. "Now I remember," he said, nodding.

"Do you?" Tanik asked. "What do you remember?"

"Not much," Gatticus replied. "I remember that I was on the *Deliverance* until someone cast me away in a transport with the goal of stranding me in deep space."

"Yes..." Tanik replied, frowning. "That was an unfortunate incident."

"Do you know who did it?" Gatticus asked.

"Of course. It was Darius Drake, the leader of the Revenants. You discovered that he was trying to take over the ship, and he needed to silence you before you could warn the crew."

Gatticus accepted that with a nod. "I see. And now you want my help defeating him? What do *you* have against him?"

"Oh, it's not a personal quest. I'm just not eager to see the galaxy go from one tyrannical government to the next. Since you knew him, Darius has moved on from his ambitions of being the uncontested captain of his own starship and crew. Now he's planning to become emperor of the entire galaxy. A law unto himself."

"And you mentioned that you need to develop a virus to target a certain strain of fungi in order to stop him."

"Indeed I do," Tanik replied.

"That should be easy enough to accomplish with either nanites or biological agents," Gatticus replied. "The hard part will be sneaking a pathogen past the nanites already present in people's bloodstreams...."

"The fountain of youth," Tanik said. "One of the Cygnians' more ironic legacies. They used nanite injections to wipe out disease and make us immortal and then began to hunt us like animals." Tanik snorted at that. "Do you have an idea to get by the nanites?"

"Perhaps," Gatticus said.

"Good. Why don't you put a team together and get started? The sooner we can come up with a way to defeat the Revenants, the better."

Gatticus nodded. "Before I agree to help, I need you to release the others—" He jerked a thumb over his shoulder to indicate Yuri, Trista, and Buddy.

"Very well," Tanik said.

"Wha..." Trista's voice trailed off. "What did you..."

Yuri gave a low growl and walked by Gatticus. "You!" He said, jabbing a finger at Tanik. "You did something to us."

Tanik spread his hands and smiled. "My apologies. Old habits. I won't do that again. Promise," he said, and held up a hand as if he were about to swear an oath.

"Much better," Gatticus said. "Now we can begin."

"Begin what?" Trista demanded.

Gatticus started for the exit, but Tanik stopped him—*physically* stopped him—with an upraised hand. It was like running into a wall. Gatticus shook his head, dazed by the sudden impact with the invisible barrier. "Do you want my help or not?" he demanded.

"One more thing," Tanik said, looking as though he's just been struck by an epiphany. He began waving his hands through the air, and a shimmering sphere of light appeared. The center of it quickly cleared, revealing a rooftop amidst a crowded city of skyscrapers, all silhouetted against fading purple skies. The streets below were crowded with all different species of aliens, and what looked like a long, orderly line of Cygnians.

"Darius has dropped his guard, which gives us a brief window of opportunity to reach him."

"Why would you want to do that?" Gatticus replied. "If he is as dangerous as you say—"

"Because it's the only way for you to see for yourselves what the Revenants are like. Don't worry, we're not going to confront him. Not yet. Now quickly, follow me."

"What... what is that?" Gatticus asked, pointing to what had to be a hallucination. *Are androids even capable of hallucinations?* he wondered.

"It's a wormhole," Tanik replied, and then he walked straight through. A moment later he appeared walking on the rooftop on the other side.

Gatticus hesitated, trading glances with Trista and Yuri.

"I'll stay here," Yuri said. "In case it's a trap." Trista frowned at him. "We can't all go," Yuri explained.

She gave in with a nod. "Fine. Come on, Gatticus."

"Can I stay, too?" Buddy asked in a quavering voice.

"Whatever happened to, *Tograns are loyal companions?* Remember that?"

"Loyal, yes. I didn't say anything about being blind and stupid."

Gatticus smiled at their exchange as he stepped through the shimmering sphere of light.

CHAPTER 27

"What's going on down there?" Trista asked as she peered over the low wall around the rooftop. "Why are all those Cygnians just standing around like that? They're unusually passive."

"Because the Revenants are controlling them. That's not all. Look—" Tanik pointed to a podium where a one-armed man stood in front of a particular Cygnian. This one *was* trying to attack, but it seemed to be restrained by unseen bonds.

"Behold!" the one-armed man said in an amplified voice. "This Ghoul is immune to our influence. He thought he could use that immunity to kill me. What should his punishment be?"

The crowd below began murmuring amongst themselves.

"I say we should repay his violence in kind. He removed my left arm, so we will remove the left arms of every Cygnian in this courtyard! Revenants! Draw your swords!"

A shriek of metal answered that command, and strangely glowing blades appeared on either side of the Cygnians. Two lines of soldiers stepped toward the Cygnians, but even with the threat of mutilation bearing down on them, none of the aliens made any kind of move to defend themselves.

"Why are they just standing there?" Trista asked.

"They've all been turned into mindless slaves," Tanik replied.

"Ready weapons!" the one-armed man ordered.

The soldiers raised their glowing swords, poised to strike. They were all now standing on the left side of the Cygnians.

"Cut off their arms!"

The swords fell in unison, and so did the monstrous aliens, all of them slumping to the left as they suddenly lost both their left arms. None of the Cygnians screamed or cried out in pain. Trista's lips twisted into a grimace. As much as she hated the Cygnians, it made her sick to her stomach to watch them all be mutilated before her eyes. Her eyes flicked over the group of aliens struggling to pick themselves up out of the dust. Some of them were much smaller than the average, and Trista realized that they were just children.

"This is Revenant justice at work," Tanik whispered.

"Stop it!" a young girl screamed. Trista's eyes were drawn to a small figure darting across the street to reach the one-armed man.

"Who's that?" Gatticus asked.

"That is Darius's daughter, Cassandra."

Trista watched her climb the podium to confront the one-armed man. That had to be the girl's father, Darius. Cassandra launched into a heated argument with him. Trista couldn't make out any of what they were saying to each other.

Darius endured her tirade for just a few seconds before gesturing offhandedly at her. With that gesture, she flew off the podium at high speed, as if she'd just been hit by a charging bull, and disappeared from sight.

Trista looked to Tanik in shock. "He did that?"

Tanik nodded. "To his own daughter. Imagine how he'll treat everyone else in the galaxy."

Darius returned his attention to the one Cygnian who had yet to have his arms removed — the one in front of him that was restrained by unseen means.

Darius flourished his sword and walked around the Cygnian, slicing off arms and legs at random. The alien screamed with a shrill, thundering noise that set Trista's teeth on edge.

Darius returned to his starting point to face the Cygnian hovering before him. Now the creature had just one leg and one arm left out of six.

"Now beg for my forgiveness!" Darius bellowed.

The Cygnian screeched something unintelligible at him, and Darius's sword flashed out once more, taking off the Cygnian's head in a burst of glowing embers. The body collapsed to the ground, suddenly released from the invisible vice that held it.

"Let the festivities continue!" Darius said.

The crowds cheered, and a shimmering portal appeared at the end of the line of crippled Cygnians—a wormhole just like the one Trista had traveled through to follow Tanik and Gatticus. She glanced behind her to see that the portal leading back to Yuri's flagship was gone.

"All right, you've proved your point about the Revenants," Trista said. "Take us back."

Tanik slowly shook his head. "I can't."

"What do you mean you *can't?*" Buddy asked before Trista could.

"As long as that portal down there is open, I can't open one of my own," Tanik explained. "But don't worry, Tarsus is the perfect place for us to develop our virus."

"You trapped us here?" Trista demanded.

"Not intentionally." Tanik spread his hands in a shrug. "But I knew it was a possibility. I didn't know how long our window of opportunity would last, and you needed to come here and see this. There will be a chance for us to leave later, after Darius and his fleet have moved on."

"And how long is that going to take?" Trista demanded.

"Hopefully not long," Tanik replied. "I trust you're both satisfied that the Revenants need to be stopped."

Trista looked to Gatticus. His jaw was set, and his eyes hard. "I am," he confirmed.

Trista was also convinced, but she wasn't sure if they should trust Tanik. He reeked of hidden agendas.

"Trista?" Tanik prompted.

She wasn't in the mood to play coy. "What about you?" she asked.

Tanik smiled thinly at her. "What do you mean?"

"Let's say it works. We make this virus for you,

and it neutralizes the powers of the Revenants. That will make you the only one with any unusual abilities. That leaves you in the perfect position to take control of the Union yourself."

Tanik's smile broadened. "You don't trust me."

"Nope," Trista replied.

"That's okay. We'll get there in time. As to your concerns, once Darius has been defeated, and the threat of the Revenants dealt with, you have my permission to infect me, too."

"And I suppose we're just going to have to take your word for it," Trista said.

"I'm afraid so, yes."

Trista frowned and crossed her arms. "That's—"

"Fine," Gatticus cut her off. "We need each other's help. Trust will grow in time."

"My sentiments exactly," Tanik replied. "Now let's go find a place to get started."

CHAPTER 28

Cassandra awoke with a start. Purple sky and white streaks of cloud swam into focus, followed by illuminated lines of air traffic. Her head pounded with a fierce thumping, as if something was trapped inside her skull and trying to bludgeon its way out.

"Cass! You're okay!" Dyara's face appeared, blotting out the sky. "I was just about to call for a medic."

"What happened?" Cassandra pushed herself up onto her elbows to take in her surroundings. Her dad was standing on a podium some thirty feet away, giving what was probably meant to be a rousing speech about the future of the empire.

Dyara hesitated, her eyebrows pinching together. "You don't remember?"

"I remember arguing with my Dad, and then...

nothing."

Dyara grimaced. "He threw you into a brick wall, Cass."

"What?" Cassandra blinked in shock. "By accident?"

"I don't think so. He didn't even come to check on you afterward. I'm sorry, Cass."

"You're lying," Cassandra said, flinging sudden tears away from the corners of her eyes.

"You were right." Dyara rubbed her back like the mother she'd never really had. "It's not him. It's the Sprites. Don't take it personally. I don't even think he's aware of what he's doing."

Cassandra couldn't talk past the knot in her throat. Her head was pounding, her throat hurt, her chest ached, her back felt like one giant bruise, and to top it all off, her dad no longer cared if she lived or died. Just a minute ago he'd almost killed her himself.

The one person she'd always been able to count on, who'd always been there for her no matter what, was now a monster. Cassandra couldn't take it. She broke down in tears, sobbing violently.

"Hey, it's okay," Dyara pulled her into a hug and held her, kissing the top of her head. Somehow that just made it worse. It should have been her dad holding her and kissing her head, doing his best to make her world right again. But this time *he* was the thing that was wrong with it.

"We have to do something, Dya," Cassandra mumbled between sobs. "We can't leave him like this!"

"Shhh. It's okay."

Cassandra pushed her away, suddenly angry. "It's not okay!"

Dyara winced. "You're right, it isn't."

"I went to see if he was okay, and he told me to leave him alone!"

"I'm sorry, Cass. I know how this must hurt."

"Did your father ever throw you away like a bag of garbage?"

"No," Dyara admitted.

"Then you don't know what it's like."

"Maybe not, but I can imagine. We're going to fix this, Cass. We're going to do everything we can to fix it."

"Fix what?" a gruff voice demanded.

Cassandra felt the blood drain into her feet with the sound of her father's voice. She turned to see him glaring down at her and Dyara with a deep frown wrinkling his brow, as if she was the one who'd done something wrong. Blood fell in fat drops from his open arm socket to the ground, but he didn't seem to notice.

"Your arm," Dyara said quickly, standing up to take a look at it.

It was a gruesome wound, with ragged bloody flesh around a hollow white socket of bone and cartilage. His green eyes were ablaze with anger and pain, and he was visibly swaying on his feet.

"Why are you crying?" he demanded.

The lump in Cassandra's throat returned, and fresh tears streaked down her cheeks.

"Stop it," he demanded.

"You need to see a medic," Dyara urged, and grabbed his other arm to get his attention.

Darius pulled away sharply. "I'm fine."

Dyara scowled at him. "Well, your daughter's not!" she snapped. "You threw her into a wall!"

"She looks fine to me."

"Are you insane?" Dyara demanded.

"She needs to learn respect," Darius replied. "She interrupted me in front of my soldiers, yelling at me and scolding me as if I'm the child and she's the parent."

She'd been yelling at him because he'd just had his arm ripped off and he'd been more interested in getting revenge than getting his injuries seen to. Cassandra couldn't take it anymore. She got up and stormed away.

"Where do you think you're going?" he called after her.

"Away from you!" she screamed, and with that she broke into a run, sobbing as she went.

"Cassandra, wait!" Dyara called after her, but she just ran faster, drawing on the ZPF to hide her presence from detection. She dived through the dispersing crowd and down the nearest street. Buildings blurred by her as she ran, and Tarsians stole curious glances at her as she went. Cassandra could sense Dyara trying to follow her, but she wanted to be alone. Her father had been all she'd ever had, and now he'd turned into a monster that she didn't even recognize anymore.

Time seemed to race and crawl at the same time. Night fell with a sudden plunge into jagged shadows and glowing neon lights. Shady-looking pedestrians seemed to melt out of the walls of adjacent buildings.

After an indeterminate period of time had passed, Cassandra stopped running. It was then that she realized she was alone on a dark, and seemingly abandoned street. Run-down buildings rose to all sides of her, and the street ended in a shadowy alcove up ahead.

"Are you lost?" a voice asked from somewhere behind her.

That voice was familiar.

Cassandra spun around to see a man in a dark cloak standing behind her, blocking the only way out. Only his eyes were visible—yellow-green eyes, glowing faintly in the dark. A red neon sign portraying a woman in a suggestive pose flickered on and off beside him, illuminating his silhouette with a crimson glow, but not his face, which remained shadowed by the hood of his cloak.

"Imagine meeting you here," the voice went on. Now Cassandra was certain she recognized it.

"Tanik?" she whispered, taking a guess at who it must be.

The hood came down, and Tanik's bald head gleamed red in the light of that flickering sign. "Hello, Cassandra."

She began backing away slowly and reaching for her sword. She drew it with a metallic shriek and aimed it at his chest.

"Stay away from me!" She summoned a shield and a pale white light pooled in the alley around her.

Tanik made no move to follow her. "I'm not the enemy, Cass," he said, holding up his hands.

"Yes, you are!" she screamed. "You lied to me, and you used me to blackmail my father!"

"I saved your life," Tanik replied, finally

taking a step toward her. "And I kept you away from him for a good reason. You've seen what he's become. He just threw you against a wall. He could have killed you."

That comment sliced straight through to Cassandra's heart. She felt her throat closing up again, and fresh tears leaked from her eyes, making them ache.

Tanik took a long step toward her. "You've seen what he's become. But he's your father, so you *want* to believe that he's the good guy."

"You held a knife to my throat!"

Tanik accepted that with a nod. "Yes. We were in a delicate situation. I had to use whatever feelings Darius had left for you in order to save my wife and what was left of her people, the Keth."

"You manipulated us into starting a war with the Cygnians," Cassandra insisted, reaching desperately for some other reason not to trust Tanik. Her world felt like it had turned on its side, and everything she'd ever known and trusted was now sliding off into an uncertain abyss.

"If that's true, then why did he go on to finish that war?" Tanik asked, taking yet another step toward her.

"Stay where you are!" Cassandra shouted, but her voice sounded small and frightened to her ears.

Tanik held up his hands in surrender. "Okay, you win. I'll leave you alone." He turned and started walking away, leaving her feeling more frightened than ever. A cold, fetid breeze blew through the alley, and a loud *bang* sounded, followed by low growls and wet, tearing sounds. Cassandra's eyes darted about, trying to find the source of the noises. Remembering to use her awareness, she reached out and found five luminous presences down at the end of the street, hunched over something—tearing into it with their hands and teeth.

Cassandra shivered and looked away, back to Tanik's retreating form. His words echoed through her head, his arguments starting to make sense. What if her dad really was the bad guy? After all, he was the one who had gone to Ouroboros to attack Tanik, not the other way around. Even after more than two months had passed, Tanik and the Keth still hadn't tried to get revenge for that attack. And now Tanik had found her, but rather than try to capture her and use her to threaten her father again, Tanik had only tried to reason with her.

A sudden scrabbling of feet sounded from the end of the alley, followed by ragged panting sounds, drawing near—

She stole one glance behind her and then ran at

top speed to catch up with Tanik. "Something's coming!" she breathed, and grabbed his arm in a fierce grip.

Tanik turned around and thrust a hand toward the darkness. A violent gust of wind whipped down the alley and unseen creatures screeched in protest, their claws skittering as they fled.

"You're safe now," Tanik assured her, as those sounds retreated into the distance.

Cassandra peered into the darkness for a few seconds longer before sheathing her sword.

Tanik favored her with a reassuring smile. Now that his face wasn't lit red by that flickering sign, he looked less frightening—even the lumpy scars running down the side of his face inspired pity more than fear.

"My dad wasn't always like this," Cassandra said. "There has to be a way to get him back."

"It's not his fault," Tanik said, nodding. "I warned him that he needed to stop using the Sprites, but he wouldn't listen, and Admiral Ventaris urged him to continue. The feeling of power and euphoria they induce makes them as addictive as any drug. Before long he couldn't resist using them. But they do more than manipulate their hosts' by stimulating opioid receptors. They also change brain chemistry, and make a person crave power."

"How do we undo all of that now?"

"I think I might know a way," Tanik replied.

Cassandra's heart leapt with eager anticipation. "How?" Her eyes darted back and forth, searching his.

Tanik wrapped an arm around her shoulders, gently turning her and walking with her back the way she'd come. "Let's go meet my team."

"Your team?" A flicker of suspicion crawled through Cassandra's gut. "Are they Keth?"

"No, not Keth. A human and a Togran—he's cute. You'll like him. And there's someone else. Someone you should recognize."

Her suspicion gave way to curiosity. "Who's that?"

"Gatticus Thedroux."

Cassandra stopped walking suddenly, and Tanik's arm slid off her shoulders. "No way! How did you find him?"

Tanik turned to her with a grin and shrugged. "Mysteries of the universe. He won't remember you, though, I'm afraid. He had an unfortunate accident."

Suspicion returned with a cold rush, and Cassandra's eyes narrowed. "My dad said you were that accident."

"Yes. I admit it," Tanik said. "He tried to stop me from going to rescue you and the others from the Crucible, and I overreacted."

"He tried to stop you? Why would he do that?"

"Because he was an Executor in the Union, and I was commandeering a Union Carrier to go rescue conscripts from their secret war with the Keth. We were on opposite sides of an old conflict."

"And now?"

"Now, we're good friends, but—" Tanik held a finger to his lips. "He doesn't know that I was the one who sent him away, and if you don't mind, I'd like to keep it that way. We need his help to get your father back to his old self."

Cassandra didn't like being forced to keep secrets, but she couldn't afford to alienate Gatticus if he was the key to getting her father back. "How is he going to help me get my dad back?"

"By re-engineering Cygnian nanites as a virus to target the Sprites in people's bloodstreams."

"Could that work?" Cassandra asked, hope soaring in her chest.

"Oh yes, I'm certain that it will," Tanik replied. "We'd better go join the others before your father comes looking for you. We don't want him to find out about our little project before we can use it to help him."

Cassandra nodded quickly. "Let's go."

CHAPTER 29

Commander Kanos of the Marine battalion stopped at the foot of Darius's throne and saluted. "We've searched the entire city, sir. It's possible your daughter found a way to reach one of the surrounding settlements."

Darius leaned forward and glowered at the man. "On foot?"

"She may have found transport with one of the locals. Or stolen a vehicle. We have also been unable to sense her in the zero-point field. It is possible that she does not want to be found."

"She's a child. This isn't about what she does or doesn't want. Find her, Commander, or I will hold you personally responsible for her disappearance and anything that happens to her while she's gone, do you understand me?"

"Yes, sir," Commander Kanos replied. He

clicked his heels together and saluted once more.

"Dismissed," Darius said, and waved him away.

The commander and his soldiers made a hasty retreat. The giant doors at the end of the throne room shut behind the Marines with a resounding boom as they left. The morning sun painted golden squares on the marble floors, window frames tracing dark squares of shadow between them. Darius rotated his throne to look out through the floor-to-ceiling windows beside him. The sun was just now peeking over the tops of the nearest buildings. Cassandra had been missing all night. At first, he'd thought she'd return after a few hours, once she calmed down and realized what a brat she'd been. But that hadn't happened, and she was still actively hiding her presence from him, making it difficult to find her. Darius scowled. Cassandra was going to be in a lot of trouble when his troops finally found her.

The doors at the end of the throne room burst open, drawing his attention to the fore. Dyara came striding in and stopped at the foot of his throne. She stared up at him.

"She's still not back, is she?" Dyara asked.

Darius scowled. "Who let you in here?"

"Forget about that and listen."

Darius could tell this was going to be a tiresome conversation. Reaching over to a compartment in the side of his throne, he withdrew a flask of living water and took a long sip. The Sprites tingled on his tongue and in the back of his throat, clearing his mind and sharpening his thoughts. *Much better*, he thought, his eyes half-closing with bliss.

"Look at you!" Dyara said. "You can't even function without them, can you? You've driven your own daughter away, I can't stand to be around you—who's next?"

Darius waved a hand at her, and she braced herself with the ZPF for a kinetic attack. He arched an eyebrow at her and a wan smile curved his lips. "Someone's jumpy," he remarked.

"Can you blame me? The last time you waved your hand like that, you threw your daughter into a wall."

A flash of anger tore through Darius with her accusation. "That was an accident."

"An accident?" Dyara blurted. "If that's so, then why did you justify it afterward? And why was I the first to check on her? Face it, you've lost all control over yourself. The Sprites are controlling you now."

Darius took another sip from his flask but said

nothing.

Dyara saw that and went on through gritted teeth, "If you don't wake up and do something now, it'll be too late. Fight back! You're not completely gone yet. I know you're still in there somewhere."

Darius gave her a stony look. "Are you done?"

Dyara gaped at him. "Don't you have anything to say for yourself? Your daughter is gone! She's out there somewhere." Dyara gestured to the walls of windows flanking the long hall-shaped throne room. "She's lost in an unknown city, on an unknown world. She could be in trouble, or hurt, or abducted by a gang of criminals. The Darius I know would have been out there looking for her all night, but instead, you're in here brooding and drinking *that*."

"She's actively hiding her presence from me and the other Revenants," Darius replied. "If she were in trouble, she'd let us find her."

"Not if she's dead," Dyara replied.

"She's not dead."

"How do you know? Or maybe you just don't care."

Darius pointed at the doors. "Get out."

"Fine, I'll go," Dyara replied, nodding slowly, "but I'm not coming back."

Darius shrugged. "Good."

Dyara fixed him with an incredulous look. "One day you're going to wake up and realize that you've driven everyone away and you're all alone. I just hope by then it's not too late for you to do something about it."

Darius watched as she turned and walked away. He took another sip from his flask to clear his head and cool his temper. The doors to the throne room banged shut in Dyara's wake.

She was a fool. If she'd stood by him, he would have made her the governor of her own star system—maybe even more than one star system—but now she'd have nothing. Without him, she was a worthless nobody. Hopefully, Cass would learn from her example when his Marines finally found her and brought her back to the palace.

CHAPTER 30

—TWO DAYS LATER—

A loud knock sounded on the rusted metal door of the warehouse, and all eyes turned to Tanik.

"You'd better answer that," Gatticus said.

"It's probably another patrol," Trista added.

Tanik looked to Cassandra. "Go to the basement, just in case."

Cass got up from the aging brown couch where she'd slept for the past three nights. She knew the routine.

Tanik walked back through the abandoned warehouse to the front door. When they'd first found the place, it hadn't even had a door. They'd had to fashion one from some old metal sheets that they'd found lying around. They'd had to improvise and scrounge all of their amenities. Trista remained thoroughly unimpressed, calling it a *kakhole*, but so far they'd managed to elude discovery by Darius's soldiers. The trouble was that the patrols kept coming, either having forgotten that they'd already checked this warehouse, or having been ordered to search the same places repeatedly.

More knocking sounded on the door just as Tanik reached it. "We can detect your heat signatures!" a muffled voice said. "Open the door, or we'll cut it open!"

Tanik lifted the metal latch on the inside and pulled the door open to a width of a few feet, revealing a full squad of Revenants outside, all of them wearing glossy black plates of armor, but no helmets.

"You live here?" the squad leader asked. He was a gray-furred Korothian with sharp green eyes.

Tanik nodded slowly, making his own eyes wide and frightened. He held his hands up, revealing ragged holes in his baggy shirt. He'd found a change of clothes in the warehouse. They smelled like sour milk, but they made him look the part of a homeless drifter. The others had refused to trade their clothes for smelly rags, but it didn't matter. Only Tanik needed to look the part. No one was actually going to search inside the warehouse. "The moon is falling!" he said in a sudden shout. "It's falling!"

The soldier's hand dropped to the hilt of his sword, and he tried to peer around Tanik. "Is there anyone else in there with you?" he asked.

Tanik nodded gravely. "The Phantoms."

The soldiers looked suddenly alarmed. "There's Cygnians hiding here with you?"

"There goes one!" Tanik said, pointing to a giant insect crawling through the dust at the man's feet. "It's a baby."

"He's crazy!" one of the other soldiers said, shaking his head.

"We're going to have to search the whole place," another added. "I can detect at least one other person in there."

"Probably just another homeless wretch," said the first.

The leader glanced back at his squad. "We have our orders." He turned back to Tanik and nodded. "Step aside."

Tanik smiled and shook his head. "Not safe. Phantoms will eat you."

"Dumb goff," the man muttered. "I said step aside!" He drew his sword, and both he and the blade began radiating the pale white glow of a shield.

Tanik reached into the ZPF and took hold of their minds. In the next instant, they all wore vacant expressions with hollow eyes. He planted a false memory in their heads of having searched the warehouse and found nothing but poor, crazy bums living in squalor, just as they were expecting.

Before he released their minds, Tanik backed away and shut the door, so that when they came back to their senses they wouldn't remember him standing there, barring the entrance.

By the time Tanik returned to the others in the abandoned offices where they'd set up their research and living facilities, Tanik could already sense that the soldiers had moved on. He dropped down onto the brown couch where Cassandra had been sitting earlier and reached out to her telepathically, telling her that it was safe to come back upstairs.

"That's three patrols in as many nights," Trista said, shaking her head. "They're not going to give up looking."

"Eventually they will," Tanik replied. "Darius isn't your average concerned parent." Cassandra arrived at just that moment, making what Tanik . had been about to say awkward, but he went on anyway. She couldn't afford to be naive if she was going to play her part in Darius's downfall. "He's only looking for her because she's making him look bad by eluding capture, and because it annoys him to be thwarted."

Cassandra was leaning against the wall, looking at her feet and picking at her finger nails, as if she hadn't heard what he'd said.

"Cass, come sit down," Tanik said to her. He patted an empty cushion beside him with the stuffing bleeding out of it. "It's safe now. I sent them away."

"I don't know why you make me go downstairs every time if they never even come inside," Cassandra complained as she flopped down on the couch beside him.

Tanik gave her a long-suffering smile. "Because I like to be careful. Some Revenants are stronger than others, and planting false memories is delicate work. I can't be certain that I'll always get it right."

"I still say we should leave. Look at this place!" Trista threw up her hands in disgust. She was sitting on a rusty, unpadded chair at a lop-sided table that they'd propped up with a loose brick. The walls of the office were badly cracked, paint peeling away in big papery sheets. The overhead lights and equipment were all patched into a solar-charged emergency power cell that Tanik had found in the basement, and the bathroom facilities were buckets. Food and water had to be sourced outside by creative means, all the while dodging Revenant patrols.

"I'm sure we can do better than this," Trista went on. "Maybe you can use that mind control power of yours to convince a real laboratory to let us use their facilities. I bet it would make the work go a lot quicker, too. What do you think, Gatticus?" She glanced over her shoulder to where he sat statuesque in front of a glowing black and white holoscreen.

Gatticus gave no reply. He was plugged directly into the computer console. Lines of code scrolled rapidly down the holoscreen as he wrote new instructions for his test batch of nanites. He was trying to get them to recognize Sprites in a sample of blood that Tanik had given him earlier.

Buddy hopped up on Trista's shoulder, gnawing on a leg bone from lunch. "Forget lodging, what about food? Why don't you get a restaurant to send a nice fillet of fish for each of us? No, make that two fillets, or..." Buddy's expression grew contemplative, and he tapped his chin with one small finger. "You could probably get a whole hover-truck full of fish delivered here, couldn't you?"

Tanik looked back to Trista. "For now, this is as safe as we're going to get. Darius will move on before long in order to keep consolidating his empire. He'll leave his men here to keep looking for Cass on their own, and as soon as he does that, I'll open a wormhole back to the Coalition fleet so that we can finish the work there."

Trista frowned, obviously unsatisfied with that plan. "What happens if Darius comes poking around here personally? You said he's immune to your mental tricks, and from what I hear, he's not going to be happy to see you."

"He won't come," Tanik replied. But deep down he wasn't so sure. And after their last two confrontations, he harbored no illusions about how a third would go. If they met again before Tanik had a chance to finish engineering his virus, he would be killed, and there would be no one left to oppose Darius.

PART 3 - CORRUPTION

CHAPTER 31

—THREE MONTHS LATER—

"The virus is ready," Gatticus said as they entered Yuri Mathos's quarters.

"Is that true?" Yuri asked, and slowly turned from the wall of viewports behind his desk. "Tanik?" Yuri prompted, re-directing the question to him.

He nodded. "Yes." Since leaving Tarsus and returning to the Coalition Fleet they'd perfected the nano virus—or rather, Gatticus had perfected it while the rest of them hovered over his shoulders asking stupid questions. He'd been able to demonstrate how his re-engineered nanites could target and kill the Sprites in an infected blood sample.

"Then we are ready to deploy our weapon?"

Yuri asked.

"Not yet. We need a live test subject," Tanik explained. "Preferably someone you won't miss in case there are adverse side effects."

"We were thinking about the captured Cygnian on board," Trista put in.

Cassandra frowned. "Just because she's a Cygnian doesn't mean we can use her as a guinea pig."

"A what?" Tanik asked.

"It's an expression. The point is, even Cygnian prisoners should have rights."

Tanik smiled patiently at her. "We need to know if our virus is dangerous. The fastest way to learn that is to infect a living host. Or would you rather that we infect your father with an untested pathogen that might kill him?"

Cassandra appeared to hesitate. "No, but there has to be another way."

"There isn't," Tanik replied. "Not one that we have time for, anyway. The Empire's inauguration ceremony is less than a month from today. We won't have another chance to catch all of the Revenants in one place."

"Our prisoner has shown no signs of having special powers," Yuri said. "If the virus is intended for Revenants, then how does testing it on a non-

Revenant help you?"

"Anyone who's been to the Crucible has the Sprites in their blood," Tanik explained. "Non-Revenants maintain much lower blood levels of them, but they're still present. If we can clear the Sprites out of that Cygnian's system, then there's no reason to think that we won't be able to do the same with actual Revenants."

Yuri nodded. "All right, let's go see how your virus works on a live test subject."

* * *

The Cygnian prisoner lay in the far corner of her holding cell, curled up and sleeping like a dog, blissfully unaware that a silvery cloud of nanites had been pumped into her cell through the air filtration system.

In theory, the nanites would do nothing to harm the Cygnian herself, but that was the point of this test—to make sure. Not that Tanik particularly cared if the virus accidentally killed its hosts, but he had to maintain the appearance of caring, and he needed to know for his own sake if the virus could be dangerous to him in the event that he became exposed.

"There they go. Look—" Gatticus pointed to the holoscreen in front of them. It was relaying a live video feed from the prisoner's cell. The air shimmered faintly beside the gill-like respiratory canals in the sides of the Cygnian's neck, indicating the presence of the tiny machines.

Two of the Cygnian's four eyes cracked open as the nanites effectively flew up its nose. The alien's mouth popped open, and it sneezed thunderously. A shimmering wave of nanites blew back out into the room, but they promptly turned around and zipped back in. The prisoner didn't appear to notice.

"How long before the virus takes effect?" Yuri asked.

"A few hours at least, a day or two at most. It's a question of how many Sprites there are versus how many nanites, and whether or not the virus can successfully spread its instructions to existing populations of nanites in the host's blood."

"So why did I come down here?" Yuri demanded irritably. "Let me know once you've got some real results to show." He turned and walked out of the brig's security station, shaking his head and muttering to himself. It wasn't even a minute later that some *real results* began to present themselves.

"Something's happening—look!" Cassandra whispered sharply.

Tanik peered more closely at the holoscreen.

The Cygnian's eyes were wide and darting around the cell, as if she were suddenly afraid for her life. She leapt to her feet and began pacing frantically around her cell, growling and hissing unintelligibly.

"What's she doing?" Trista wondered.

In the next instant, the alien stopped at the door and began trying to claw her way out. "That's never going to work," Trista said. "We de-clawed her." Next the prisoner tried gnawing on the door handle with ragged black gums. "We also removed her teeth," Trista added.

Cassandra gave her a horrified look. "That's barbaric."

"We had no choice," Trista replied. "Cygnians can claw or chew through six-inches of solid alloy plating like it's paper. We would never have been able to hold her here safely otherwise."

"What's she doing now?" Buddy interrupted.

The prisoner was slumped against the door, pawing it feebly with one claw-less hand.

"She doesn't look too good," Cassandra pointed out.

"No, she doesn't," Tanik mused. He fixed Gatticus with a frown. "I thought you said you had perfected the virus?"

"I did."

"Then what's going on in there? She looks like she's dying. It won't do us any good to solve the problem of the Revenants if we kill everyone in the process."

"Let's not make any assumptions yet," Gatticus replied.

Trista's eyes darted around the security station. "What if that virus gets out and infects us? Is her cell airtight?"

"Don't worry," Gatticus said. "It's not infectious."

"We just saw it infect that Cygnian!" Trista replied.

"I set it to infect one host, no more," Gatticus replied. "And as an added safety measure I can deactivate the nanites remotely if I need to."

"You'd better do that before it kills her," Cassandra said.

"Not yet," Tanik said. "Gatticus is right. We shouldn't jump to conclusions yet. We need to know the full extent of the side effects if we're going to fix whatever is wrong with our virus."

"What if those side effects kill her?" Cassandra demanded.

"We'll do our best not to let it get that far," Tanik replied. "After all, we may need her for subsequent tests."

Cassandra's eyes narrowed swiftly at that. "You don't care about the Cygnians, either. You're just like my dad."

Tanik arched an eyebrow at her. "Do you want to save your father or not?" That seemed to suck the air out of her lungs, and whatever retort she might have offered went with it. Her shoulders slumped, and she looked away. "That's what I thought," Tanik said. "Gatticus, keep an eye on the prisoner's life signs."

"Of course."

"And try not to let the virus kill her," Tanik added. "I'll be in my quarters if anyone needs me. Let me know if there are any changes in her condition."

"You will be the first to know," Gatticus replied.

"Good." Tanik turned and walked out of the security station. The doors slid shut behind him with a muffled *thump.* He blew out an impatient sigh and shook his head. He hoped this wasn't a significant setback. They didn't have a lot of time left before the inauguration, and if Gatticus couldn't get his virus working soon, Tanik would have to think of some other way to stop Darius.

Perhaps he could try stealing and smuggling a ZPF bomb to the inauguration. He wouldn't even have to get it down to the surface. He just had to get someone to deliver it *close* to the planet and then set it off.

But Darius would likely be expecting such an obvious attack. Worse yet, he'd almost certainly have a vision or a dream about it. The problem with plotting against Revenants, especially powerful ones, was that subtlety and trickery were the only way to get around their sixth sense of predicting the future.

Even Tanik's plan to distribute Gatticus's nano-virus would have to be layered with multiple levels of decoys in order to succeed, and that was assuming Gatticus could get the virus to work.

Tanik scowled. He should have paid more attention to his visions of Darius sitting on a throne ruling over a New Union. So far that future didn't look like it was going to be easy to change.

CHAPTER 32

Darius sat on his throne, listening to his Revenant governors arguing amongst themselves. He'd had tables and seats arranged on both sides of the throne room to create a temporary forum for them to air their grievances and report on the state of their star systems. The objective was for him to get an idea of the overall condition of his burgeoning empire without having to meet with each of his governors individually. He planned to share the positive highlights from their reports when he delivered his inauguration speech in three weeks' time. But so far those highlights were more negative than positive.

The primary problem seemed to be that he'd appointed just one hundred and ten governors out of almost twenty thousand Revenants. The basis of those appointments had largely been their relative strengths. He'd appointed the most powerful Revenants, thinking that they would be the best-equipped to hold on to power. What he hadn't accounted for, however, was that the other nineteen thousand would begin plotting to usurp his appointed governors just as soon as he left their star systems. At the moment there were twelve seats empty out of the one hundred and ten, and Darius was hearing rumors that the missing governors hadn't shown up because they'd been killed by their own enforcers.

Darius frowned angrily and leaned his chin on his fist as he listened to the surviving governors argue about different solutions.

"We should disband the enforcers entirely," Governor Wilks said while smoothing down frizzy strands of blonde hair that had escaped the bun on top of her head. She had the floor at the moment, evidenced by the fact that she alone was standing, but it didn't seem to matter. The others were all interrupting her at random.

"That won't solve anything!" said a Dol Walin governor, waving a flipper-like hand in her direction. His pale lavender skin had flushed dark purple, and his glossy blue eyes were flashing and darting to either side of his snout. "If anything that will only hasten our demise. Either we share power with them equally, or they'll find some way to take it by force."

Murmurs of agreement followed that statement.

"So instead of one governor per star system, we'll have two hundred?" Governor Wilks demanded. "How do you even share power equally with that many people?"

"Give everyone their own jurisdictions and the power to vote on decisions that affect their star system," the Dol Walin said. "If everyone has an equal number of constituents and an equal number of votes, no one will be able to complain."

Someone barked a laugh at that. Darius saw that it was one of the ghostly white-eyed Vixxons. "In an ideal situation, that might work, but there will still be plenty of discrepancies. Some jurisdictions will be more affluent or important than others regardless of their number of inhabitants. You can't divide the empire up into perfectly equal parts, and even if you could, differences would emerge over time, and new power struggles would occur."

"At least it should be enough to prevent outright assassinations," the Dol Walin argued. "And we'll have sanctions in place to deal with rogue elements. Right now we're vulnerable because the Empire is in its infancy and the fleet is spread too thin to police all of our worlds."

"And what happens when we do have fleets in place?" a human governor with dark skin and a bushy black beard demanded. Darius tried but failed to put a name to the face. "That will only make it easier for a star system to break away! Any one of us could take control of a fleet with non-Revenant crews and make them do whatever we want. A lone enforcer could have such a fleet execute an orbital strike on his governor's palace! There's a reason the Augur used the Luminaries to keep us under control. Their influence united us and kept us all from turning on each other."

At that, the room burst into chaos, with all of the governors shouting denials and angry retorts. None of them were sorry to see the Luminaries go. They were finally free, and they had no interest in becoming slaves again. Darius's policy of spreading them out across the galaxy ensured that not even he could control them, and that had been a large part of what had convinced them to go along with his plans to re-unite the galaxy under his rule. The implication that they *needed* to be controlled by him from some central location was probably more true than false, but it was definitely not a popular idea.

"Enough," Darius raised a hand for silence, but no one listened. Standing up from his throne, he added the weight of his mental influence to that suggestion, making it an order they couldn't refuse.

Silence fell like a shadow over the echoing throne room, and all eyes turned to Darius. His governors' expressions were glazed and staring, as if they'd all suddenly forgotten what they were arguing about. Darius relaxed his hold on their minds, giving them back enough of their faculties to listen, but not enough to argue.

"These petty struggles will end just as soon as the Empire is established because I will identify rogue states and crush them myself. If you are afraid of your enforcers, I suggest you increase your security and figure out who you can trust. Get your houses in order. We have three weeks left until the inauguration. Between now and then I expect you all to come up with a list of positive progress that you've seen since entering office. This meeting is adjourned."

Chairs pushed out in unison, and the resounding thunder of a hundred pairs of boots hammering marble tiles followed the governors out of the throne room.

Once the last of them left and the doors

slammed behind them with an echoing thud, Darius turned his throne and sat scowling out the windows at Tarsus City, the capital of his empire. He watched as the sun sank and lengthening shadows went inching across the roofs of shorter buildings. The fading sun cast everything in a golden hue, and stars began to prick through the sky between faint wisps of cloud.

Darius tore his thoughts away from the view and considered the problem at hand. All this vying for power and petty rivalries were symptoms of a deeper problem. The Revenants didn't want to be subordinate to anyone. Eventually the infighting would reach Darius in the form of an assassination attempt, or an on-going series of them.

Darius let out a heavy sigh. Now he understood why the Cygnians had appointed androids to rule their Union. Subordinates who could be programmed to obey would give far less trouble.

But taking back the power he'd given to the Revenants would just pit them against him. He couldn't do that without first finding a way to eliminate them as a threat.

There were ways of doing it, especially now that the inauguration put them all in one place. A well-placed ZPF bomb would take out the entire planet in the blink of an eye. Poof, no more Revenants. But surely they would foresee the threat coming and decide to flee the planet. Furthermore, Cassandra was still here somewhere—unless she'd found a way to leave the planet. He couldn't risk killing her in the process of eliminating the others. Darius scowled and shook his head. He should have let Tanik kill the Revenants when he'd had the chance. Of course, back then it would have been premature. He'd needed them and their fleet to consolidate his empire. In fact, he probably still needed them to keep local populations in line.

Darius sighed again. He never imagined that ruling an interstellar empire would be so complicated.

* * *

"How long has she been like this?" Tanik asked, nodding to the holoscreen.

"Since this morning," Gatticus replied.

The Cygnian prisoner was sitting down, staring at the door to her cell. She was awake and alert—a significant improvement over the past day, which she'd spent drifting in and out of sleep, refusing to eat or drink.

"What do her test results show?" Tanik asked.

"No fever, no signs of respiratory or cardiac

distress. The swelling in her brain has subsided. She's made a complete recovery twenty-nine hours after infection."

"And the Sprites?" Tanik asked.

"The virus appears to have eliminated all of them."

"So it worked?"

Gatticus nodded.

"And it didn't kill the host," Tanik added.

"No, it didn't, but it's important to note that the Cygnians are a much hardier species than most. If the virus put her at death's door for the past day, there's no telling how it will affect other species — or for that matter how it will affect Revenants, whose blood concentrations of the Sprites are much higher. We won't know what to expect until we test it on them."

Tanik scowled and shook his head. "There's no time for that, and even if there were, how do you propose we test all the other species? We can't abduct a dozen other test subjects, and something tells me we're going to be short on volunteers from Yuri's fleet. Besides, we'll never get the data that we really need, which is how the virus will affect Revenants."

"Correct. I just thought you should know the risks involved."

"Is there any way to mitigate the side effects?"

"If we slow the rate at which the Sprites are killed, the effects should be diminished. Slow them enough, and the host might not even notice that they are feeling poorly until their powers begin to fade."

"What kind of time frame are we talking about?"

"For a Revenant? Who knows. For this Cygnian, setting an elimination period of three to five days would likely have eliminated most of her symptoms."

"That's too long," Tanik replied, shaking his head. "We're going to have to risk it. We can't afford to make the elimination period longer, or we'll risk giving the Revenants enough time to neutralize the virus before it can do its job. The Cygnians might be resilient, but so are the Revenants. It won't kill them."

"I hope you're right," Gatticus said.

"Make sure you create enough of the virus to infect at least twenty thousand people."

"Twenty thousand?" Gatticus blinked in shock. "I'll need several hundred kilograms of nanites for that."

"Then you'd better get started. We leave for Tarsus in two days. Can you do it?"

Gatticus nodded absently. "If Yuri cooperates, I should be able to make it in time."

"Good..." Tanik trailed off, nodding to the Cygnian. "Has she demonstrated any behavioral changes?"

"Such as?"

"Reduced aggression, increased tolerance for other species, reduced impulsivity...?"

"There's no way to be sure from here," Gatticus replied.

"True," Tanik said. "Let's go open the door. I'm going to have a chat with our prisoner."

"Are you certain you want to do that?"

"Why not? She's not contagious, is she?" Tanik asked.

"No, but she may try to kill you," Gatticus replied.

"With no claws and no teeth?" Tanik snorted. "I'll be fine. Let's go."

CHAPTER 33

"What is your name?" Tanik asked.

A series of growls and hisses followed.

"I am Queen Rassura. Who are you?"

"Tanik Gurhain. You are not trying to kill me. Why is that?"

The Ghoul bared her ragged, toothless black gums at him. "With what teeth?" Then she held up a hand and fluttered six claw-less fingers. "And what claws?"

Tanik nodded. "Futility wouldn't stop the Cygnians I know. The Cygnians I know are driven by emotion and instinct, not reason. What makes you so different?"

"Why should I answer your questions?" Queen Rassura countered. "What do I get out of it?"

"You could save your people," Cassandra said, stepping forward quickly. "They're not all dead.

Not yet."

Tanik shot a warning look at her. The Cygnian drew herself up onto her hind legs and hissed loudly. "What do you mean we're not all dead *yet?*"

Cassandra cleared her throat, probably about to describe her father's xenocidal rampage through Cygnian space, but Tanik put an arm in front of her chest, and pushed her back.

"What she means is that the Cygnians are losing the war, but there might be a way to negotiate peace if your people were more reasonable."

"And how do you propose to make us more reasonable?" Queen Rassura asked, while stepping forward and looming over him with all four of her massive arms poised to rip him apart.

This time Tanik didn't need to push Cassandra back. She backed up all by herself, and he could hear Trista, Yuri, and Gatticus all doing the same thing. Calling them here for this behavioral test had been Gatticus's idea. Tanik hoped it wasn't about to get one of them killed. That would really mess up his plans.

"We administered a treatment that was designed to eliminate an alien parasite in your blood," Tanik explained. "It made you sick."

"I remember," Queen Rassura growled, and her hands curled into fists.

Tanik went on blithely. "The parasites made you sick with toxins that they released when they died. We believe that while they were alive, these parasites were influencing your behavior, making your species more aggressive and impulsive."

"You are mistaken," Queen Rassura replied. "We would have noticed such changes in our behavior."

Tanik shook his head. "Not if the onset was gradual. The proof is in the fact that you are talking to me rather than attacking."

The Ghoul's body tensed, and her legs bent. *Here it comes...* he thought. But then she appeared to relax, her eyes narrowed, and she gave an ugly, toothless smile. "You are trying to trick me. It will not work."

Tanik couldn't believe it. "Yes, you are clearly too smart for that," he said, and began backing away, forcing the others to leave the Cygnian's cell.

"Release me!" the Ghoul snapped in a throaty roar.

"Soon," Tanik replied, nodding. "We will take you home to your people as soon as this is all over."

"How do I know that?"

"You will just have to trust us," Tanik said.

Queen Rassura narrowed her eyes at him once more, but still she made no effort to attack. They all managed to leave her cell and shut the door behind them without incident.

"I think we have our answer," Tanik said, turning to face the others in the corridor. Yuri and Trista nodded slowly, while Gatticus gave no reply. Tanik glanced at Cassandra. "This is proof that we can save your father."

She offered a trembling smile and wiped sudden tears from the corners of her eyes. "When do we leave?" she asked.

"In two days. As soon as Gatticus has finished preparing enough nanites to infect all of the Revenants."

"I'm going to need all of the booster shots you have," Gatticus said, looking to Yuri. "And access to the fleet's manufacturing facilities to make more."

Yuri's pointed black ears twitched, and he hissed with displeasure, but he gave in with a nod. "Very well."

"How are we going to get the virus into position to infect everyone?" Trista asked. "Orbital patrols will be searching inbound transports, and security at the inauguration is going to be on high alert."

"I'll take care of it," Tanik explained. "Remember the patrols that Darius sent looking for his daughter? I'll do the same thing again. It won't be a problem."

"Why don't you just use a portal to get us there?" Trista asked.

"Because Darius already has one open, and I can't open one big enough for a transport, so we're going to have to go to Tarsus the conventional way."

"All right, let's say it all works out just like you're planning," Trista said. "What happens after we've infected everyone and you're the last Revenant standing? You really expect us to believe you're just going to let us infect you and take away your powers too?"

"She makes a good point," Yuri said.

Tanik favored each of them with a paper thin smile. "So what do you suggest?"

"How about we infect you now?" Trista said. "You can be our next test subject. That will also tell us how it works on a Revenant, which we're only guessing at right now."

"It will work," Tanik replied, waving his hand to dismiss those concerns. "Regardless, you can't afford to infect me yet. You're going to need my help to smuggle the virus past security and orbital patrols."

"Well, isn't that convenient," Trista replied.

"What if we infect him with a dormant version of the virus," Gatticus suggested. All eyes turned to him.

"How would that work?" Yuri asked.

"Simple. I set a timer to activate the virus during the inauguration. We could also use that version to infect Darius prior to the event, just in case he doesn't get infected with the others."

"Timing would be critical," Tanik mused, while stroking his chin between his thumb and forefinger.

"The event has been widely publicized," Gatticus replied. "It won't be hard to time the activation sequence to coincide with the ceremony."

Tanik nodded. "True. And you're right, we can't assume that Darius will be infected with the others. He might see the crowd reacting to the release of the virus and manage to escape before it reaches him."

"Great. It's settled then," Trista said. "Gatticus will infect you before we leave."

Tanik noticed that she was watching him carefully, trying to gauge his reaction. "Why not do it now?" he replied, smiling back at her. "Gatticus has the virus ready. All he has to do is set a timer. That shouldn't take him more than a minute or two, right Gatticus?"

"Less than that," Gatticus confirmed.

"Then let's do it," Tanik said.

Trista's eyes narrowed in suspicion, and her lips flattened into a dissatisfied line, but she relented with a sigh. "Okay, but we still have a lot of details to work out. So maybe the plan won't fail because you're planning to betray us, but it could still fail by sheer lack of planning."

"There'll be plenty of time to work out the details while we're en route to Tarsus," Tanik replied.

"But I won't be there for that," Yuri pointed out. "Where's my role in all of this?"

"Defeating the Revenants will create a power vacuum. We'll need to set up a legitimate government as soon as possible to avoid chaos. That will be your job. We'll arrange a rendezvous before we leave, and as soon as it's safe, I'll send for you."

Yuri nodded. "I will be waiting."

"Are there any other questions or concerns?" Tanik asked, his eyes flicking from face to face.

"Just one," Cassandra said. "How do we know

the virus is safe?"

"The girl makes a good point," Yuri added. "Thanks to Queen Rassura, we know that it makes non-Revenants sick. How do we know we won't be releasing a deadly pathogen that later goes on to kill billions?"

Tanik turned to Gatticus. "Well?"

"The virus won't be able to spread from one host to another, and it's not self-replicating, so it won't be as dangerous as a biological pathogen. As an additional measure of security, I will be able to deactivate the virus with remote access codes.

"Aha!" Trista said. "So what's stopping Tanik from deactivating the virus to protect himself?"

Tanik spread his hands in a placating gesture. "I don't have the codes."

Trista frowned. "You expect us to believe that?"

"He's right. Only I know the codes," Gatticus replied. "And I am immune to the Revenants' mental influence, so there is no way for him to steal the codes from me."

"He could still coerce you," Trista pointed out.

Gatticus shook his head. "I would not allow it. If he tried, I would activate the virus prematurely, and neutralize him as a threat."

Trista still didn't look satisfied.

Tanik fixed her with an innocent look. "You see? There's no reason for you not to trust me. Why don't we all go to the med bay now? You can watch while Gatticus injects me with the virus."

"Maybe someone else should do it," Trista replied. "Just in case you've found some way to get to him."

"My programming is impossible to alter," Gatticus replied. "The Cygnians made sure of that."

"He's right," Yuri added. "We've tried re-programming Executors before. It triggers a complete memory wipe and an SOS call to anyone close enough to hear."

"Well, how do we know he hasn't found some other way to beat the virus? Maybe he's been developing a vaccine or something."

"If you're looking for reasons not to trust me, I'm sure you'll find them," Tanik replied. "But if I really am planning to keep my powers and betray you all, then the solution is simple. Have Gatticus deactivate the virus before it runs its course, and let Darius and his Revenants deal with me. It'll be one against twenty thousand, and I'll never stand a chance." Tanik spread his hands in invitation. "Either way, you're still holding all of the cards."

Trista still didn't look convinced, but Tanik

suspected that was a product of stubborn pride and an old habit of distrusting everyone but herself.

After a protracted silence and a brief staring contest with him, she gave in with a huff and shook her head. "I suppose it will have to do. Let's get down to the med bay and get this over with." Trista turned and started down the corridor, heading for the nearest bank of elevators.

"After you," Tanik said, smiling politely as she breezed by him. Buddy pulled his cheeks open and stuck out his tongue in a childish gesture of contempt, but that only made Tanik's smile stretch into a grin.

CHAPTER 34

Darius stood on the speaker's podium before a crowd of tens of thousands of Revenants and ordinary citizens. The palace courtyard and surrounding streets were crowded to the point that not a single gap remained. Hovering camera drones buzzed in the air, zipping around above their heads. The inauguration ceremony was being recorded for subsequent distribution to news networks throughout the known galaxy. This was a moment that would go down in galactic history.

Darius smiled and took a deep breath. As he did so, unintelligible whispers crowded in at the edges of his hearing. The sound gave him pause, and he hesitated. His eyes darted through the crowd searching for a threat. He recognized that sound. It was a warning from the Sprites, but what were they trying to warn him about? The crowd began murmuring amongst themselves, feet and clothes rustling as they waited for him to speak. Perhaps it was nothing. Just his imagination.

"Welcome, everyone!" Darius said. "This day we come together with one heart and one mind to celebrate the end of the Cygnians' rule over us. They are defeated, and they are never coming back!"

The crowd roared and screamed in response, and Darius smiled winningly for the cameras. He waited for everyone to settle down, but the commotion showed no signs of stopping. If anything, the screaming was growing louder. A moment later, Darius saw why. The crowd was thinning out rapidly; people were dropping in waves.

Darius stumbled back a step, his eyes darting to find a cause. He summoned a shield to protect himself, but there was no discernible threat anywhere. No sign of anything...

Then he spotted the silvery clouds undulating through the crowd, glittering like sand in the sun. People fell wherever the clouds went. But not everyone was reacting the same way. Some collapsed in fits, while others ran away screaming, stampeding like wild animals, only to collapse a few seconds later. Someone had released a nano virus into the crowd.

Darius turned and ran from those silvery clouds of death as they came drifting toward him. Just then, a blinding wave of agony stabbed through every fiber of Darius's being. He sank to his knees with gritted teeth. A splitting headache began, and he pressed both of his hands to the sides of his head, wailing in agony. He couldn't see through the tears streaming from his eyes, or hear through the ringing in his ears. In the next instant, every muscle in his body went into spasms, and he collapsed on his back, flopping around like a fish. The pain intensified, forcing raw unintelligible noises from his lips and making him chew through his own tongue.

He tried to fight back by drawing on the ZPF, but he'd lost his connection to the zero-point field. Darkness swirled in, promising a release from the pain, and Darius welcomed it.

* * *

Darius awoke bathed in sweat. He sat up, shaking with rage and echoes of the agony from his dream. *No, not a dream—a vision,* he realized.

Someone was going to release a nano virus at the inauguration ceremony. He'd have to call it off. Or change the venue and double down on security. Or... maybe he wouldn't do any of that...

Darius recalled his recent meeting with his governors. The Revenants were turning on each other and vying for power in a self-destructive spiral of backstabbing and treachery. It was only a matter of time before they turned on him, too. If someone was planning to release a nano virus at the inauguration, maybe it wouldn't be such a bad thing.

Yes, having someone wipe out all of the Revenants for him would be a blessing. But who was that someone? Who would *want* to wipe them out? There was, of course, one obvious answer—Tanik Gurhain and the Keth. It would make sense if the virus was their doing, but whoever planned the attack they couldn't know that the Sprites had warned him in advance. The ceremony was in three weeks. He had more than enough time to put precautions in place. Afterward, it should be a simple matter to identify the pathogen and develop a vaccine. In the worst case, he'd simple isolate Tarsus from the rest of the empire and turn it into a quarantine zone.

The trick would be taking precautions in such a way that wouldn't scare off his enemies or alert the other Revenants to the threat. Darius smiled. If everything went according to plan, after the inauguration he would be the last living Revenant in the galaxy.

CHAPTER 35

—NINETEEN DAYS LATER—

Everything was ready. Trista was below decks, loading supplies and the cargo of nanites into her ship, the *Harlequin*. The others were either sleeping or out enjoying their last few hours of freedom aboard Yuri's flagship before transferring to Trista's transport for the last leg of the trip to Tarsus.

That gave Tanik the perfect opportunity to handle some last minute business of his own. He was floating above the deck, meditating, with his arms and legs crossed and his eyes shut. He cast his mind out across the light years in search of his people. It wasn't long before he found them on the desolate, gray world where he'd left them. Keeping that planet fixed firmly in his mind's eye, he summoned a wormhole to reach it. A moment later he opened his eyes to see a shimmering sphere of light. It rapidly expanded and cleared to reveal a dusty gray expanse of dirt and pebbles leading up to a gleaming facility of boxy metal modules and interconnecting tunnels.

Tanik uncrossed his legs and extended them to the deck. His mag boots clicked smartly as they yanked him down and pinned him in place. He mentally checked via his ESC to make sure the door to his quarters was locked before striding through the portal to reach the other side. Gravity added sudden weight to his bones, and a sharp pain erupted in the small of his back. His knees almost buckled in response.

A frigid wind blew across the barren gray expanse where he stood. Tanik shivered and hurried to the front doors of the facility. Once there he used the vidcom to announce himself, while simultaneously announcing his presence through the ZPF.

The doors swished open a few seconds later, revealing both Feyra and her father, Vartok. Feyra grinned and rushed out to greet him, throwing her arms around his neck and showering him with kisses.

Vartok remained where he was, barring entry

to the facility. "Have you succeeded in defeating the Revenants yet?"

Tanik shook his head, and Feyra withdrew, looking suddenly crestfallen. "But you're back, and it's been so long. I just assumed..." she took a quick step back and looked to her father for his reaction.

"Feyra is right. It has been far too long. We have waited patiently for your return, and I believe I made myself clear the last time we spoke. If you failed again, you would have no place among our people."

"I have not failed," Tanik replied. "I have come to report my progress. I have finished developing the virus that will wipe out Darius and the other Revenants once and for all. I will release it at the inauguration ceremony, and I have foreseen that it *will* succeed."

"Foresight does not guarantee success," Vartok chided. "There are too many moving pieces to ever see the future with certainty."

"I am a master of seeing how those pieces fit together. You already have the proof of this. I used my Foresight to lure the Augur to his death, and I will use it again to lure Darius and the Revenants to theirs."

"Time will tell, but I fail to see why you would come here just to tell us that you are about to succeed. What is the purpose of that?"

Tanik shook his head. "I came because I need your help. I am infected with the virus—"

Feyra recoiled from him and ran back to her father's side. Vartok flinched and scowled. "So you came here to infect us, too?" he demanded. "Have you lost all capacity for reason?"

"The virus is dormant," Tanik said. "It's no threat to you or even to myself. Yet."

"I see. I thought you were supposed to develop a vaccine."

"And I will, in time, but for now I need the people around me to trust me. The easiest way to earn their trust is to make them think that they're the ones in control. The virus inside me is set to activate itself automatically in just a few days. I can delay that timer by freezing myself in a cryo pod, but there's an android who has the activation codes. He'll activate the virus as soon as he realizes that the timer failed to do so. That's where I need your help. Once Darius succumbs to the virus, and his wormhole collapses, I need you to open one of your own and come join me. Find the android and destroy him, and then we'll finish whatever is left of the Revenants together."

"You seem to have forgotten that none of us can open portals anymore."

"That will change when the Revenants are knocked out by the virus."

"Assuming you are right, why would we risk exposing ourselves to your virus?" Vartok asked, his eyes narrowing to thoughtful slits.

Tanik gestured vaguely to the facility behind him and Feyra. "There are exosuits in there. If you put them on before you travel to Tarsus, then nothing will happen to you. And you need to take the risk because the virus will not kill the Revenants. All it will do is incapacitate them and take away their powers. After that, we will have a window of opportunity to kill them ourselves and finally have our revenge."

Vartok's eyes lit with interest, and he began nodding. "It will be satisfying to kill the Revenants ourselves. Very well, we will help you, but your plan had better work."

Tanik inclined his head to that. "Thank you, master."

"What does this android look like, and where can we find him when the time comes?"

CHAPTER 36

"**W**e have ten minutes until we drop out of warp. We'd better go strap in," Trista said.

Cassandra turned to face her from where she stood by a broad, curving viewport in the *Harlequin's* crew and passenger lounge.

"Not yet," Tanik replied. "Let's go over the plan one last time. Gatticus you have the virus?"

Gatticus patted his stomach and nodded. "All set." He had two canisters of the virus stored in his utility compartment, each of them disguised to look like auxiliary power cells. The canisters would disperse their contents into the air one minute after their seals were broken, at which point the virus would fly through the air and infect the nearest viable host, just like the one they'd used on the Cygnian prisoner. The difference was, this batch of the virus was programmed with a timer to only activate in two days' time, during the inauguration ceremony. Gatticus had the access codes to remotely adjust that timer in order to coincide with the ceremony, or to simply activate the virus if the timer failed.

Tanik turned to Cassandra next. "What's your story going to be when Darius asks where you've been hiding all this time?"

"I've been hiding in an abandoned warehouse on the outskirts of the city. That's where I found Gatticus, who was also hiding there."

"Good. And you remember what I taught you about shielding your thoughts? We can't afford for Darius or one of the other Revenants to find out about our plan by seeing it in your mind."

"I remember," Cassandra said. Since successfully testing the virus on that Cygnian prisoner, Tanik had been working with her on the skill of shielding her mind. It had gotten to the point where she could compartmentalize certain thoughts and memories while revealing others, which would make it look to her father like she wasn't trying to hide anything. As for Gatticus, he'd created an altered set of memories to coincide with their cover story. Once he switched data sets, their lies would become his truth, and he would forget all about their plot until Cassandra spoke the code word—Gakram—to reactivate him. That was a precaution against the possibility that the Revenants might scan his data core to verify their story.

"Gatticus, how did you come to be in the warehouse?" Tanik asked.

"Would you like me to answer the question from my current data set, or the altered data set?"

"Do the cover stories differ between data sets?" Tanik asked.

"They do not."

"Then use your current data."

"Very well. When I woke up after being cast away from the *Deliverance*, I found myself drifting in an Osprey with no fuel and no memory of how I'd come to be there. I cobbled together a comm probe from pieces of the transport and used it to make contact with Trista, a freelance pilot at a nearby fuel depot. She took me to Tarsus in exchange for fair payment."

Trista snorted. "Yeah, and I'm still waiting for that payment, by the way."

Tanik ignored her and nodded to Gatticus. "Go on."

"I went into hiding as soon as the Revenants took over, because I was afraid of what the people of Tarsus would do to me if they learned that I used to be an Executor for the Cygnians. Several months later Cassandra found my warehouse while trying to hide from Revenant patrols. I recognized her from my time on the *Deliverance*, so I helped her to hide, but she eventually grew tired of hiding and convinced me to turn myself in with her at the palace."

"And after that?" Tanik asked.

"After we turn ourselves in, I will find a way to give one of the canisters containing the virus to Cassandra."

"Good. Cassandra, what will you do with the virus?"

"I'll sneak it into his room the night before the ceremony."

"And I'll leave mine in another strategic location, in case hers fails," Gatticus added.

Tanik nodded along with that. "Trista, what about you?"

She gave a dramatic sigh. "We've been over this a hundred times. My job is to sprinkle the courtyard with the little kakkers the night before. But you still haven't told me how I'm supposed to do that with fek knows how many guards watching me from the palace."

"Let me worry about the guards. I'll make sure they don't see you. You just make sure that no one sees they're standing on a thin layer of micro-machinery the next day."

"But you're not even going to be there," Trista fumed. "So how are you going to deal with the guards?

"Don't worry. I'll be somewhere nearby. That will be good enough."

Trista snorted dubiously. "Better be. If I turn out to be the unwitting patsy in this plan, I'll sing like a *caropian* war beetle and tell everyone that you were behind it."

Tanik smiled tightly at her. "I wouldn't expect anything less."

"And *I* will bite off each of your fingers and gnaw the meat from your bones while you watch!" Buddy declared from Trista's shoulder.

Silence hung in the air following that threat. Tanik regarded the furry ball of lard with his eyebrows raised.

"Too much?" Buddy asked, glancing up at Trista.

"No, that sounds about right," she replied. "Let's go strap in. We've got two minutes left before we arrive at Tarsus."

Tanik nodded and waited for her to lead the way to the cockpit, doing his best to act even-tempered and reasonable, when in reality he was boiling with rage and vengeful thoughts. Trista had been nothing but trouble since they'd met. If it weren't for her and her suspicions, he never would have had to agree to be infected with his own virus. He was going to take special delight in killing her when the time came.

* * *

"Stand by for docking," a gruff voice said over the comms.

"Standing by," Trista replied.

Cassandra watched over her shoulder as an Osprey from the Tarsus Orbital Defense Fleet lined up its lower airlock with their upper one. A moment later the two airlocks met with an audible *clunk* and a barely perceptible jolt.

Trista turned her chair away from her controls. As she did so, Buddy popped out of his custom-sized acceleration harness and sailed gracefully through the zero-G environment to land on her shoulder.

"I still say we should have found a way to hide the three of you," Trista said, nodding to Tanik. He stood leaning against the cockpit door, beside his empty seat. There was no point in any of them staying strapped in right now. Trista had been ordered to kill all thrust and forward momentum until the authorities could conduct a physical inspection of their ship and cargo.

"Hiding won't be necessary," Tanik said.

"What if someone recognizes you?" Trista countered. "Or Cassandra? She's been missing long enough that by now the entire system should have seen her face."

"Remember the warehouse?" Tanik replied. "None of the patrols even set foot inside to search it, but I made them think that they had. This will be the same."

"You're just lucky none of them recognized you. Those scars on your face are hard to forget."

Tanik nodded agreeably. "And my influence is equally hard to resist. The only person we need to worry about seeing me is Darius himself, and he is in the executor's palace on the surface."

Trista didn't look convinced, but she said, "I hope you're right."

"I am." Tanik flashed a tight smile and left the cockpit without another word.

Trista blew out a sigh and shook her head. "I don't trust him."

Cassandra considered that with one eyebrow raised. "Why not? We've already infected him with the virus, and Gatticus can activate it any time. There's nothing he can do to us."

Trista sighed. "Call it a hunch. No one gives up

power willingly. He's planning something. I'd bet my ship on it."

Cassandra wasn't about to believe her without a good reason, but something deep inside of her urged her to listen. "Even if he is planning something, what can we do about it?"

Trista snorted and shook her head. "I don't know about you, but I'm going to be ready to run to the deepest, darkest corner of the galaxy if I so much as *suspect* that things are about to go kakside up."

Cassandra thought about it. As far as backup plans went, that wasn't a bad one. "You have any extra seats?"

"Sure, why not. It might be helpful to have someone with your powers around."

"If I still have them after we release the virus."

"Here's a tip. Wear an exosuit to the inauguration. Or pretend you're sick and don't go. You might have noticed that no one asked you to infect yourself ahead of time. All you have to do is avoid getting infected with everyone else."

"Hey, that's a good point," Cassandra said. "Why has no one asked me to get injected with nanites like they did with Tanik?"

"Because you're just a *kid*, kid. No one sees you as a threat. You're too young and innocent."

"Thanks... I guess."

"Don't mention it." Trista turned her chair back to the fore and stabbed a button on one of her consoles. "Hey, Tanik, how's it going back there?"

When no answer came, Trista stabbed at her console again and said, "If you don't answer me I'm going to—"

"Everything's just fine," Tanik replied, his voice coming from directly behind them.

Cassandra jumped and whirled around at the same time as Trista spun her chair back to look.

"Where's the boarding party?" Trista asked. "Don't tell me they're busy tearing my ship apart without any supervision!"

"No, they're standing in your airlock, staring at a wall."

"What... how? No, never mind. Why make them stare at the wall?" Trista asked.

"Because anyone watching that patrol ship will expect a delay while our vessel is searched, and you don't want them traipsing through your ship, so I thought staring at the wall would be a nice compromise."

"What happens when someone tries to contact them, and they don't reply?" Trista asked.

"They're not unconscious. They actually think they're searching the *Harlequin* right now. They're in a trance. It's something like sleepwalking, but without the walking part. They can still reply to their comms if they need to."

"I'll take your word for it," Trista said. "How long is this going to take?"

"Half an hour seems about right," Tanik said.

"So what are we supposed to do while we wait?" Trista asked.

Tanik shrugged but didn't offer any suggestions.

"I'm hungry," Buddy put in. "What's to eat?"

"You're always hungry," Trista said.

"I'm also hungry," Tanik replied.

"Me, too," Cassandra added softly.

"Where's the galley?" Tanik asked.

Trista fixed each of them with an incredulous look before throwing up her hands in exasperation and releasing her acceleration harness. "Next time you should all wait until someone starts shooting at us. That'd be a great time for a snack!"

Buddy perked up at the suggestion. "Actually, I do get hungry when—"

"Shut it, fur ball."

Tanik smiled and winked at Cassandra while Trista stormed out of the cockpit ahead of them.

As they followed her to the galley, Cassandra found herself staring at the back of Tanik's bald head and thinking that Trista was wrong about him. She had to be. Tanik was genuinely trying to save her father and the other Revenants from themselves—and save the rest of the galaxy from them. Why else would he work so hard to earn their trust? He was making the people who'd come to search their ship stare at a wall for half an hour, so he could definitely make Trista and Cassandra follow him around blindly if he wanted to. He didn't need them to trust him if all he needed was to make them go along with his plan.

Cassandra nodded to herself, reassured by that logic. Tanik was on their side. He didn't have any hidden agendas.

CHAPTER 37

The palace loomed large and terrifying in the distance. Four spires rose high from the corners of the *I*-shaped edifice, tracing shadows against the night. The closer she got, the more Cassandra felt her footsteps dragging. She hadn't seen her father in almost four months. What would she say to him when she returned? And more importantly, how would he react? The last time she'd seen him, he'd thrown her into a wall and knocked her unconscious for daring to talk back to him. What would he do to her now for daring to run away from home? Not that the Tarsian Palace could really be called a home, much less *her* home.

"Is everything all right, Cassandra?" Gatticus asked, glancing briefly in her direction.

"No," she admitted, and gave her head a quick shake. "I'm scared."

"Because of the mission?"

Cassandra's eyes flared in alarm, and she looked around quickly to make sure none of the shadowy pedestrians walking by them had taken a sudden interest in their conversation. But none of them had. They were all walking with their heads down and faces hidden. "Because of my dad," she explained. "He's not the same anymore. Not since he started drinking that glowing water."

"I see. If it makes you feel better, you are not alone. Substance abuse changes people, and those changes can be frightening for their loved ones."

"Yeah," Cassandra agreed. "The worst part is that he doesn't seem to notice his own behavior. He's nothing like he used to be."

"I am sorry for your loss," Gatticus said.

Cassandra fixed him with a puzzled look. Her *loss*. That was a strange thing to say about someone who was still alive, but Gatticus was right. In a lot of ways, her father was dead.

They walked on in silence until the palace walls came into view, at which point Gatticus reminded her to watch her tongue and stick to the script Tanik had given them. "I'm preparing to switch data sets now," he added. "Do you remember the activation word?"

Cassandra nodded. "Yes."

"Don't use it until you're sure that it's safe," he added.

"I'll be careful."

Gatticus fell silent once more, and they walked on ahead for a few more minutes. Dead ahead, Cassandra glimpsed the palace and the moonlit courtyard through the bars of a giant metal gate.

When they were just a few dozen meters away, Gatticus glanced at her. "It's not too late to turn back. We were safe in the warehouse."

Cassandra arched an eyebrow at him. His memory swap must have taken effect already. "We can't hide there forever, Gatticus." Turning back to the fore, she saw two Revenant soldiers in black armor come swirling out of the shadows around the palace gate. A giant red and white hologram blazed to either side of them, advertising the time and date of the inauguration. It would be held in the courtyard tomorrow evening.

"Halt," one of the soldiers said as they came within a dozen feet of him. "The palace and courtyard are closed. Assuming you have legitimate business here, you'll have to come back tomorrow."

"Do you know who I am?" Cassandra asked.

"Should I?" the soldier challenged, his gaze inscrutable behind his helmet. His head dipped up and down as he looked her over. "You are a Revenant," he concluded.

He must have seen the sword sheathed on her back.

"I am the Emperor's daughter, Cassandra Drake," she replied.

The two soldiers glanced at each other, then back to her. They hesitated, probably comparing her face to whatever records they had. A split second later, both soldiers dipped their heads in a shallow bow. "My apologies. It has been many months since you left, My Lady. Your father will be pleased to see that you have returned." The soldier's helmet turned a few degrees to the side until he was staring directly at Gatticus.

"And who is..." Suddenly both soldiers drew their swords. "You brought an Executor with you?" They must have sensed the void where his presence in the zero-point field should have been.

"I am no longer an Executor," Gatticus replied. "And the Union no longer exists. You have nothing to fear from me."

"He is an old friend," Cassandra said. "My father and I owe him our lives. His name is Gatticus Thedroux. Go ahead and ask. My father will want to see him too."

"One moment please." The soldier appeared to

freeze. A few moments later he began nodding in response to whatever conversation was going on inside his helmet. "You have both been cleared to enter the palace, but we'll need to scan you first."

A fan of blue light flickered out from the top of the gatehouse, passing over her and Gatticus from head to toe. As it finished, a green light winked on above the gate, and a pleasant chime sounded. In the next instant, the gate began to rumble open, sliding up like the portcullis of an ancient medieval castle.

"This way, My Lady," the soldier said, and gestured to the rising gate. "Your father is eager to see you both."

Cassandra's stomach fluttered with a conflicting mixture of hope and dread. Maybe she'd been worrying for nothing? Maybe her dad wasn't as far gone as she'd thought.

* * *

Darius watched as his daughter and *Gatticus,* of all people, approached his throne with the guard who'd received them at the palace gates. He'd considered receiving them in a less forbidding environment, but Cassandra had wasted a lot of time and resources by making them search for her. She didn't deserve a warm welcome. As for Gatticus, he was an android that could be programmed to commit any crime, and Darius couldn't simply read his thoughts to determine his agenda like he could with Cassandra. Androids and other non-biological lifeforms were uniquely dangerous in that respect.

"So, the prodigal returns," Darius declared as his daughter and Gatticus stopped at the foot of his throne. The soldier who'd escorted them bowed and silently retreated to one side. "How did you manage to remain hidden all this time?"

Cassandra stared up at him, her jaw thrust out defiantly, her blue eyes hard. "If you couldn't sense me, what makes you think any of the others could? It was not that hard to hide."

Darius snorted. "I suppose that makes sense. Why did you come back?" As he asked that question, Darius reached out for Cassandra's mind and rummaged through her thoughts and memories to find the answers he was looking for. "You were hiding in an abandoned warehouse," he said, his eyes half-lidded as he focused on her mind rather than his conventional senses. "No food other than what you could steal... no clothes. No plumbing." He smirked. "Is that what I smell?"

Cassandra said nothing to that, but he could see her lips trembling. A tear streaked down one cheek. "Still angry with me, I see." He turned to look at Gatticus next. "How did you two meet? In fact, how are you here at all? The last time anyone saw you was just before Tanik sent you on a one-way trip into deep space."

"Who is Tanik?" Gatticus looked to Cassandra, and she regarded him in turn with wide, blinking eyes. The android returned his gaze to the fore and shook his head.

Darius waved a hand to dismiss the question. "A mutual enemy."

Gatticus nodded slowly.

"What do you recall from your time on the *Deliverance*?"

"Nothing. I remember waking up stranded in deep space with all of my recent memories corrupted by physical damage. The transport's log showed that it had been launched from a Union carrier named the *Deliverance*."

"I see," Darius replied. "And how did you find your way out of that predicament?"

Gatticus went on to explain about creating a comm probe and getting rescued by a freelance pilot.

"Why come to Tarsus?" Darius asked.

"It seemed like a good place to get lost in the crowd. I couldn't be sure who in the Union wanted me dead, so I couldn't return to my old posting.

After the Revenants came, I had even more reason to hide, for fear of reprisals from angry citizens."

"And you're not afraid anymore?" Darius asked.

"Your daughter convinced me to turn myself in with her. She said that you owed me your life, and because of that you would make sure nothing happened to me."

"Indeed, that is true," Darius said. "In fact, I would like to reward you with an appointment in the Empire—as soon as I determine whether you can be trusted."

"You are welcome to scan my data core," Gatticus suggested.

Darius nodded and gestured to the soldier who had escorted his daughter and the android from the palace gates. "Take Gatticus to the data center for scanning."

"Yes, my lord," the man said and hurried to Gatticus's side at the foot of the throne. He bowed and Gatticus mimicked that gesture before turning to follow the soldier out.

As they left, Darius fixed his daughter with a stern look. "So? What have you got to say for yourself?"

Cassandra looked like she was grinding her teeth. He could feel anger and indignation rolling off her in waves. In spite of that, she bowed her head, and said, "I'm sorry for running away."

"And?" Darius prompted.

"Sorry for disrespecting you in front of your soldiers."

"Good." She could harbor all the simmering anger and defiance she liked, just so long as she knew that he was an unacceptable target for those emotions. Let her take it out on her subordinates.

Darius stood up from his throne and walked down the steps to greet her properly. He couldn't quite bring himself to hug her. Instead, he wrapped his arm around her shoulder and turned her back toward the entrance of the throne room. "It's late," he explained. "We have a big day tomorrow with the inauguration. I assume that's part of the reason you chose to come back now?" he asked, looking to her for confirmation as they walked through the throne room together.

Cassandra nodded but said nothing.

"Wise of you. You are just in time for me to introduce you to the galaxy as my right hand. Your authority will be second only to my own."

"What about Dyara?" Cassandra asked.

Darius hesitated, and his upper lip twitched into a sneer at the mention of her name. "She chose to forfeit any privileges she might have had."

Cassandra stopped walking just before they reached the doors, and Darius's arm slid off her shoulders. "What did you do to her?"

He fixed her with a cold look. "I didn't do anything. She left the palace by her own choice soon after you did. Unlike you, however, she has not yet recognized her mistake."

"Maybe I should talk to her," Cassandra said.

"Perhaps. There'll be time to track her down after the ceremony. Right now we must rest. Tomorrow will be a very busy day."

"What about Gatticus? When will you be done scanning him?"

Darius regarded her with eyebrows raised. "Why do you ask?"

"He... made me feel safe while we were hiding together. I don't know if I'll be able to sleep without him in the room."

Darius frowned, disappointed by Cassandra's weakness. "You are perfectly safe here. No harm will come to you."

"I'd feel better if Gatticus were there, and if I don't sleep well, I might fall asleep during the inauguration."

"Forget Gatticus!" Darius snapped. He shook his finger in her face in lieu of a more violent response.

Cassandra flinched, and tears sprang to her eyes. "What are you going to do? Throw me into another wall?"

Darius had to work hard to keep his anger in check. "I would if I thought it would knock some sense into you."

Cassandra held his gaze for a long moment before giving in with a nod and wiping the tears from her eyes. "I'm sorry."

"That's better," Darius growled. He gestured to the doors of the throne room, and they burst open, sending the guards on the other side sprawling. He stormed out, setting a brisk pace for Cassandra to follow. That had the added benefit of getting her out of his sight. He took deep breaths to cool his temper as he went. Cassandra knew just how to provoke him. It was as if she did it on purpose! Good thing he'd never had more children. Cassandra was more than enough to deal with.

CHAPTER 38

Cassandra lay awake in her bed, staring at the dark, fuzzy ceiling. Her mind raced with anxious thoughts. How was she supposed to infect her dad now? Gatticus had the virus, and he was locked up in the data center being scanned to make sure he wasn't a threat—even though he was.

What if they found Gatticus's hidden memories and learned about their plot to infect the Revenants? What if they found out that she was involved? Her father would lose it if he found out that she was secretly plotting against him. The frosty reception she'd got from him only reinforced her fears. He was dangerous and unpredictable. She couldn't rely on whatever lingering affection he might feel toward her. If her father found out she was working with Tanik, he might kill her himself.

Cassandra shivered. Her chest ached, and her throat hurt. All kids were afraid of monsters. She wasn't any different. For a long time her monster had been cancer, but now the monster was her father.

She rocked her head from side to side on her pillow. It was wet with tears. She had to get him back. She had to try. He'd risked everything to save her when he followed her into cryo storage to wait for a cure to her illness. Now it was her turn to risk everything for him.

Cassandra got out of bed and crossed her room to the door. There was no need to get dressed first. She was still wearing the clean uniform she'd put on after taking a much-needed shower. Cassandra waved the door open.

No guards were there to greet her—a sign that she'd earned her father's trust. Her mental shield must have worked. Cassandra nodded to herself, encouraged that she might succeed. She was going to need her father's trust to have any hope of infecting him with the virus tonight.

But first things first, she had to get down to the data center and convince whoever was in charge of scanning Gatticus to let him go. Her dad wanted her to step into her role as his second-in-command, inspiring fear and obedience wherever she went.

Well, he was just about to get what he'd asked for.

* * *

The soldier guarding the data center stepped sideways to block the door. "The android has been isolated for scanning. You can't take him out without an express order from the Emperor himself."

"I am the Emperor's daughter," Cassandra intoned and took a menacing step toward the man. "If I say he should be released, then you will do as I command."

The soldier crossed his arms over his chest. "Not without permission from your father."

"Have the scans been completed?"

"That's not the point."

"Have they or not?" Cassandra demanded. It was a gamble, but it had been at least two hours since they'd arrived at the palace. How long could a data scan take, anyway?

"Your father gave the order to put the android in isolation, and your father has to be the one to release him."

"The Emperor is a busy man, and you would do well to refer to him as *Emperor*."

The soldier frowned. "Of course."

"What's your name—never mind—" Cassandra reached into his mind and snatched the answer from his thoughts. "Corporal Kellar, I'm going to count to three. If I have to say *three* and you still haven't opened that door, I'm going to knock your head into that wall until your skull caves in. And you're not going to fight back, because my father is the Emperor and if you hurt his little girl, even in self-defense, he'll do something much worse than crack your skull. Do we understand each other?"

Corporal Kellar's hazel eyes widened, and his Adam's apple bobbed up and down. "Yes, My Lady." He stepped aside and keyed the door open. "The android is powered down in the archives room. Second door to the right."

Cassandra's gaze sharpened, and she took another step toward the Corporal. He leaned away in response. "So the scans are done," she guessed.

"I really can't say. I'm not privy to that information. The chief analyst is in charge, and he already went to bed. I just guard the door."

Cassandra considered that. "If that's the case, they might not have even started scanning him."

"Again, I really can't—"

"Say. Of course," Cassandra said, cutting him off with a wave of her hand. "I'll find out for myself." She breezed through the door and down a long, dark aisle between stacks of blinking blue and white data cubes. The data center was deserted. She walked down the aisle until the stacks ended and a hallway with doors began. The second door to the right had a glowing plate on the door that read *Archives.* Cassandra tried waving the door open, but it was locked with a key code. She flicked a scowl over her shoulder, aimed for the Corporal back at the doors of the data center. Reaching around, she drew the sword from the sheath on her back and summoned a shield. The blade began glowing a dim, ghostly white, and she plunged it through the door, drawing a circle big enough for her to step through. She kicked the center, and it caved inward. Ducking through into a dark room, she found Gatticus standing right behind the door, his face and expression limned in an eerie green light from the screen of a nearby data terminal.

"Gatticus?" she asked.

But he gave no reply. His expression was blank and staring. A thick conduit snaked from his hip to the terminal. The screen was filled with scrolling green lines of text. Cassandra walked over and read what she could from the screen. The text was scrolling by too fast to read, but at the top was a static line that read: *Scan 5% Complete.*

She blinked in shock. If they'd started scanning

him an hour ago, that meant it would take another twenty hours to finish! By then the inauguration would be over.

She couldn't afford to wait that long, and she couldn't take Gatticus out of the data center while he was obviously still being scanned. *That will just make my dad suspicious of* me. There had to be another way. Maybe she could smuggle the virus out without taking Gatticus with her. Cassandra scanned the room, looking for security cameras. She didn't see any. Walking around in front of Gatticus, she pulled up his shirt and touched his navel to open the utility compartment. A synthskin-covered panel popped open, revealing two gleaming metal canisters, each about the size of her fist. Too big to hide in the palm of her hand, but maybe small enough to hide in one of her pockets.

She grabbed one of the canisters and shut the compartment. Slipping it into her left pocket, a conspicuous fist-sized bulge appeared. Why hadn't she thought to bring a bag, or a jacket? Cassandra cast about, looking for something to put the virus in. She scanned the shelves in the archive room. They were filled with data cubes. If she hollowed one of them out with her sword, she could put the virus inside. She could say she was removing the cube because she wanted to learn a new skill. Cassandra walked up to the nearest shelf and used her extra-sensory implant to scan the labels of the data cubes.

She found security tapes from the palace, personnel files, Tarsian history, records of meetings... and then she hit the jackpot. One of the cubes was someone's personal library, labeled *Useful Books*. Cassandra checked the contents. The cube was filled with books on business, psychology, organizational management, accounting... as well as a host of other dry topics. She made a face but pulled the cube off the shelf. Holding it carefully in one hand, she summoned the weakest shield she could and used her sword to slowly carve a chunk out of the cube. Acrid smoke poured into the room, making her gag. When she was done, she sheathed her sword and quickly stashed the piece she'd carved out under the nearest set of shelves.

She waited a few seconds for the cube to cool before putting the canister containing the virus inside. It fit well enough, but she had to hold it in with her hands, and now no one could actually check the label or the contents to figure out what was stored on the cube. Cassandra frowned. If she'd thought about that, she could have picked any old cube off the shelf.

Cassandra spared one last glance at Gatticus before hurrying out and back through the data center. When she reached the door, there were four more soldiers waiting for her, in addition to the guard she'd had to deal with earlier.

"Where's the android?" the soldier with the most stripes asked. Cassandra wasn't good at recognizing rank insignia, but she thought he might be a sergeant. "And what's that in your hands?" he asked, jerking his chin to indicate the data cube she was holding.

CHAPTER 39

"**I** am the Emperor's daughter, and you're questioning me?"

The sergeant shrugged. "I can get the emperor himself to do it if you prefer. Are you going to answer me, or do I have to wake him up?"

"I don't think you want to wake him," Cassandra replied, hoping that was true. "You know how he can get."

"Then let's spare each other the unpleasantness. Why did you feel the need to break into the data center to see the android? And what's in that data cube?"

"His name is Gatticus," Cassandra replied. "And I had to break in because the guard at the door couldn't tell me anything about the status of his scan. When I found him, I saw that his scans aren't done yet, so I left him in the data center. I found the cube there with Gatticus. It contains some books that I'd like to feed into my neural mapper."

"You can access the library from any terminal in the palace," the sergeant pointed out.

"These books aren't in the library," Cassandra replied.

"I can't let you withdraw sensitive information from the data center. How do I know that cube is filled with books? I can't access its contents, ID code, or label. It could be anything."

Cassandra's heart was hammering in her chest and ears, but she tried not to let that show. Instead, she fixed the man with her most defiant glare. "You can, and you will let me take whatever I want from wherever I want. Tell my father if you must, but I'm taking the cube."

"I see." The sergeant replied. "As you wish. The Emperor *will* hear about this in the morning."

Cassandra gave the man a thin half smile and then breezed by him and his squad. She sucked in a deep breath as she went, struggling to calm her racing heart. Her palms were slick with sweat, and her legs were shaking.

But she'd done it. She had the virus. Now all she had to do was find a way to get it into her father's room. Unfortunately, his room would probably be guarded, too, and the door would almost certainly be locked. She needed some excuse to wake him and get into his room to plant the virus.

Cassandra racked her brain for an idea as she walked through the palace to his room. Somehow, Tanik hadn't thought to develop their plan beyond this point. He'd left her with the vague and complicated task of infecting her father without offering any specific ideas for how to do so. Cassandra thought about that as she climbed a broad, winding staircase up to her father's room. She could have taken an elevator, but the stairs gave her more time to think.

Think, Cass! she urged herself, as if inspiration were a door that would open if only she knocked hard enough.

* * *

Cassandra came up with an idea to get the virus into her father's room just before she reached the tenth floor. His sleeping quarters and private space encompassed the entire floor.

Instead of going up there, she stopped on the floor below and started down the corridor from the stairwell. This floor contained the sleeping quarters for the palace staff. Using her Awareness to keep track of her father, Cassandra tried to find the point directly below his bed. He was lying there now, presumably fast asleep, which gave her a window of opportunity. If she could get below him, she could cut a hole in the floor and push the canister with the virus up under his bed. There it would be safely out of sight, but still close enough to infect him while he slept.

As she drew near to the point below her father's bed, Cassandra saw that it was located somewhere on the other side of the door to room #12. And she could see with her connection to the ZPF that there was someone sleeping inside that room.

Cassandra grimaced. Even if she could get that person to let her in, how would she explain the need to cut a hole in their ceiling? She had to find another way. Maybe she would have a chance to infect her father tomorrow.

But there were no guarantees of that. She needed to get him alone and pin him down in one place long enough for the canister's timed release to let the virus out.

Cassandra continued down the corridor, checking the surrounding rooms for occupants with her Awareness. The room two doors down was empty. Cassandra tried the door controls. The door swished open, revealing a bed and a closet.

She stepped inside and shut the door. The room looked unused. She went to check the closet and found it empty. Glancing up, Cassandra used her Awareness to figure out what part of her father's room was above her...

She saw a luxuriously appointed bathroom and smiled. *Perfect.* When he got up in the middle of the night, or the next morning, the nanites would sense him and do their job. Unfortunately, he'd be awake so he might see a glimmer of nanites in the air. There wasn't much to do about that. At least he wouldn't be able to sense them in the ZPF.

Cassandra placed her hollowed-out data cube on the bed and shut her eyes, reaching out once more to guide herself to a point directly below the garbage can that sat between the sink and toilet. Opening her eyes once more, she found herself standing right in front of the door. She drew her sword and summoned a shield to enhance the blade. Hopefully, it wouldn't make too much noise as it cut through the floor....

* * *

Darius saw the exact same scene unfolding again, but this time he saw it from a disembodied, third-person perspective. He saw the crowds screaming, falling, scattering, and he saw the shimmering clouds of nanites undulating in the air.

He saw himself put on the helmet that he'd arranged to be hidden inside the lectern on the speaker's podium. His bulky black and gold ceremonial robes hid the fact that he was already wearing a suit of power armor and an oxygen tank. The helmet was all he needed to add in order to properly isolate himself from infection.

This time as the shimmering silver clouds raced toward him, Darius saw himself stand his ground, waiting for them to arrive. Even before the nanites reached him, he collapsed in agony, just as he had in his previous vision. Just then his daughter came striding out from the back of the podium. She was wearing a suit of armor like him. That wasn't strange by itself. He probably would order her to wear a suit in order to avoid infection. Cassandra walked up to him, but she showed no signs of concern over his thrashing, or for the screaming crowds in the courtyard. She just stood there, watching as he died.

"It's okay, Dad," he heard her say. "It will be over soon."

It wasn't until his glowing green eyes rolled up in his head and his back arched with a final spasm that she began to show signs of distress. "Dad?" She dropped to her haunches beside him and shook him by his shoulders. "Dad! Answer me!"

When he didn't even twitch, and the last stragglers in the courtyard collapsed in spasming heaps, Cassandra looked up and slowly shook her head, surveying the massacre. "What have I done?!" she asked in an anguished voice. "Tanik!" she screamed. "Tanik! You lied to me!"

Darius woke up with a roar and burst out of his bed. Whispering voices chattered urgently in his ear. The air seemed to tremble around him. A second later he realized that *he* was trembling, not the air.

What had he just seen?

Darius wasn't surprised that Tanik was behind the virus. What surprised him was that his own daughter was also involved. Moreover, somehow Darius's planned countermeasures were not going to be enough. Could the virus eat through his armor? But no, that didn't make sense. Cassandra hadn't been affected by it, and in his vision she'd been wearing a suit just like his. There had to be some other explanation. Maybe he was going to get infected by the nano virus before he put on his helmet, and if Cassandra was involved, then she might be the one who was going to infect him.

As that thought occurred to him, the whispers returned, but softly. *Confirmation?* he wondered.

Darius reached out with his Awareness, trying to sense any lurking threats in his quarters. He couldn't detect anything immediately wrong with his surroundings, so he reached out further, searching for his daughter...

But he couldn't find her anywhere in the palace. He expanded his awareness to search the entire city, but he couldn't find her beyond the walls of the palace either. She had to be hiding her presence from him again. Where was she and what was she doing that she felt the need to hide?

"Lights, 25 percent," Darius said, glancing around quickly as a dim golden hue suffused the room, peeling back the shadows. There was no one in there with him that he could see, and he could still sense the guards posted outside his door. Furthermore, his door was locked from the inside, and he was the only one who could open it to let Cassandra or anyone else in. His quarters had to be secure.

The whispering voices of the Sprites returned, but this time he heard them retreating from him rather than echoing in his ears. He turned toward the sound and saw a faintly glowing tendril of light trace a path toward the bathroom. He started in that direction.

But after taking just two steps, those whispers

became urgent shouts, and the tendril of light raced away from the bathroom. Darius got the message. There was something in there. Something dangerous. A shimmering cloud of nanites, perhaps?

Darius considered his options. He could open a wormhole and leave immediately, or simply go out the front door and sleep somewhere else, but if he did that, he might alert Cassandra to the fact that he was on to her, which might scare Tanik off, too.

No, there was a much simpler solution. He crossed over to his closet and opened it to reveal his ceremonial robes and the accompanying set of power armor. He put the suit on and then went to the front doors of his quarters and waved them open. The guards turned at the sound of the doors swishing open. "Give me your helmet," he said to one of them.

"My helmet, Lord?"

"Now," Darius snapped.

The guard twisted his helmet off, revealing short red hair and pale blue eyes. Darius took the helmet and quickly slipped it over his head. It sealed against the collar of his suit with a faint *hiss*. Darius mentally pressurized the suit and opened the valves to the oxygen tank on his back. Now safely isolated from the environment, he turned and went back inside. Shutting and locking the door behind him, he set out to investigate whatever threat was lurking in his bathroom.

CHAPTER 40

Cassandra used the ZPF to float the canister containing the virus up through the hole that she'd carved in the ceiling. She placed it in a shadowy corner behind the garbage can in her father's bathroom, and then beat a hasty retreat from the room before the nanites could activate and hone in on *her*. They weren't programmed to be discriminating. They would infect the nearest person, whoever that was.

Once Cassandra was back in the stairwell, she took a moment to check on her father with her Awareness. He was up and moving about. She saw his luminous silhouette walking through his room. It looked like he might be heading for the bathroom, but it was hard to be sure. Cassandra thought about using her Awareness to cast her mind into the room with him and see what was going on up there, but with her father awake now, it was too risky to do that. She would just have to trust that her plan would work. Maybe Gatticus could confirm that for her later, after his scan was completed—*if* it was finished before the ceremony, that is.

Cassandra turned and hurried down the stairs to her room. She'd been out long enough already. It was time to get back to bed before she attracted more attention to herself.

* * *

Trista walked up to the palace gates in her exosuit, pulling a power-assisted trolley with two hundred kilograms of dormant nanites in a metal crate. The crate was actually an agricultural unit that she and Tanik had purchased earlier that day, using what little funds and credit she still had to her name. It was designed to spray fertilizer or pesticides, but it would work just as well for micro machines.

"Halt!" the nearest guard said as she stopped in front of the gates.

"Hey there," Trista said, trying to sound casual rather than kakking-her-pants nervous.

"Turn around. This area is restricted."

Trista wrinkled her brow. "Ah, I've got a work order to spray the courtyard with pesticides tonight—something to do with a weaver bug infestation?"

"I don't have any record of that," the guard said. "I'll have to call it in. One moment."

Trista smiled and held her breath. Tanik was supposed to be lurking somewhere within earshot of the gate, standing by to work his magic and get her past security. After a few seconds, she let her breath out in a sigh and glanced around, as if bored by the wait.

Tanik... where the fek are you?

"Everything checks out," the guard said. "Stand by for a scan."

Trista nodded as a fan of blue light flickered down from the top of the gate. Once it reached her toes, a green light snapped on, and a pleasant chime sounded. The gate rumbled up into the tower above it, and both guards nodded.

"Proceed," one of them said.

Trista grabbed the handle of her trolley and pulled it along behind her into the courtyard. Moonlight gleamed on the flagstones. Here and there light glowed in the windows of the palace. She hoped no one was watching the courtyard, but even if they weren't at the moment, someone was bound to glance out a window in the next hour and a half while she seeded the courtyard with nanites.

She hoped Tanik was up to the task of *blinding their eyes,* as he claimed.

Pulling her trolley into position at one corner of the courtyard, Trista took a moment to survey how much ground she had to cover. The palace was actually a sprawling complex, with dozens of buildings rising around the central I-shaped structure. A miniature city within the city. The courtyard itself had to be at least a couple of hundred meters on each side. She ran the numbers through her extra-sensory chip and came up with an area of about 40,000 square meters. That was a lot of ground to cover in an hour and a half. She was going to have to hustle.

Trista activated the sprayer, and a water-based solution of nanites sprayed out onto the flagstones to either side of the trolley. She grabbed the handle and turned the trolley to push it in front of her. Setting a brisk pace, she walked down the side of the courtyard. Even with the trolley's power-assist, it was tiring work. Within just a few minutes she could hear her breath echoing raggedly inside her helmet. Her lungs and muscles burned. She glanced up at the palace periodically, hoping that Tanik would be able to handle his end of things. He had assured her that he could blind the eyes of any number of observers—with the exception of the emperor himself.

Trista took a short break in the shadow of the steps leading to the palace. Her heart hammered in her chest as much from fear as from the exertion. She peered up at the towering structure and tried to guess which of the handful of illuminated windows belonged to the emperor. She hoped none of them. Tanik *claimed* that he was sound asleep.

Sucking in a quick breath, Trista grabbed the handle of the sprayer and went back to pushing it through the courtyard.

* * *

Darius stood in his quarters, safely encased in his suit of armor. He'd already found the silver canister in his bathroom. He'd seen the faint shimmer of nanites in the air, and found the hole in the floor under the garbage can. Now he stood at the wall of windows in his living room, using up the air in the oxygen tank on his back while he tried to decide what to do about this development. Cassandra would pay for her betrayal, but he couldn't confront her about it. Not yet. He had to wait and pretend he was none the wiser if he wanted to catch Tanik, too.

A hint of movement in the courtyard below the palace caught Darius's eye. He frowned and closed his eyes, casting his mind out and using his Awareness to get a better look. In his mind's eye he floated just above the courtyard and watched as someone in an exosuit pushed a metal crate along. Liquid was spraying from the sides of the crate, wetting the flagstones and making them gleam brightly in the moonlight.

So this was how the nanites he'd seen in his visions had gotten into the courtyard—yet another part of Tanik's plot revealed. He could sense that the person in the courtyard was a woman, and not a Revenant, but Tanik had to be somewhere nearby in order for her to have made it past security.

Darius thought about trying to flush him out now and hunt him down, but that wouldn't help him deal with the other Revenants. He needed Tanik's plot to wipe them out first. Besides, now that he'd found the means by which Tanik and Cassandra had planned to infect him, there was no longer any danger to himself.

But Tanik needed to believe that Darius was also infected, or else he would run away and hide again. He would have to pretend to succumb to the virus.

Darius's lips curved into a cold smile. He would lure his enemies out and kill them. Cassandra was now one of those enemies. It was ironic that he'd spent so much of his life trying to keep her alive, and now he was going to kill her.

His smile turned to a scowl. She could have had everything. Instead, she'd chosen to throw it all away and join his enemies. What a brat she had become. Her betrayal cut deep. His whole body trembled with rage just thinking about it. Somehow he had to keep a lid on that anger until the ceremony. He resolved to avoid Cassandra as much as possible. The less he saw of her, the better.

CHAPTER 41

Back in bed, Cassandra stared at the ceiling. She couldn't sleep. Not after all her sneaking around. There was too much going on and too much at stake. If her dad didn't get infected by the virus, he was going to stay the way he was. She might never have another chance to reverse the damage that the Sprites had done to him. And even if her dad did get infected, there was no guarantee that it would work. They hadn't tested the virus on Revenants.

And then there was the added problem of the soldiers she'd run into at the Data Center. What would they tell her father in the morning? They could get her into big trouble, or worse, make him suspicious enough to investigate what she'd been up to. If he found out about the virus she'd planted in his room, he'd kill her.

Cassandra took a deep breath and let it out in a ragged sigh. She shut her eyes for the umpteenth time and tried to will herself to sleep.

A metallic *thunk* sounded somewhere in her room. Cassandra's eyes flew wide. *What was that?* She strained to listen, but all she heard was the quiet whisper of air cycling into her room from the climate control system.

Thunk, thunk.

Cassandra sat up and reached out with her Awareness, searching for the source of that sound. Within seconds, she found a small, crouching presence up near the ceiling, behind an air vent in the wall beside her bed. That presence was familiar. Cassandra got out of bed and walked up to the vent. Peering up at it, she whispered, "Buddy?"

"Heya, Cassy," he whispered back.

"What are you doing here?" She stood blinking up at the vent in confusion.

"I came to get an update."

"Tanik sent you?"

"Yes."

Cassandra snorted with annoyance, thinking about how she'd had to cut a hole in the floor of her father's room in order to smuggle the virus in. And all this time, Buddy could have snuck it in through the vents! But thinking about it some more, she guessed that Tanik hadn't given Buddy that task because he wasn't a Revenant. He couldn't hide his presence, and her father would have sensed him coming.

"So? Have you got anything to report?" Buddy prompted.

Cassandra filled him in with all the recent events, and how as far as she could tell, she'd been successful.

"Great," Buddy said. "I'll be sure to tell Scarface the good news. Anything else before I go?"

"There is one other thing," Cassandra said. "Gatticus is not going to be there for the ceremony. He's still being scanned, and I don't think he'll be reactivated until after it's all over, so if the timer doesn't work, Gatticus won't be around as a backup."

"Got it. I'll tell the others. See you."

"Wait," Cassandra said. "What about Trista? Did she manage to do her part?"

"She did. She's already back at the *Harlequin*, making plans to run for it if this doesn't work."

Cassandra nodded. "If it comes to that, I'll try to join you."

"Great! Good night, Cassy."

Cassandra smiled, wishing she could give his head a pat. He hated that, but his reaction was too funny. She could have used the comic relief right now. "Good night, Buddy," she said, but she could already hear him scampering away through the ducts—*thunk, thu-thunk, thunk...*

* * *

Tanik sat in the galley of the Harlequin, smiling as he listened to Buddy's report. He especially liked the news about Gatticus being out of commission. That meant he wouldn't have to wait for the Keth to take the android out before he could come out of hiding.

"Good work," Tanik said. "You're sure no one at the palace saw you?"

Buddy shook his furry head and blinked huge black eyes. "No one saw me."

"Someone probably sensed or heard you," Tanik said. "But they probably dismissed you as harmless vermin. You're lucky. It's a blessing to be so easily overlooked."

"Vermin! Overlooked!" Buddy drew himself up on his hind legs and bared his teeth in a snarl.

Tanik watched him with a curling smile.

"Settle down, Furball," Trista said, and scooped him up in her arms. Buddy hissed at Tanik when they came to eye level with each other.

"He wasn't *calling* you vermin, right Tanik?"

"Of course not," he replied, shaking his head.

"And the important thing is, everything is going according to plan," Trista went on.

"Yes."

"So my part's done?" Trista asked, with eyebrows raised. "I can go?"

"You can leave immediately if you like."

Trista's eyes narrowed in thought, as if she were considering the idea.

People like her were the real vermin, scurrying away from danger, hiding in the shadows, and profiteering from illegal enterprises—not to mention being a royal pain in Tanik's backside. He hoped she would decide to stick around so that he'd have the chance to kill her for all the trouble she'd given him, but if not, he would put out a warrant for her capture later—after *he* became emperor in Darius's stead.

Tanik smiled and stood up from the acceleration couch where he was sitting. "Well, I'll take my leave of you now," he said. "Thank you for your help."

"Yeah? And where are you going, Scarface?" Trista asked, her eyes pinching into slits.

Tanik regarded her with eyebrows innocently raised, as if he couldn't imagine why she would be suspicious of him. "Elsewhere. I assumed you would be leaving soon, but I have to stay to make sure everything goes as planned."

"Right. Well, good luck with that," Trista said.

"Thank you," Tanik replied, smiling thinly at her as he turned to leave. Now all he had to do was find a cryo lab where he could convince the technicians to freeze him until just before the ceremony began. That would stop the timers of the nanites in his blood, which relied on his metabolism to supply their power.

As Tanik exited the rear airlock of Trista's transport and started across the landing pad, he saw a rosy glow cresting over the top of the surrounding spaceport. It was dawn already. That meant he had about twelve hours before the ceremony began. More than enough time to freeze himself, wake up, and then make his way to the courtyard to confront Darius. He needed to save a few hours so that he could find a way to extract or disable the nanites in his blood. It wouldn't take twelve whole hours to kill Darius. Maybe one or two, but it was nice to have the extra time just in case.

Tanik smiled at the thought of the confrontation. Darius had no idea what was coming for him. Tanik had planned it all out meticulously. Not only would Darius pay, but so would the Keth—with the exception of Feyra, of course. He would make sure he saved her.

Tanik's smile grew into a twisted grin. They had all underestimated him. They were blinded by their arrogance. Perhaps Darius was the more powerful Revenant, but Tanik was the smarter one, and he'd take savvy over raw strength any day.

CHAPTER 42

—TWELVE HOURS LATER—

Cassandra stood at the back of the podium, watching as her father went out to greet the massive crowd in the courtyard below the palace steps. There were tens of thousands gathered there. More than half of them were Revenants, who had no choice but to attend. The others were probably local Tarsians, and maybe a few interstellar travelers who'd come from other planets to be a part of history. Ultimately, it all made her father look a lot more popular than he probably was, but it was an impressive display all the same.

Cassandra glanced to one side, her eyes tracking down below the front steps of the palace, to the alley where she'd stashed her oxygen tank. She'd decided to wear a complete suit of power armor to the ceremony. She figured that if her father had asked about it, she could always say she was guarding against possible assassination attempts. But the oxygen tank was harder to explain, so she'd smuggled it into an alley beside the podium. It hadn't been hard. Everyone in the palace had been so busy preparing for the inauguration that they hadn't even seemed to notice her. She kept expecting one of the soldiers she'd met last night to tell her father about her illegal entry to the Data Center. If they had, he hadn't paid any attention to them, because he'd never confronted her about any of it. In fact, she'd barely seen him all day.

Cassandra took a deep breath, and listened to it whistling in through the air intakes in the back of her suit. Right now those vents were open, but as soon as she saw her father or the crowds reacting to the virus, she'd shut the intakes and run down to grab her oxygen tank. She could hold her breath for a few minutes, and there would still be some air inside her suit. She hoped she'd have enough time to retrieve the tank and connect it to her suit. If not, she'd get infected along with everyone else. That wasn't necessarily a bad thing. She wasn't planning to be the last Revenant in the Galaxy. She'd expose herself to the virus willingly when the time came. But if something went wrong, she might need her powers to escape.

Cassandra frowned as a new set of worries crowded her thoughts. There was no way to know if her dad had actually been infected last night. And if not, this would all be for nothing. Her dad would find some way to defeat the virus and then re-infect the Revenants with Sprites. She pushed those negative thoughts from her head and directed her attention back to her father and the cheering crowds.

He had his hands raised for attention. "Welcome, everyone!" he said. "This day we come together with one heart and one mind to celebrate the end of the Cygnians' rule over us. They are defeated, and they are never coming back!"

The crowd went crazy, screaming and roaring with delight. It went on and on, and...

Cassandra's brow furrowed as she realized what was really happening. The crowd wasn't screaming with delight, they were screaming in pain. The virus had already been activated. People were dropping by the hundreds, others scattering and running in confused circles.

Cassandra drew in a deep breath and sealed the air intakes of her suit. Peripherally, she saw her father sink to his knees, but she didn't have time to check on him. She raced across the podium and down the steps to reach her air tank. Finding it right where she'd left it in the alley, Cassandra snapped it into place along the magnetic docking plates on her back. Using her ESC, she mentally opened the tank's valve and re-opened the intakes for her suit, which would now be sucking in air from the tank rather than outside.

By the time she finally let out the breath she was holding, her lungs were burning, and her brain was buzzing with the urgent need to *breathe!*

Gasping for air, she turned and hurried back up the steps to check on her father. She kept a hand on the hilt of the sword sheathed at her hip—just in case. She found him collapsed and spasming on the podium at the base of the lectern. He had a *helmet* on, and she noticed what looked like a suit of power armor lurking beneath his robes. She blinked in shock, realizing that he'd somehow *known* this was coming. He must have had a vision. But that vision hadn't been enough to warn him about the virus she'd smuggled into his bathroom.

"It's okay, Dad," she said, standing over him. "It will be over soon."

He glared up at her, his eyes full of rage and pain, but said nothing. As she watched, his back spasmed, arching and lifting him off the ground.

His teeth flashed white in a rictus of agony.

Worry burst like fireworks in Cassandra's head. Apprehension swirled. She looked up to see that the crowds in the courtyard weren't faring any better. There were still a few people running around screaming and swatting at the nanites like they were bugs, but for the most part, everyone had already collapsed and fallen eerily silent.

Cassandra looked back to her father just in time to see his eyes roll up in his head. "Dad?" She dropped to her knees beside him and shook him by his shoulders. "Dad! Answer me!" But he showed no signs of a response. His breathing was shallow and irregular.

Cassandra looked up in horror and checked the courtyard once more. Even the ones who'd been running around in crazed circles had all collapsed now. This wasn't at all what she'd been expecting. She'd expected them to get sick, but not for them to all fall into a coma! "What have I done?!" she cried. "Tanik!" she screamed. "Tanik! You lied to me!"

In that same instant, she saw a shimmering portal open up at the foot of the stairs. More than a dozen people came walking out, all of them wearing exosuits, and all of them shielded with the muted white glow of the ZPF. They were brandishing glowing swords. She caught a glimpse of their glowing eyes and translucent white skins. They were Keth.

Cassandra stood up and drew her own sword, determined to protect her father from them.

"Stay back!" she said, summoning a shield of her own and pointing her sword at the invading aliens.

They stopped at the foot of the steps. "Where is the one called Gatticus?" one of them asked.

"I'm not telling you anything!" Cassandra replied in a trembling voice, even as she wondered how they knew about the android. But she figured it out a split second later. Tanik had told them. Of course he had. Why else would they be here now, and how else would they have known to prepare for the threat of infection by wearing exosuits?

A flicker of movement drew Cassandra's gaze to one side, and she saw someone else come striding into the courtyard from an adjoining alley. This person was also wearing a suit, and his presence was all too familiar. It was Tanik. Somehow he'd managed to neutralize the virus that they'd infected him with. This had all been a setup.

"Tanik!" Cassandra screamed. "What have you done?!"

The Keth turned, waiting for him to arrive at the foot of the stairs. Tanik walked steadily through the courtyard, heedless of all the people he was stepping on along the way.

In the next instant, Cassandra felt firm hands land on her shoulders, and one of the Keth cried out in alarm. Twisting around to look, Cassandra saw her father, back on his feet, and smiling coldly at her.

"Hello, Cassy," he said.

CHAPTER 43

"**D**ad! You're okay!" Cassandra said.

"No thanks to you," Darius replied. It was all he could do not to kill her right then and there, but he had more pressing concerns right now. He hadn't predicted that Tanik would bring the Keth to Tarsus. He never should have allowed his own wormhole to collapse. He'd been so focused on giving a good show to draw Tanik out of hiding, that he'd forgotten about the risk of dropping his defenses—even momentarily.

Darius released Cassandra's shoulders and took a long step sideways to get out from behind her. Drawing his sword and summoning a shield, he stood gazing down on Tanik and the Keth.

"It's a trap!" one of the Keth said.

"Yes," Tanik replied. "But not for us."

"Are you certain of that?" Darius asked.

"You said he would be infected with the others," the tallest of the Keth said. "You lied!"

"I didn't lie. Obviously, that part of the plan failed, but look around you! All of the others are dead. Darius is alone!"

"Dead?" Cassandra exclaimed. "What do you mean they're *dead?*"

Darius saw her backing away from the courtyard, shaking her head in denial. Clearly Tanik hadn't told her everything about his plot. He'd taken advantage of her naiveté again. A small part of him was relieved. She hadn't actually been plotting to murder her own father. Perhaps he wouldn't have to kill her, after all. Darius returned his gaze to the foot of the stairs.

"Your arrogance blinded you!" Tanik said, stepping in front of his people. "You foresaw all of this, and you let it happen anyway because the other Revenants were a threat to you. But what you failed to consider is that you might need their help. Now you're all alone to face fourteen Keth warriors, and me. With the Revenants gone and fewer people than ever sharing the same power source, we're far more formidable than we were the last time you fought us."

"Then so am I," Darius replied.

"It's still fifteen against one."

"Fifteen against two!" Cassandra said.

Darius turned to her with eyebrows raised, and nodded approvingly. She'd made a mistake by siding with Tanik against him, but at least she was on the right side now. "Cassandra, run!"

She gave a shallow nod, and together they ran back inside the palace, as much to get away from whatever lingering contagion might remain in the courtyard as to escape the Keth.

* * *

"Is it true?" Cassandra asked once they were inside the palace.

"Is what true?"

"That you knew about the virus."

"This is not the time or place to discuss anything," Darius replied.

That wasn't a denial. Cassandra stared at her father in shock. He stood barring the entrance of the palace, watching as the Keth came striding up the stairs with Tanik in the lead.

Cassandra had a bad feeling that Tanik had been telling the truth. How else would her father have known to prepare? He'd had a helmet within easy reach, and he was wearing a suit of power armor under his robes. "Did you know the virus would kill them?" Cassandra pressed.

Her father's helmet turned. "No."

Cassandra searched his glowing green eyes and reached out through the ZPF to test his thoughts. He wasn't lying, but she could tell that he wasn't upset that the Revenants were dead. He was just glad to have them out of the way.

"You need to make up your mind, Cass," Darius growled, and stabbed his finger into her chest. "Are you with me, or are you against me?"

Cassandra backed away from him, shaking her head. "I'm neither."

Darius's eyes flashed darkly. "Then get out of here while you still can!"

Cassandra's face screwed up in misery. "Fine!" she yelled back at him. "Get yourself killed, too—I don't care anymore!" She turned and ran through the entrance hall of the palace, putting as much distance between herself and her father as she could. She didn't even know where she was going. She just had to get away.

It was over. The whole thing had been a setup from the start. Tanik had used her, and her father didn't want her around, so why bother anymore? All she'd wanted was to save him, but he was clearly beyond saving.

As Cassandra left the entrance hall, she heard the first rumblings of a powerful storm booming in the distance. But no, the skies were clear outside.

This was more like an earthquake, or rubble crashing. Maybe Tanik and the Keth were tearing the palace down around Darius's ears. Cassandra caught herself using his name in her thoughts, but somehow that felt right now. He wasn't her father or her *dad* anymore. He was Emperor Drake.

Another *boom* rumbled somewhere behind her, followed by crashing rubble sounds. Cassandra stopped running, but not because she was having second thoughts about leaving the emperor to fend for himself. Rather, she was wondering what her next move should be. Whoever won, she didn't want to be around for it. She thought about Trista's offer.

Reaching out for the other woman's mind, Cassandra found her still waiting at the spaceport. *Wait. I'm coming*, she said, speaking through Trista's thoughts.

Cass? Is that you? came Trista's confused reply.

Yes.

Cassandra broke the connection, and turned in a quick circle to get her bearings. She was still on the first floor of the palace, halfway down the corridor leading from the entrance hall to the gardens at the back. She could slip out through the gardens easily enough and then make her way to the walls. She'd have to climb or jump over them, but that wouldn't be a problem for her. Cassandra started running again, heading down the corridor to the gardens. A second later she skidded to a stop as something occurred to her.

Gatticus. She couldn't leave him behind. Darius would destroy him for his part in everything, and Tanik... she had no idea what he would do with the android if he won, but she didn't trust him any more than her father at this point. They were both mass murderers.

Spotting a bank of elevators up ahead, Cassandra started running again. Once more she heard that booming sound, followed by more crashing noises. This time the whole palace shivered. Cassandra grimaced and glanced at the ceiling as concrete dust trickled down. *Don't cave in yet*, she thought as she hammered the elevator call button with the heel of one hand.

* * *

"Darius!" Tanik yelled from the speaker's podium outside. "If you're planning to hide in there, I'd think twice about it."

Hide no, Darius thought, but at least in the entrance of the palace there was no easy way for the Keth to surround him. They could break in through windows on the second floor and circle around, but that would take time, and at least he would have some warning with the sound of breaking glass.

Darius glared at his enemies through the metal lattice frames of two 12-foot glass doors. Tanik stood off about a dozen meters from the palace, with the Keth clustered behind him. They didn't seem to be in a hurry to press their advantage. Darius flexed his hand on the hilt of his sword and smirked. They were probably hesitating because they were scared.

Darius waved the doors open. "Come and get me!" he yelled, beckoning to them with his free hand.

In lieu of a reply, Tanik raised his hands toward the palace. The building shivered, and bits of rubble rained down. Moments later, a titanic *boom* sounded, followed by the rumbling of settling debris. Darius reached out with his Awareness to find that Tanik had just torn down one of the palace's four spires. It lay broken in the courtyard—a mountain of debris strewn over the masses of dead Revenants.

In the next instant, Darius saw a giant boulder come sweeping toward the entrance of the palace. He reached out to stop it, but the debris had too much momentum, and there wasn't enough time. He leapt out of the way just as a massive rock came crashing through the doors with an explosion of shattered glass and stone.

Darius landed to one side of the rubble, blinking in shock, his ears ringing with the violence of the impact. He half expected to see the Keth come storming through in the wake of that attack. Instead, he heard and sensed boulders breaching different parts of the palace. Moments later, Darius sensed the Keth entering the building. They were going to surround him after all. It was just a matter of time.

Scowling, Darius walked around the debris in the entrance hall to face Tanik once more. Only three of the Keth remained with him.

"Cowards!" Darius yelled, his voice amplified by the speakers in his helmet. He flourished his sword and set his feet in a wide stance, but they didn't budge. Tanik was probably waiting for the others to circle around and block off any possible avenue of escape. Darius couldn't afford to wait around until that happened.

Reaching for the mountain of rubble lying in the courtyard, he picked it up with his mind and threw it at his enemies. They saw it coming and managed to deflect the debris into the walls of the palace. The entire building shook under the assault, but Darius didn't stick around to see the front walls cave in. He turned and vaulted up the stairs to the second floor, using his Awareness to track the nearest Keth.

There were two of them, just coming into view at the end of a long corridor. They locked eyes with Darius, and he rushed toward them. In a matter of seconds, they were crossing blades in the tight space. Two swords flashed against his one, both trying to sneak past his guard. Darius grabbed one of the Keth in a mental hold, freezing his limbs and body. In that same instant, he gave the second one the hardest telekinetic shove he could. She flew into the wall at the end of the corridor, hard enough to make a physical impression, and then slumped to the ground—unconscious or dead. Turning back to the one that he'd frozen, Darius's swept his sword through the alien's midsection. The Keth's glowing amber eyes widened in horror just as his abdomen vanished with an explosion of fiery ashes and a greasy puff of smoke.

Darius walked over to the unconscious Keth and skewered her with his sword, punching a charred hole in her stomach to make sure she was dead.

Two down. Twelve to go, he thought, just as Tanik and the three Keth reached the top of the stairs.

"Now who's the coward?" Tanik chided. "Stand and fight!"

Darius darted down the next stretch of corridor, running through the palace at top speed and tracking the next Keth. He had to reduce their numbers before he stopped to face Tanik.

CHAPTER 44

Cassandra found the door to the Data Center unguarded, but locked, when she arrived. The lock didn't last long under her blade. After cutting it open, she ran down the aisle of blinking blue and white data cubes to reach the Archive Room where Gatticus should be. There was still a hole in the door from last night when she'd broken in. She found Gatticus in the exact same state as before— powered down and plugged in at the hip to the nearby data terminal. Her gaze darted to the holoscreen. Now the progress line above the scrolling green lines of text read: *Scan 79% Complete.*

She couldn't wait here for it to finish. Chewing her lower lip, Cassandra studied Gatticus more carefully. He had to have an on/off switch somewhere. She ran her hands over his body to look for hidden access panels, but couldn't feel any buttons or switches lurking under his clothes and artificial flesh. There had to be some way to turn him on!

Maybe if she pulled the data cable out of his hip, he would automatically restart. She yanked the cable out, and the text on the holoscreen stopped scrolling.

Cassandra looked at Gatticus's face. His expression was still frozen, his eyes a lifeless gray. She checked the port where the cable had been plugged in. *Bingo!* There was a likely-looking button there. Just as she stabbed it with her finger, she felt the hair on the back of her neck rise in warning. Faint, whispering voices tickled her eardrums. Something was wrong.

Gatticus jerked to life, and Cassandra glanced at him. Was *he* the threat she was sensing? Just them, a shadow ran into the room brandishing a glowing sword. Cassandra tried to draw hers to block, but there wasn't enough time. Gatticus put out his arm to block the blade, and Cassandra fell backwards in her hurry to get away. Gatticus's arm evaporated in a flash of molten metal, and he retreated hurriedly.

Their attacker advanced, backing them up against the data terminal and boxing them into a corner. Cassandra saw the pale, sparkling face of a Keth male behind the faceplate of his helmet. She finally managed to draw her sword and summon a shield to protect herself. "Stay back!" she said, shaking the glowing blade at the alien.

Instead, he took another step toward her and raised his blade for another strike. Cassandra reached into the ZPF and threw every single data cube in the room at him to create a distraction. They bounced off his exosuit and ricocheted off the walls and shelves. The assault seemed to give him pause; he stood there frozen and just out of reach, his mouth gaping open in shock.

Cassandra's brow furrowed. Her attack shouldn't have been more than a temporary distraction. Then she noticed the glowing blade poking through his stomach, rapidly burning a hole.

The Keth fell on his face, revealing his attacker.

"Dyara?" Cassandra could hardly believe it. "How did you...?"

The dark-haired woman rushed forward and wrapped her up in a hug. She withdrew a second later and glanced over her shoulder, as if expecting another Keth to come barging in. Looking back at Cassandra she said, "I sensed your distress and came to find you."

"But Darius said you left the palace...."

Dyara hesitated briefly before nodding. She was probably surprised to hear her call Darius by his name. "I did leave, but I didn't go far because I had a vision that you would return, and that your father was going to try to kill you."

Cassandra swallowed thickly. "Oh."

"What's going on in the palace?" Dyara asked. "How did the Keth get here? And what happened to everyone in the courtyard?"

"Hang on." Turning to Gatticus she nodded and said, "Gakram."

The android flinched, and his eyes blinked rapidly for a few seconds. She gave him a moment, then asked, "Do you remember why we came to the palace?" Her eyes searched Gatticus's as she waited for his reply.

"We came to infect your father with the virus."

"What virus?" Dyara asked.

Cassandra explained everything as quickly as she could. When she was finished, she added, "It didn't work. Darius didn't get infected, so we need to get out of here before he finds us and kills us."

Dyara looked torn. "Whoever wins, Darius or Tanik, it's not going to be good for anyone. Unless they somehow manage to kill each other, there's still going to be an evil dictator on the throne. We have to stop them."

"How?" Cassandra asked. "Darius is too strong, and Tanik has the Keth on his side."

"I might have an idea," Gatticus said.

Both Cassandra and Dyara looked to him. "Go on," Dyara said.

"I have a second canister of the virus in my utility compartment. If we can get it close to Darius and release the contents, he'll be infected just like the others were."

"That's not a bad idea," Dyara said. "And if we're lucky, we should be able to infect Tanik while we're at it."

Gatticus nodded. "That is possible, yes. The virus will infect anyone it finds nearby. There is enough of it to infect multiple people."

"But what about their suits?" Cassandra asked. "They're all wearing exosuits, and Darius is wearing power armor."

"That's a good point," Dyara said. "We'll need to get past those barriers somehow."

"You might not have to," Gatticus said. His gray eyes found Cassandra, and he nodded to her. "How much air is left in your tank?"

She checked her HUD. "I'm down to twenty-seven percent, with almost thirty minutes left."

"Then Darius's tank won't have much more

than that—unless you started using yours before he did?"

Cassandra shook her head. "About the same time."

"So we wait until he runs out of air," Gatticus said. "At that point, he'll have to remove his helmet or open the intakes in his suit. That's when we release our virus and infect him."

"Cass, you should open your suit's intake vents," Dyara said. "Save what's left of your air for when we release the virus. If it killed the others, you don't want to get infected either."

Cassandra nodded woodenly, and an icy trickle of dread coursed through her gut. "We're going to kill my dad."

Dyara fixed her with a sympathetic look. "Cassy, I know he still looks like your father, but..." She trailed off, shaking her head. "He's long gone. In a lot of ways he's already dead."

Cassandra's eyes burned with the threat of fresh tears, but she knew Dyara was right. She'd already come to the same conclusion herself. She wiped a solitary tear from the corner of her eye, and said, "Let's do it."

CHAPTER 45

Tanik sensed Darius cutting the Keth down one after another as they chased him through the palace. Before long he'd killed them all—except for the three following him.

"Tanik!" Feyra's father, Vartok, roared. "I'm holding you personally responsible for the deaths of our people! You were supposed to have taken care of Darius before we arrived!"

"I am not all-powerful," Tanik replied. *Arrogant old fool,* he thought, grunting as he vaulted up a winding staircase. Darius was heading ever higher. Eventually, he was going to have to come back down, or else jump out a window.

They reached the uppermost level, level twenty, and still, Darius was above them. "He's on the roof!" Tanik shouted as he led Feyra, her father, and her father's favorite concubine, Elisana, up the final flight of stairs. They burst through the metal door at the top to find Darius waiting for them at the other end of the roof. He was standing in the eye of his own personal hurricane. Thick clouds of rubble from the tower Tanik had torn down were whipping around Darius's head at high speed. Violent winds generated by that maelstrom buffeted Tanik, threatening to send him tumbling back down the stairs.

"It's the end of the line, Darius!" Tanik shouted to be heard over the wind. "Nowhere left to run!" They cautiously approached the swirling storm of wreckage.

"What makes you think I want to run?" Darius shouted back. And in that instant all of the debris changed directions, sling-shotting around Darius as if he were a planet. Chunks of wall with jutting metal rebar hurtled toward Tanik and the others at high speed. They used their powers to redirect all of the projectiles that they could, but the smaller rocks broke through and pelted them with bruising force. One about the size of a hover car slipped by and slammed into Vartok's chest, sending him flying off the roof.

"Father!" Feyra cried.

Tanik pretended to be equally alarmed and outraged. He could sense Vartok's life force ebbing away as he fell. His chest had caved in with the blow. The last of the debris flowed harmlessly around them. Vartok's concubine didn't seem at all disturbed by his sudden passing, but Feyra was out of her mind with rage. "I'm going to kill him!" she screamed. Without warning, she broke ranks and rushed Darius.

"Feyra, wait!" Tanik raced after her, but he reached her side after she'd already engaged Darius. Thankfully, she had far more experience wielding a blade than Darius did, so there were no immediate consequences of her facing him alone.

Tanik tried to circle around behind Darius, but he kept turning as he parried Feyra's attacks so that he was always facing them both. Tanik snuck in a jab at Darius's ribs, but Darius pushed off from Feyra's blade in time to block the attack.

Tanik flicked an irritated glance over his shoulder to find that Vartok's concubine was no longer with them. She'd decided to flee rather than try to avenge her master.

Tanik blocked an attack from Darius, and feinted left before slicing low for his legs. Darius back-flipped over that attack just as Feyra darted around to get behind him. While their enemy was in the air, he slashed down and sliced off her sword arm. Feyra screamed and collapsed, clutching her smoking stump.

A hot flash of fury tore through Tanik's being, and he gave Darius a violent telekinetic shove just as he landed. It didn't knock him off his feet, but it did stagger him. Tanik put himself between Darius and Feyra before Darius could think to finish her off. He launched a furious flurry of attacks, forcing Darius to backpedal around the roof.

The self-appointed emperor smiled wickedly behind his helmet. "It's just you and me now, Gurhain. Do you remember how that went the last time? Because I do. How are the legs?"

Tanik gritted his teeth and screamed, intensifying his attacks and using every technique he could think of to put Darius off balance, all the while bracing himself against possible kinetic attacks and using his Awareness to look for more incoming debris.

Darius was a better swordsman than Tanik had anticipated, and what he lacked in technique, he seemed to make up for with speed. This was not going to be easy.

But just as he thought that, Tanik sensed two new arrivals emerge on the rooftop. He spun away from Darius, panting and gasping for air, to see *three* familiar faces: Cassandra, Dyara, and Gatticus—whom he couldn't sense.

Maybe he wasn't alone after all.

"Cassandra!" he yelled, his voice amplified by his helmet. "You have to help me stop your father!"

She gave no reply, but he could see her slowly shake her head. Convincing her to help him after he'd lied to her wasn't going to be easy. He needed some last-minute trick of manipulation. Some new argument to convince her.

"The Keth are dead!" he tried, thinking that this time the truth would work. He backed steadily away from Darius, using the zero-point field to drag Feyra away with him. He stayed between her and Darius to shield her from possible attacks. "I'm no match for him by myself!"

"You lied to me!" Cassandra shouted back.

"About what?" Tanik demanded, glancing over his shoulder at her as he drew near. "I didn't know the virus would be deadly any more than you did! It was untested."

Tanik reached Cassandra's side and sheathed his sword to check on Feyra. She was barely conscious, her breathing shallow. Her arm stump was cauterized from the heat of Darius's blade, so there was no danger of bleeding out, but Tanik knew from experience that the loss of a limb was excruciating. Feyra was probably in shock.

"You didn't tell me you were planning to bring the Keth here," Cassandra said. "And I don't believe for a second that you didn't know the virus would kill the others."

"He manipulated you!" Darius said, casually strolling across the rooftop to join the conversation. "And he's trying to do it again. I'm not the bad guy here."

Tanik looked up sharply and shook his head. "All I want is peace."

"Then why did you bring a sword and an army?" Darius replied. "We'll never have peace as long as you're alive."

Tanik stood up and drew his sword once more. He sidestepped away from Feyra and began circling around the roof in an effort to keep the fight away from her. Darius pivoted on the spot, tracking his movements. Then he threw his sword like a boomerang. It came spinning toward Tanik, glowing impossibly with a shield. ZPF shields began and ended with physical contact with the wielder so Tanik couldn't understand how he was able to do that, but he didn't have time to figure it out. He raised his sword to block the incoming weapon—

But it missed and went spinning *around* him, back toward Darius. It never reached him either.

Tanik watched in horror as the glowing blade went sailing toward Feyra. "No!" Tanik shouted. He reached for the weapon, using all of his strength to pull it off course. It worked. The sword went skimming harmlessly along the rooftop, drawing molten furrows as it went.

"Look out!" Cassandra screamed.

Tanik whirled around just in time to see a second blade sailing straight for his chest. A searing heat erupted there, and his mouth popped open in an airless scream as the sword sailed out through his back. It went whipping back around and smacked into Darius's waiting palm. In his desperation to save Feyra, Tanik had inadvertently narrowed his focus and blinded himself to the real threat. Feyra's sword.

Tanik sank to his knees with acrid black smoke rising from the charred hole where his heart used to be. The smoke grew rapidly thicker, obscuring everything in sight. He saw Darius approaching, but only dimly; then came a blur of light and another flash of heat erupted in his neck. He saw the world tip and turn around him and glimpsed his headless body collapse just a split second before his oxygen-starved brain gave up the fight.

CHAPTER 46

Cassandra watched with wide eyes as Tanik's head rolled across the roof. The Keth woman he'd been trying to protect was still alive, but unconscious from the loss of her arm.

Silence rang but for the wind whistling around Cassandra's helmet.

"You!" Darius roared and jabbed a finger in her direction. "You tried to warn him!"

Cassandra glanced at Gatticus. He still had the virus locked in his utility compartment. He couldn't take it out now without Darius realizing what they were up to. Furthermore, he still had his helmet on. He hadn't run out of air yet.

But he has to be close, Cassandra thought.

Darius advanced on her with his sword raised and simultaneously summoned the one he'd thrown at the Keth woman into his other hand.

"Darius, calm down," Dyara said, and stepped between them.

"Get out of the way," Darius growled.

"No."

Cassandra saw her father's chest heaving with rage and eyed the swords in his hands. Drawing her own blade, she joined Dyara in staring him down.

Darius let go of both swords, but they didn't drop to the ground. Instead, they hovered in the air to either side of him while he reached up and twisted off his helmet. Shaking out a mane of long, sweat-matted brown hair, he grabbed his swords once more and sucked in a deep breath.

Now's our chance! Cassandra thought, even as Gatticus began backing away from the developing confrontation.

Darius smirked. "You know, I don't even have to fight you. I could just take control of you both and make you walk off the roof."

Cassandra's eyes widened with alarm. He was right. He was a Luminary, the last one now that Tanik was dead. "Dad..." she tried.

"Don't you *Dad* me." She felt his mind reaching for hers, pushing past her defenses and taking control of her will. Dyara's eyes glazed over in an instant, but Cassandra fought back with everything she had, using the mind-shielding techniques that Tanik had taught her. She could feel Darius's surprise, and his subsequent outrage as she pushed him out.

"You've gotten stronger," Darius said. "It's a pity you chose to fight against me. Together we could have been unstoppable—father and daughter, ruling the galaxy forever."

"We still can!" Cassandra said, hoping he would buy it.

"Liar!" he screamed, and began advancing on her once more.

Cassandra glanced sideways at Dyara and grimaced at the sight of her blank, staring eyes. "Snap out of it, Dya!"

Dyara turned and smiled, her sword flashing up toward Cassandra's face.

She leapt back and the blade blurred by mere inches from her nose. "Dyara!" Cassandra screamed, backpedaling hastily to put some distance between them.

"You're going to have to kill her," Darius said. "She won't stop."

Cassandra reached for Dyara's mind in a desperate attempt to break Darius's hold on her, but it was no use. Darius was too strong.

Dyara leapt into the air, covering the distance

between them in a flash. Her sword swept down, and Cassandra brought hers up to block. The force of the blow was too much for her. It knocked her on her rear. Cassandra lay gazing up into Dyara's staring brown eyes, helpless to get away. She cringed and gave Dyara a telekinetic shove. The woman stumbled back a few steps, giving Cassandra the chance she needed to jump back to her feet.

In that instant, Cassandra saw Gatticus creeping up behind Darius with the canister. She had to keep him distracted and facing her. He couldn't sense Gatticus, but he could still see the android with his eyes if he turned around.

Dyara came striding back in, her blade flashing back and forth in a deadly zigzagging motion. Cassandra parried and blocked, backpedaling the whole way to buy time. "I don't want to fight you!" she said.

Darius just laughed. "If you don't fight, you'll die."

Dyara's attacks were too determined and too strong to resist. Darius was right. She had to strike back, or she was going to die before Gatticus even had the chance to release the virus.

Cassandra darted around Dyara and swept her legs out with a kick, while simultaneously aiming a diagonal slash for her sword arm.

Dyara lost her footing and fell at just the right moment. She only partially blocked Cassandra's blade, and it sailed on to nick a flaming chunk out of her side. Dyara fell screaming, and her vacant stare gave way to wide, pain-filled eyes and flaring nostrils. Darius had broken the connection.

Cassandra dropped her sword and fell on her haunches by Dyara's side. She could see where severed ribs ended, and the hole in Dyara's side began. She could see... organs. Air whistled in and out of one of Dyara's lungs. The damaged lung pressed against jagged black ribs, squeezing out through the hole and blowing noxious curls of smoke into Cassandra's visor.

She rounded on Darius with a hateful glare. "You did this!"

He held up his hands in a shrug, both of them still clutching swords, and offered her a smug smile. "I didn't do anything. That was you. Now finish her off and prove your loyalty to me. Then I'll forgive you, and we will rule together as the last two Revenants in the galaxy."

Cassandra gaped at him. His green eyes were blazing with an unholy light. His pallid, gray skin glowed in the light of his shield and danced with the endless scurrying of the Sprites. He was like some demon from the pits of Hell. *This* was not her father.

Cassandra turned back to Dyara. "Do it," Dyara said through gritted teeth. "Kill me."

"No." Cassandra shook her head and defiantly thrust out her chin as she looked back to Darius. "You'll have to kill us both."

Darius's face fell dramatically. "Very well," he said, and began striding toward her.

Cassandra picked up her sword and leapt to her feet, backing away hurriedly. Where was Gatticus? He should have been able to infect Darius by now!

She fetched up against the door leading down into the palace. Desperate to escape, she turned and tried to pull it open.

But it wouldn't budge. Cassandra's mind raced. Had someone locked them out?

"Where do you think you're going?" Darius crowed.

Cassandra faced him and tried to push him back with a telekinetic shove, but Darius just kept coming. He was too strong. If he reached her, there was no way she could defend herself against two swords. Cassandra tried to run, thinking she could jump off the roof and use the ZPF to slow her fall.

But she found herself pinned to the door.

Darius held her there, making it impossible for her to run. Cassandra pushed back against the invisible hand holding her, using every ounce of strength she had, but Darius pushed harder still—so hard that she could barely breathe.

Darius stopped within easy reach of her, his expression full of dismay. "I had such high hopes for you, but you have been an utter disappointment. All those years, I went to such lengths to save you, and this is how you repay me? With betrayal?" Darius slowly shook his head. "I saved your life, and now I'm going to take it away. I hope for your sake you find your way to an afterlife with a god who's more patient than I."

Cassandra's eyes blurred with tears as she watched Darius raise both of his swords for the kill.

"Darius! Catch!" Dyara said in a gasping voice. In the next instant, a silver canister appeared spinning in the air between them. Cassandra hurriedly shut the air intakes of her suit and re-opened the valves to her air tank.

Darius's eyes pinched in confusion, then widened in horror and recognition at the sight of the silver canister. He sucked in a horrified breath and stumbled away just as the nanites streamed out in a silvery cloud. He took in a whole lungful of them before trying to cough them back out.

But even as he did so, they zipped back in, flying up his nose and through his ears. Darius's nostrils flared, and his glowing eyes flickered. His face turned bright red, and pinpricks of blood appeared like freckles all over his face.

The weight on Cassandra's chest lifted, and she sagged, gasping for air. She stood staring in horror at Darius, even as an agonized scream tore from his lips.

Gatticus came striding into view, and Cassandra rounded on him. "What is it doing to him? Why is he bleeding?"

Gatticus just looked at her and shook his head. "I don't know, but he doesn't have long."

CHAPTER 47

Cassandra held Darius's head in her lap, her tears falling in a puddle inside her helmet. Spasms rippled through his body, muscles and tendons standing out like cords. He gasped, struggling to speak. "C-Cass," he stuttered. "I'm s-sorry."

She looked up at Gatticus. He stood off to one side, watching with a frown. "You have to stop the virus! He's changing back. He's going back to his old self!"

Gatticus just looked at her. "His pupillary response indicates that he is being deceptive. If I deactivate the virus now, he might kill you."

"But it's killing *him!*"

"You knew that would happen," Gatticus replied.

"Because I thought we couldn't save him!"

Darius's whole body tensed and he cried out

once more, his eyes rolling in his head.

"Gatticus! Deactivate it now!" Cassandra pleaded.

"Very well."

Darius relaxed suddenly, and the pained expression left his face—replaced by a flash of rage. He leapt to his feet and gestured to Gatticus with one hand, lifting the android into the air. "You're going to wish you hadn't done that, robot."

Darius made a fist, and Gatticus's body and face began to deform, crumpling inward like tin foil. "Dad! Stop!" Cassandra put a hand on his arm, trying to force it back down to his side, as if that could affect what he was doing with his mind.

"Gatticus, reactivate the virus!"

But a distorted slur was all he gave for a reply.

Darius's rage paled to shock. He blinked and dropped his arm all by himself, his attention dipping to the gleaming black sword jutting from his chest.

"What?" he asked, and sank to his knees, shaking his head. Gatticus fell in a heap, and struggled to rise with a grinding whine of damaged joints and servomotors.

Cassandra was equally confused—until she remembered Dyara. She spun around to find the woman had dragged herself to within fifteen feet of them. She'd propped herself up on one elbow to watch them.

"How could you!" Cassandra screamed. "You killed him!"

"I'm sorry, Cass," she said in a husky whisper.

Cassandra scowled and shook her head, too furious to speak.

"Get it... out," Darius gasped.

She hurried to remove the sword. It slid out of his back with a sickening squelch of blood, and Darius collapsed once more. Cassandra held him to her chest, his blood slipping through her fingers in a slick, sticky river. "You can't die!"

"The empire is yours now," he rasped.

Cassandra refused to accept that. "No. You're going to live."

"Be..." Darius sucked in a ragged breath and grabbed her hand in a painfully tight fist. He coughed up a clot of blood that ran down his chin in a crimson stain. *Be better than me,* he finished, using whatever vestiges of power he had left to finish his sentence inside Cassandra's thoughts. Darius's gaze slid to hers just as the light left his eyes. His expression froze, with death stealing what little color was left in his face.

"No!" Cassandra screamed. She had to get him

to a hospital. She reached into the ZPF and called to Trista, telling her to come pick them up on the roof of the palace.

Trista responded affirmatively.

"Gatticus! Use your hands!" Cassandra said, suddenly remembering that he'd been able to use his hands to shock people back to life on other occasions.

Gatticus was already down on one knee, still struggling to get up after the damage Darius had inflicted. His jaw hung open at an odd angle. His nose was crooked, and one of his eyes drooped. The other one swiveled to regard her, then dipped to Darius. A blue fan of light flickered out as he performed some kind of scan. He shook his head with a sound of grinding metal.

Cassandra's eyes opened like two faucets, and she fell over backward, sobbing herself senseless. When the O^2 indicator on her HUD began blinking, warning that she was running out of air, she didn't even care. She wanted to suffocate. If she died, there was a chance that she might still be reunited with her dad in some kind of heaven.

But Gatticus refused to let her. He limped over and twisted off her helmet. Cassandra's lungs heaved reflexively, forcing her to suck in a deep breath. She just lay there, blinking tears and staring in horror up at the cold blue sky.

She was dead in ways that went far beyond the physical. The roar of landing thrusters rumbled, making the air shiver, and Trista's transport hovered down into view. Moments later, Trista and Buddy came bounding out of the airlock.

"What happened?" Trista shouted as she ran across the roof. Cassandra didn't have the strength for a reply.

"Who are yoo—oh, Fek!" Trista exclaimed, as she reached Dyara and saw her injuries. Cassandra felt a flash of bitter satisfaction at that. Dya deserved it. She'd killed her father!

But then she remembered Darius's last request—*be better than me*—and for the first time in the past many months, she understood the darkness that had overtaken him. Anger and rage over losing her, the necessity of war, and the cold, slithering whispers of the Sprites themselves had all twisted him into something that he never should have become.

Despite the pain of losing him, Cassandra experienced a moment of clarity, and her anger gave way to shame and guilt. She had to fight back if she was going to avoid her father's fate.

"Cassy!" Trista said. "Are you okay?" She rose on wooden legs and nodded stiffly. "Come on."

The other woman wrapped an arm around her shoulders. "We have to get Dya to a hospital."

Cassandra let Trista lead her across the rooftop toward the *Harlequin*, but then she remembered something. "Wait..." Cassandra whispered, and dug in her heels.

"What's wrong?" Trista asked.

Cassandra's gaze flicked around the rooftop, looking for the unconscious Keth that Tanik had been trying to save, but she was nowhere to be seen. "Someone's missing."

"We'll find them later," Trista said, and pulled her toward the waiting transport once more.

Gatticus limped up beside them, dragging a useless leg with a persistent scraping sound.

Trista spared a glance at him. "You look like you got hit by a hover truck."

Gatticus nodded with that assessment and gestured vaguely in Darius's direction.

"Can't talk, huh?" Trista said. "Well, don't worry. We'll fix you up."

CHAPTER 48

—ONE YEAR LATER—

Cassandra sat in the throne room of the palace, listening with half an ear to reports from her ministers, generals, and admirals. The galaxy was in ruins, with all the different species fighting each other over the scraps. The Revenants had provided a temporary sense of order, analogous to what the Cygnians had established during their reign. Fear had kept everyone in line, and when a group of conquering heroes with supernatural powers had arrived, that same system of ruling by fear had continued. Without it, people were succumbing to the madness and violence of the Sprites simmering in their veins. Thanks to the Crucible and the Cygnians' practice of exposing everyone to the Sprites when they came of age, the same disease that had consumed Darius was raging to a lesser extent inside every sentient being in the galaxy.

The Sprites were the disease, but a modified version of Gatticus's virus was the cure. The original virus had pacified the surviving Cygnians, spreading across their lonely prison world in short order and making them the most civilized species in the known universe. The Sprites were the real enemy in all of this.

Cassandra battled them daily. Now she knew what horrors her father had faced, and succumbed to, during his rise to power. Power itself was addictive, and the Sprites were always there begging for more—whispering, urging, and tempting her to fill herself more fully with them, to *become* them.

Dyara was a voice of reason, the guiding light that kept her sane and accountable. Even so, somehow it was therapeutic to sit where her father had sat and to know the demons he had faced. It helped to reinforce the fact that *he* wasn't the one who had done and said all those horrible things.

The General who had been speaking a moment ago trailed off suddenly, seeming to realize that she was no longer listening.

Cassandra smiled her thanks for his report

and waved him away. "Admiral Mathos, how is our fleet doing with its task?"

The black-furred Lassarian stepped to the fore and bared his teeth in a predatory smile. "We have seeded twelve new worlds with the virus, and they are now willing to discuss joining the empire—on the condition that we protect them from their more militant neighbors."

Cassandra nodded. "That won't be a problem, will it?"

"I hope not, Empress," Yuri replied. "The civil war still rages, but our fleet is strong."

Cassandra breathed a sigh that rasped through her respirator. She had to wear that mask, and her isolation suit at all times. It was the only way to protect herself from infection. Likewise, her right-hand, Dyara, also needed to keep her abilities—at least for now. Cassandra could hear her breath rasping in and out of her mask from where she stood to one side of the throne.

Cassandra would have gladly given up power and subjected herself to the virus, but there was at least one Keth still out there somewhere, and dozens of Revenants, whose bodies had been suspiciously missing from those found in the courtyard—despite Darius's decree that attendance was mandatory. They'd probably foreseen the coming massacre, just as Darius had.

"Gatticus?" Cassandra prompted.

"My Lady?"

"How is the production of the new Executor models coming along?"

"Very well. We've filled twenty-one new orders just this week."

"Good, and the Marine bots?"

"Forty-two thousand units are on their way to support the Executors on allied worlds," Gatticus replied.

"Excellent, and how are we doing with the relocation of the Cygnians?"

"They've been cooperative. There have been no incidents so far."

"I still believe it's a mistake to let them live," Yuri growled. "Much less to give them a suitable world where they can rebuild."

"My father would have agreed with you," Cassandra said, thrusting out her chin in disdain for that objection. "And that is why *I* do not. The Cygnians were more affected by the Sprites than most species. It isn't their fault that they did the things they did."

Silence answered that rebuke, and Yuri bowed his head in apology. "Yes, My Lady."

Cassandra's gaze roved on, past her mob of

generals, admirals, and other military leaders, until she found a particular individual, Evos—an artist, a Dol Walin sculptor who had nothing to do with the dark and ugly business of war.

She nodded to him. "How's progress on my monument coming along?"

"It is nearly complete, Empress," he replied in his watery voice. "With your permission, perhaps you would like to come and see it before the official unveiling?"

Cassandra's eyes crinkled with a genuine smile that Evos couldn't see behind her mask. She nodded to him. "Yes, I would like that very much." She glanced at Dyara who was standing silently to one side of the throne. "Shall we?"

"After you, Empress," Dyara replied.

* * *

Cassandra sat in the front seat of Evos's hover car as he flew circles above the palace courtyard to show off his work. He and hundreds of others just like him had been working tirelessly on this project for the past six months. There, standing in front of the palace, with arms wide open to welcome all who might come through the palace gates, was a two-hundred foot statue of her father, serving as a massive headstone to conceal his actual grave. The sculptors had done amazing work. The statue looked just like him—but not as he had been in death, rather, the way she remembered him. Kind green eyes, a warm smile, and an expression that radiated nothing but love.

"Take us down," Cassandra said, her voice sounding hoarse even through the distortion of her mask. "I want to read the inscription."

"Of course," Evos replied.

Dyara leaned forward from the back seat and placed a comforting hand on Cassandra's shoulder.

As soon as they landed in the courtyard, Cassandra strode out to the base of the statue. There was a solid gold plate as tall as her that read:

Here lies Emperor Darius Drake, Destroyer of Worlds, Savior of The Galaxy.

"Be better than me." -Emperor Drake 2015 AD - 1521 AU.

"Cryptic. Do you think people will get it?" Dyara asked, stopping beside her to read the inscription as well.

Cassandra turned to her. "Maybe not, but they can always read about it in the history books. In my time we had a saying about good intentions. My father had plenty of those, but the truth is you can't do evil in order to accomplish something good. You've got to start with the good."

"Wise words. Maybe that should be on the inscription, too," Dyara said.

"Yes," the sculptor agreed, coming to stand with them at the foot of the statue. "I agree. Start with the good."

"But where is it?" Cassandra asked, slowly shaking her head.

Dyara placed a hand on her shoulder once more, and their eyes met through the visors of their helmets. "We'll find it. It's easy to look at the mess and see everything that still needs fixing, but that just blinds you to the things that are already fixed. We've made a lot of progress, and we'll make a lot more before we're finished."

Cassandra nodded. "You're right. I just wish..." she turned back to the statue and peered up at it. "I wish he was here to see it."

"Maybe he is," Dyara said, and jerked her chin to indicate the pale blue sky.

Cassandra followed Dyara's gaze. There, gleaming against the blue, she could have sworn she saw something—a glowing, sparkling mass of Sprites. As she watched they swarmed into the shape of her father's face. Whispering voices crowded in at the edges of her hearing, and for the first time, she heard them plainly, as if the Sprites had suddenly learned to speak her language.

I love you, Cassy, they said, and then that shimmering face in the sky smiled.

GET MY NEXT BOOK FOR FREE

Rogue Star: Frozen Earth
(Coming August 15th, 2018)

Get a FREE digital copy if you <u>post an honest review of this book</u> on Amazon and <u>send it to me here.</u>

Thank you in advance for your feedback!
I read every review and use your comments to improve my work.

KEEP IN TOUCH

SUBSCRIBE to my Mailing List and get two FREE Books!
http://files.jaspertscott.com/mailinglist.html

Follow me on Twitter:
@JasperTscott

Look me up on Facebook:
Jasper T. Scott

Check out my website:
www.JasperTscott.com

Or send me an e-mail:
JasperTscott@gmail.com

OTHER BOOKS BY JASPER SCOTT

Suggested reading order

Rogue Star
Rogue Star: Frozen Earth
Coming August 15th 2018!

Broken Worlds
Broken Worlds: The Awakening (Book 1)
Broken Worlds: The Revenants (Book 2)
Broken Worlds: Civil War (Book 3)

New Frontiers Series
(Standalone Prequels to Dark Space)
Excelsior (Book 1)
Mindscape (Book 2)
Exodus (Book 3)

Dark Space Series
Dark Space
Dark Space 2: The Invisible War
Dark Space 3: Origin
Dark Space 4: Revenge

ABOUT THE AUTHOR

Jasper Scott is a USA TODAY bestselling science fiction author, known for writing intricate plots with unexpected twists.

His books have been translated into Japanese and German and adapted for audio, with collectively over 500,000 copies purchased.

Jasper was born and raised in Canada by South African parents, with a British cultural heritage on his mother's side and German on his father's, to which he has now added Latin culture with his wonderful wife.

After spending years living as a starving artist, he finally quit his various jobs to become a full-time writer. In his spare time he enjoys reading, traveling, going to the gym, and spending time with his family.

15089165R00227

Made in the USA
Lexington, KY
11 November 2018